“My mo… getting together aga…

“Really?” Rick forced back a shaft of disappointment and concentrated on putting the tools away.

“Yeah.” The teenager shrugged casually. “They never shoulda gotten divorced in the first place, and I think Mom's finally starting to realize it. He's been having dinner with us almost every night, and they're getting along great.”

Rick told himself the concern he felt was for Marti's sake, not his own, and it was his discomfort over discussing her behind her back that caused this sudden uneasiness. Whatever the reason, he didn't want to talk about it anymore.

Unfortunately, Cameron did. “Dad says if things keep going this well, he's gonna buy her a diamond for Christmas.”

“Does your mom know?”

“Nope. Dad's gonna surprise her. Cool, huh?”

Cameron flashed a smile so like his mother's that Rick's stomach knotted.

“Cool,” he replied, hoping the boy wouldn't notice the sarcasm in his voice.

Dear Reader,

Usually, getting to know the characters I write is a long, involved process. But every once in a while, one comes to me in a flash—fully formed and completely alive.

Rick Dennehy is such a character. Several years ago, while driving through the mountains outside Gunnison, Colorado, I passed the entrance to a group of guest cabins. There, among the towering pines and quaking aspen, I saw Rick in my imagination. I knew almost everything about him in that second.

It took longer to find the right heroine. Rick had been so hurt by life, I knew he needed a woman who could understand his pain and embrace it as part of him. When I finally found Marti, I knew it was time to start writing their story.

Let It Snow is a story about the healing quality of love. About that special something that happens between two people when love finds them at the most unexpected time and in the most unexpected place.

When my editors suggested I set the story during the Christmas season, everything else fell into place. The enchantment of the holidays combines with the magic of love to bring healing to these very special people.

I hope you'll grow to love them as I have, and that this story will work magic on your heart as it has on mine.

Sherry Lewis

P.S. I'd love to hear from you. You can write to me at P.O. Box 540542, North Salt Lake City, Utah 84054-0542

LET IT SNOW
Sherry Lewis

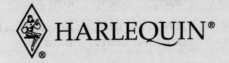

HARLEQUIN®

TORONTO • NEW YORK • LONDON
AMSTERDAM • PARIS • SYDNEY • HAMBURG
STOCKHOLM • ATHENS • TOKYO • MILAN • MADRID
PRAGUE • WARSAW • BUDAPEST • AUCKLAND

ISBN 0-373-70816-5

LET IT SNOW

Copyright © 1998 by Sherry Lewis.

This edition published by arrangement with Harlequin Books S.A.

Printed in U.S.A.

To my nephew,
Matthew Lewis Preysz,
for helping me understand all things "boy."

CHAPTER ONE

MARTI JOHANSSON lifted the last of the clean dishes from the dishwasher and stacked the plates in the cupboard. Behind her at the kitchen table, her son, Cameron, let out a heavy sigh. She could see him reflected in the window, the sour expression, the slumped shoulders, the blond hair hanging into his face. He'd been surly all through dinner, and her own temper had almost reached the boiling point.

"Give me one good reason why I can't get a car," Cameron demanded.

"One?" Marti glared at him over her shoulder. "I can give you half a dozen. Let's start with the fact that you're only fifteen."

Red blotches dotted Cameron's pale cheeks. "I'll be sixteen in three months."

"Here's another, you're still on probation."

"Like that matters." These days he stood a full head taller than Marti, and his voice had dropped low enough to match his father's. Both things made him think of himself as an adult.

Marti just wished he'd begin acting like one. "It matters, Cameron." She closed the cupboard and crossed the room to the table. "You're the one who decided it would be cool to borrow a car and go joy-riding with your friends. You're the one who didn't think it was important to turn in your homework last semester. Now you're the one who gets to pay the price.''

Cameron rolled his eyes and ticked his tongue in disgust. ''It wouldn't have made any difference if I had turned in my homework. I still would have gotten an F.''

''That's not true,'' Marti insisted. ''You're smart enough, you just don't try.''

''I *do* try.''

''Maybe in woodshop and auto mechanics, but you don't even bother in the rest of your classes.''

''I don't know what that has to do with me getting a car,'' he muttered.

''In that case,'' Marti snapped, ''I'll spell it out for you. Until you get your grades up and keep out of trouble, I'm not likely to shower you with rewards.''

Cameron planted his elbows on the table and propped up his chin with both hands. He looked so dejected, Marti felt herself weakening.

She sat where she could look into his eyes. Immediately, he averted his gaze. ''You're a smart kid, Cameron. You could get good grades if you'd only try.''

''That's what you always say. You and those stupid counselors you're always dragging me to see.'' He flicked a contemptuous glance at her out of eyes so clear and blue they made her heart ache. ''I'm not smart, I'm stupid.''

''I take you to counseling because I don't know what's gotten into you lately.''

Another glance, this one even more venomous. ''Yes, you do. I've told you a million times.''

For three years he'd complained about everything

from the divorce, to moving to California, to the teachers he'd been assigned. She didn't know which topped his list today. "Tell me again."

He kicked his feet onto an empty chair and glared at his fingernails. "I hate this place, that's what's wrong with me. I want to go home."

Of course. With the Christmas holidays approaching, she should have guessed he'd miss Colorado more than usual. But they didn't live in Gunnison anymore, and after three years, he should be able to accept that. "You *are* home," she reminded him.

"No, I'm not. This isn't home. It'll never be home."

"I know you miss Colorado—"

"It's not just that," Cameron interrupted. "I miss Dad. I never get to see him anymore."

Marti knew he blamed her for the nonexistent visits with Gil. If she hadn't decided to leave Gunnison after the divorce... If she wasn't so mean to Gil... She'd heard the accusations so many times, she didn't even bother to defend herself anymore. No matter what she said, Cameron steadfastly refused to believe that Gil was responsible for anything Cameron didn't like.

"Maybe he'll let you visit when you're off probation."

"Maybe I won't ever *be* off probation."

Another piece of her thinning patience evaporated. "Maybe you won't. Especially if you keep hanging around with Jared and Tim."

"Oh, yeah," Cameron snarled. "Blame Jared and Tim. You divorced Dad, jerked me out of my school and took me away from all of my family and friends. And now that I've finally made a few new friends here, you're trying to take *them* away, too."

"Only because Jared and Tim are always in trouble."

"So?"

"So, I don't want you doing the things they do. I don't want you to screw up your life by making stupid choices."

"I'm *not* making stupid choices," he shouted. "And I'm not screwing up my life. You're the one who's doing that."

"I'm not screwing up your life," Marti insisted. She tried to keep her voice steady, but she could feel the heat of anger creeping up her neck into her face and she knew that she was in danger of losing the battle. Again. "Moving from Gunnison was the best thing I ever did for you."

"You mean it was the best thing you ever did for yourself."

"I'm not going to talk about this now," she told him. "I want you to go to your room until you've calmed down. When you can discuss things rationally, I'll be glad to talk to you again."

Swearing, Cameron jumped up to face her. He leaned both fists on the table in a pose she knew he meant to intimidate her. "I'm not going to my room."

She stood to face him, forcing herself to hold his gaze, to meet the challenge in his eyes. "Yes, you are."

"Go to hell."

She started toward him, but Cameron spun on his heel and jackrabbited out the back door before she could reach him. She raced after him, but he jumped down the back steps and ran down the driveway before she could even make it out the door.

Gripping the doorframe, she shouted after him, but she knew it was a waste of energy. He wouldn't come back now. He'd hook up with Jared and Tim, and probably get himself into more trouble before the end of the night.

Somehow, she'd lost control of him, and she had no idea how to get it back. Their relationship seemed to get worse with every passing day. She'd tried everything to reach him. She'd talked to counselors, read books and attended parenting seminars, but he only grew more angry, bitter and hateful. Lately, she'd begun to despair of him ever making a turnaround without a miracle.

Sadly, she stared at the night sky and remembered the days, long gone now, when Cameron had climbed into her lap, wrapped his arms around her neck and pressed soft kisses to her cheek. He'd loved sitting in the rocking chair with her and curling his fingers through her hair while they watched television. He'd been her companion during Gil's absences and her only solace during that horrible time after the stillborn birth of her second child. Gil certainly hadn't been there for her. He'd been too busy drinking his nights away at the Lucky Jack and chasing around with other women.

But Cameron had been there. And Marti had done her best to put her grief over losing Chelsea behind her and get on with her life—for Cameron's sake. But Cameron couldn't see how hard she'd tried. Marti suspected he didn't want to see.

Trying not to panic, she closed the door behind her and walked back to the kitchen table. Almost mindlessly, she sat down and sorted through the day's mail, scowling at the inevitable pile of bills, junk mail and flyers. Nothing interesting there. Maybe she could find something on TV. Or she could finish the novel she'd started last week.

As she tossed the mail back onto the table, an envelope fell out of a folded advertising circular. Hoping it wasn't another letter from Cameron's school, she picked it up. When she recognized her father's bold scrawl, she sighed with relief, ripped open the envelope and scanned the single page.

Just like her dad, she thought. No chatty details, just straight to the point. An invitation to bring Cameron home to Gunnison over the Christmas holidays and one terse sentence telling her that neither of her brothers nor her sister could make it this year.

She started to set the letter aside, then stopped and stared at it for several long seconds. True, her father hadn't approved of her divorcing Gil. True, he hadn't been exactly warm and loving since she'd moved away. But maybe he was ready to put all that behind them. He *had* taken time to write, which meant he must want to see her.

She lowered the letter to the table and gave her dad's suggestion serious thought. Maybe—just *maybe*—taking Cameron back to the Lazy M Ranch for a few weeks would help her fix their relationship.

Of course, she did have obligations to consider. Her next magazine article was due before the new year, but using her laptop computer she could write anywhere. She'd done most of the research when she'd begun the series on family vacation resorts along the West coast. Besides, Cameron wasn't the only one who could use a dose of crisp Colorado mountain air. She'd missed her childhood home more than she wanted to admit— even to herself.

Leaning back in her chair, she locked her arms behind her head and smiled up at the ceiling. Her dad had offered the perfect solution to her problems. She could separate Cameron from Jared and Tim. She and her dad could patch things up. And, with luck, she just might be able to start mending her relationship with her son, as well.

WITH A SIGH OF RELIEF, Rick Dennehy closed the last file on his desk and raked his fingers through his hair. It had already been a long day, and it wasn't over yet. Afternoon sunlight streamed in through the wide window behind him, making it feel more like late autumn in Denver than the first of December. From the street two floors below, the persistent sound of a bell ringing nonstop irritated his already frayed nerves. Outside his office door, Christmas music echoed through the marbled corridors of the courthouse.

Doing his best to ignore both, he forced a smile and handed the file to his assistant. "I guess that's it, Noreen," he said, rolling down his shirtsleeves and nodding toward the teetering stacks of files they'd created on the floor. "Think you can get case administration to close all those files before the end of the year?"

Noreen shrugged lightly and added the file to one precarious-looking stack beside her chair. "I can as long as we don't run into computer problems while you're gone. If the system goes down, I'm not making any promises."

Rick scowled at her and tightened the knot in his tie.

"If the system goes down or everyone suddenly develops a case of holiday fever."

Noreen scowled back. He never had been able to intimidate her. "We might put up a few Christmas decorations and listen to music," she said, "but we still get the work done."

"Decorations and music aren't the problem," he reminded her. "It's the long lunches shopping and leaving early and talking about Christmas presents and parties that slows everyone down."

"Some of us happen to *like* Christmas."

Not Rick. Losing his wife a week before Christmas two years earlier made him dread the season and the memories it evoked. He didn't remind Noreen. She knew all about Jocelyn's accident and, thankfully, she knew better than to discuss it with him.

She leaned back in her chair, crossed her legs and studied him for a long moment. "So? Are you going to leave me a number where I can reach you?"

He let out a soft laugh. "Not on your life. I'm spending a month *away* from this place." In the Monterey beach condo of an old friend. Warm sunshine, sand and all the free time a man could want. He didn't intend to let anyone or anything interrupt his un-Christmas holiday.

"What do I do if your Realtor calls?"

Rick's smile faded as it always did when he thought of the cabins he and Jocelyn had built in the southern Colorado mountains outside of Gunnison. "I'll call Bix before I leave this afternoon."

Noreen shook her head slowly, but she didn't look at him—a sure sign that she was about to say something Rick wouldn't like. "You're really going to sell the cabins?"

"I am."

"But you love those cabins."

Correction. Rick *had* loved them. He didn't now. In fact, he'd done his best to ignore their existence since he'd come back to Denver after Jocelyn's death. Once he'd thought he might eventually go back. Now, he knew better. So, six months earlier, he'd listed the cabins and the land with a Realtor based in Gunnison. Unfortunately, in spite of the confidently grinning picture on the man's business card, Bix Mason hadn't been able to pull in even one offer yet.

Rick pushed away from his desk and scowled at Noreen. "They're just a bunch of boards sitting on a pile of dirt."

She pursed her lips in disbelief. "Yeah. Right."

"I'm selling," he insisted. "And don't worry about Bix. I'll give him a number where he can reach me." He used his sternest voice—the one he usually used only on recalcitrant debtors and troublesome attorneys.

It didn't faze Noreen. She'd worked with him before he moved to Gunnison and again since he'd come back to his job as Chief Deputy Clerk at the bankruptcy court after Jocelyn's death. They'd grown comfortable with their professional friendship over the years. She knew his boundaries, and she knew better than to overstep them.

But for some reason, she seemed to forget today. She sent him a tight smile. "I still think you ought to change your mind. Give yourself more time to think about selling."

"I don't need more time," Rick assured her.

"You haven't been back there since Jocelyn's accident—"

"I don't need to go back," he snapped. "I know what I'm doing." He leaned both fists on the desktop and glared at her. "Now, if there's nothing else, I've got a lot to do before I leave today."

Noreen slowly uncrossed her legs and tucked her pen behind her ear. "I know you don't want my opinion, but I'll give it to you anyway. You're running away, Rick. You're afraid to go back and face the place where Jocelyn died."

Rick pushed up from his desk and clenched his fists until the stubs of his nails bit into the palms of his hands. "What did you do? Get a degree in psychoanalysis while I wasn't looking?" Anger flashed through Noreen's eyes. He knew he'd offended her, but he didn't care. "Do me a favor," he said sharply. "Use your armchair psychiatry on someone else. I have work to do."

"Fine." Noreen's face had turned an angry shade of red, but she had enough sense not to argue with him. "I'll have a couple of clerks bring a cart to pick up these files."

"Good."

"And I hope you have a great time—wherever you're going."

"Thank you, I will."

He waited until she'd closed the door behind her, then sank into his chair again. Only then did he realize how badly the conversation had shaken him. His knees wobbled, his hands shook and he had trouble catching his breath. He took a minute to pull himself together, then found Bix Mason's business card in his Rolodex, lifted the receiver and punched in the number. Might as well get this part over with now. Then he could forget about Gunnison and the cabins for the rest of the month.

The phone rang five times before Rick got an answer.

"Mason Realty." It was Bix's familiar tenor. "What can I do for you?"

"Bix? Rick Dennehy here. Just checking in before I leave town for a month."

"Well, imagine that," Bix said with a laugh. "I was just looking up your number when the telephone rang."

"You were? Why? Have we finally got an offer?"

"No-o-o." Bix dragged the word out for an eternity. "Matter of fact, I was fixing to tell you I don't think you're going to get one, the shape the property's in right now. At least not one that'll clear up your loan, much less give you a little profit."

"I don't need a profit," Rick assured him. "I just want to come out even."

"Well, see, that's the thing. I don't think you're going to. Not unless you fix the cabins up some. Last winter was a harsh one, and you've got some damage to several of the cabins already. If they sit through another winter as they are, you might as well bulldoze 'em."

Rick swore under his breath and rubbed his forehead with one hand. Couldn't Bix have waited to give him this news until *after* his vacation? "Fine," he said. "Let's fix them up."

"Are you going to come down here and do it?"

"No, I'll hire someone."

"I thought you might say that," Bix said, rattling

papers near the telephone, "so I asked a couple of local guys for estimates."

Rick relaxed slightly. "How much?"

Bix quoted two bids, one far too high, the other astronomical.

"There's no way it could possibly cost that much."

"Actually—"

"*No way,*" Rick interrupted. "They're brand-new."

"They've been vacant for two years."

"Well, what in the hell—"

"Two years of harsh weather," Bix added. "You're looking at a substantial amount in material plus labor to get those things habitable again."

Rick couldn't afford to do that unless he took out another loan. "What about another contractor?"

Bix snorted a soft laugh. "How many do you think we have around here? You want to bring somebody in, you'll be looking at more than that. Trouble is, both these guys work other jobs, so you're looking at spring before you'd be ready to sell."

Rick didn't want to wait until spring. He'd expected to sell off the cabins long before now. And he sure as hell didn't want to end up owing more money than he already did. He kneaded his forehead and tried to think.

"You could save yourself a bundle if you did the work yourself," Bix said. "I mean, it's not as if you can't do it. And if you really punched it, you could probably get it done in a month. Six weeks, tops."

Not for the first time, Rick wished he'd never talked Jocelyn into buying the land and building the eight cabins. The personal price he'd paid had been far too high. He'd lost his dream and his wife and now he couldn't even get rid of the stupid things without taking another month to six weeks off work.

Unbidden, the solution presented itself to him, but he shoved it away. He would *not* give up his vacation in Monterey. He'd earned this time away and he looked forward to spending the whole month of December walking the beaches, watching basketball on television and pretending that Christmas didn't exist.

Of course, he could ignore Christmas in a remote cabin in Gunnison as easily as he could in Monterey. He could catch up on his reading in the evenings. And he could prove to Noreen—and himself—just how off base she'd been to suggest he was running away from his memories.

"Well?" Bix prodded. "What do you want me to do? You want me to hire one of these guys?"

Rick hesitated another minute. Then asked, "What about the main cabin? What kind of shape is it in?"

"Your house? It's all right. I took a couple through it just last week. You must have built it sturdier than the guest cabins."

Of course he had. He'd planned to live in it year-round, and he'd wanted it nice enough to keep Jocelyn happy. "Can you arrange to have the phone turned on for me? And the other utilities as well?"

"Consider it done." Relief tinged Bix's voice. "How soon do you need them?"

"How soon can you do it?"

"Is tomorrow soon enough?"

"Perfect."

"You're making the right choice," Bix assured him.

Rick hoped so. "I'll call you when I get there," and disconnected before he could change his mind.

RICK TRUDGED through the snow from the main cabin to his truck in the parking area outside. Late-morning sun streamed through the trees and glistened off the snow. A brisk wind ruffled the bare branches of the aspen trees and teased the exposed skin on the nape of his neck. Shivering, he unlocked the truck and climbed inside.

He'd stopped in Gunnison on his way to the cabins the day before, checked in with Bix Mason and picked up supplies for a few days. But he hadn't figured on needing to cut firewood so soon. When he'd left two years before, there had been a generous stack of wood near the kitchen door. Unfortunately it had all disappeared. With the radio calling for a serious winter storm, he couldn't put off gathering more.

And after a cursory inspection of the toolshed that morning, he'd realized the cabins weren't the only things that had suffered from neglect. Most of his tools had rusted beyond repair.

At least he didn't have to drive all the way into Gunnison today. He should be able to find what he needed at Greta's Groceries, a tiny all-purpose store a couple of miles up the highway. Greta stocked a little of everything from hunting equipment to milk.

After letting the truck's engine warm up for a minute, he followed the short tree-lined lane from the cabins to the access road he shared with Henry Maddock across the river. Once, all this land had been Maddock's property. But Maddock had run into financial trouble a few years earlier, and his misfortune had opened the door for Rick's dream. Or so Rick had believed at the time.

He'd counted himself lucky to pick up the land at a

fair price. But the old man hadn't considered the sale lucky at all. He'd resented having to sell even an inch of his ranch. In fact, Maddock had acted as if Rick was responsible for his financial problems.

As he drove Rick wondered idly whether time had mellowed the old man. They were neighbors, and Rick didn't want trouble. The instant the thought came, he laughed at himself. He wasn't staying so didn't need to worry about Maddock. The new owners would have to deal with him.

Checking the bridge to Maddock's property for traffic, he pulled onto the dirt access road, but he accelerated a little too fast and the truck fishtailed on the ice and snow. Too late, he realized a car had turned onto the dirt road from the highway just in front of him.

Cursing under his breath, he pumped his brakes and struggled to bring the truck under control. The driver of the other car slammed on the brakes and sent the vehicle into a skid. While Rick watched, helpless, it turned sideways and slid, out of control, straight toward his truck.

The driver fought the steering wheel, which only made the situation worse. Bracing himself for impact, Rick watched the occupants of the car do the same. And he tried to force away the images of Jocelyn spinning out of control in her tiny car.

Somehow, miraculously, the car slid to a stop just inches from Rick's front bumper. With his heart racing, he threw open the truck's door, and jumped out. "What in the hell?"

Obviously shaken, the driver climbed out of the car. She drew the collar of her coat tight around her neck and sent him an unsteady smile. A kid of about fifteen or sixteen slid across from the passenger side and climbed out of the car behind her. His thin blond hair, the same shade as the woman's, hung over the shaved sides of his head. He frowned at the woman and turned a distinctly hostile glare on Rick. Even with the difference in their ages and expressions, their features were strikingly similar. Probably mother and son.

Standing on tiptoe, the woman looked at the space between the two vehicles. "I'm so sorry. I didn't expect anyone to be on this road. I guess I've forgotten how to drive in weather like this."

The kid sneered as if she'd said something stupid. "You *forgot* to watch where you were going."

For some reason, his blatant hostility tempered Rick's own anger. After all, he'd been partially to blame. "You can watch like a hawk," he said with a smile, "but it won't make much difference on an icy road."

The boy flipped hair out of his eyes and snarled, "Yeah. Right." He walked to the front of the car, stopped when he realized he'd have to step into the drainage ditch to get around it and flipped his hair again. "I don't know what he's doing on this road, anyway. It's private property."

The woman mumbled something Rick couldn't hear. She studied the car for a moment, then turned a disconcerted glance on Rick. "I'm not sure how to get myself out of this."

"I can back up," Rick offered, "but I don't know how we'll get you turned around so you don't slide into the ditch."

She frowned at the car again. This time when she

looked up at him, her blue eyes caught the faint rays of sunshine and reflected back at him, as clear as the lakes in the high mountains, as light as Jocelyn's had been dark, and nearly as compelling.

Suddenly uncomfortable, Rick forced himself to look away. "I suppose we could use the truck to pull you around."

The kid sent another disgusted frown at his mother and reached for the door handle. "Maybe *you* can't move the car, but *I* can."

"Don't even try it, Cameron," she warned. "The way it's sitting, you'll only get us stuck in the ditch. Besides, you're not old enough to drive."

"So? I've driven plenty of times."

Her eyes rounded in surprise, and Rick could tell she didn't like what she'd heard.

Rick knew he should ignore the kid, but something tugged a response from him. "Your mother's right. It wouldn't matter if you had years of driving experience, you could still get the car stuck."

The kid swore and kicked at a chunk of ice. The woman sent Rick a grateful smile—nothing more than a gentle curve of her lips, but the transformation caught him off guard. He hadn't realized how young she was until she stopped scowling.

He pushed aside an unexpected twinge of something he thought must be sympathy and started toward the truck's bed for a length of rope. "Let's get your car tied to the truck."

She nodded and released her grip on the collar of her coat. "That sounds great. Thank you. By the way, I'm Marti Johansson and this is my son, Cameron."

"Rick Dennehy," he said, then turned to Cameron.

"If you'll push from behind while your mom steers, we should be able to keep the car out of the ditch."

Cameron looked as if he wanted to argue, but he didn't. He gave one curt nod and inched toward the back of the car. Rick dropped to the ground and slid under the truck. His jacket did little to keep the cold away, and the denim of his jeans did even less. Shivering, he tugged off his gloves with his teeth and secured one end of the rope to the truck's frame.

He could hear Marti and Cameron whispering, but he couldn't make out what they said until Cameron's voice rose slightly as Rick came out from beneath the truck. "If *you* don't ask him what he's doing here, *I* will."

Brushing snow from his jeans, Rick scowled. The kid's attitude was beginning to grate on him. "Maybe you ought to tell me what *you're* doing here."

"*We* belong here." The words snapped from the kid's mouth. "My grandpa owns the Lazy M Ranch."

That explained a lot. Cameron had obviously inherited his grandpa's sunny personality. "Well, then," Rick said with a forced smile. "It looks as if we're neighbors. I bought this stretch of land from your grandfather a few years back."

Marti's blue eyes widened slightly. "You're the one who built the cabins?"

"I am," he said. "Obviously, you've heard about them."

She nodded, but she looked slightly uncomfortable. "Dad's mentioned them."

In spite of the cold and his growing irritation with Cameron, Rick laughed at her tactful phrasing. "I'll bet he has."

Mischief tweaked the corners of her mouth, but she didn't elaborate. "Cameron and I flew in from California this morning. We'll be staying with Dad for the holidays."

"Then I imagine we'll be bumping into each other from time to time." To his surprise, he didn't mind the possibility.

She slanted a glance at the car and grinned up at him. "Yes, but hopefully not this way again."

Something—her eyes, her smile, her laugh—pulled an uncomfortable response from Rick. He didn't take time to analyze it. Instead, he laughed softly. "No. Hopefully not."

She fell silent, and only the rush of wind through the treetops, the echo of Rick's laugh and the almost palpable hostility from Cameron disturbed the tranquillity.

Rick cleared his throat and shifted his weight. With Jocelyn's memory so close, his laughter suddenly seemed like a betrayal. "I guess we'd better get to work," he said, "or we'll be here all day."

He tied the rope to the frame of Marti's car, climbed back into the cab of his truck and started the engine. He watched Marti say something to Cameron. In response, the boy gestured angrily toward the bridge.

Even from this distance Rick could tell Marti had to exert a great deal of self-control when she responded. He had no desire to step into the middle of a family argument, but he couldn't help wondering why the kid was so angry with her. It might be the age, he thought. Other than his limited experience with Jocelyn's nieces, Ashley and Kendra, he knew next to nothing about kids. Not that he hadn't wanted children. They just hadn't been in the cards.

Jocelyn hadn't wanted to get pregnant until her career was off and running. Every year, they'd pushed their estimated date for starting a family further away, until Rick had finally realized that Jocelyn would never feel secure enough in her career to start their family. He'd been disappointed for a while, but he'd eventually adjusted. And now, watching Cameron with Marti, he thought maybe he'd been lucky.

When Marti finally slipped behind the wheel of the car and Cameron took up his position near the trunk, Rick backed the truck slowly along the ice. The rope snapped taut and jerked the front of the car toward him. Marti worked the steering wheel while Cameron used his legs and back to keep it from sliding any farther toward the ditch.

Twice, Rick thought they'd lost the battle. He fought frustration, knowing he could do nothing but inch the truck backward and keep the rope taut. Somehow, Marti and Cameron managed to keep the car on the road and, after what felt like forever, it slid to the center of the road and out of danger.

Breathing a sigh of relief, Rick turned off the truck's ignition and climbed down to untie the rope. But this time, Cameron beat him to the job. When he'd finished, Cameron flicked a surprisingly non-hostile glance at him and tossed him the rope. But when he turned to his mother, the anger roared to life again. "So? Are we going to Grandpa's, or are you going to stay here and talk all day?"

"We're going." Marti's eyes clouded with embarrassment and her cheeks flamed, but she didn't say a word to Cameron about his attitude. She just sent Rick one last sheepish smile. "Thanks again. I can't thank you enough for all your help."

"No problem. Glad to do it." That much was true, anyway. He couldn't have left her car straddling the road. He climbed quickly into his truck, relishing the warmth from the heater, and backed out of her way.

He watched as she drove slowly across the wooden bridge toward her father's house. Even after she'd disappeared, the image of her clear blue eyes and warm, friendly smile stayed with him.

Cameron might have inherited his attitude from his grandpa, but it had obviously skipped a generation.

CHAPTER TWO

SMILING SOFTLY, Marti drove away from the encounter by the bridge and started up the narrow snow-covered road toward the Lazy M Ranch. Rick Dennehy had surprised her. Her father had been so upset at having to sell part of the Lazy M, she'd pictured the man and his wife as evil incarnate. But Rick had actually been friendly, pleasant and more than a little helpful.

Cameron scowled, as if he couldn't stand seeing her smile. "Are you going to tell Grandpa about what happened back there?"

She hesitated before answering. She didn't know why she did. The rental car hadn't been damaged, and nobody had been hurt. But knowing how her dad felt about Rick and his cabins made her apprehensive. "I don't know," she said at last. "Nothing actually happened, did it?"

Cameron's frown deepened. "No, but not because of anything *you* did."

Marti refused to let him goad her into another argument. "I never said it wasn't my fault. I didn't expect anyone else to be on the road."

Cameron responded with nothing more than a sideways glance and a roll of his eyes. He slouched in his seat and stared out at the valley through the windshield.

His constant tension exhausted her. She sent him a

thin smile and tried to change the subject. "What do you want to bet Grandpa's sitting by the window, watching for us?"

He lifted both shoulders in a listless shrug. "Probably."

"He'll be glad to see you."

"Probably," he said again. He waited a moment, then turned a challenging glance in her direction. "I'm going to spend tonight at Dad's."

Marti struggled not to respond in the same tone of voice. She'd long ago learned that rising to his bait only made him more defiant. "I think we should both stay at Grandpa's tonight. Tomorrow we can decide when you and your dad can get together."

"I don't want to spend tonight at Grandpa's."

"Maybe not, but that's what I'd like you to do. I don't want you to start out this visit by hurting your grandpa's feelings."

"It won't hurt his feelings," Cameron protested. "He won't mind if I want to see my dad. It's *you* who doesn't want me to. You're using Grandpa as an excuse."

"That's not true," Marti insisted, but she wondered if there might be a spark of truth in his accusation.

"That's why you made me move to California in the first place," he insisted. "To keep us apart."

Marti battled to keep her voice from rising. "We moved to California because we needed a fresh start. I couldn't stay here after the divorce."

"*I* could have."

"Not without me." She glanced over at him. "I'm really not in the mood to have this argument again. We've been over it at least a million times."

"Yeah, and you always say the same old thing. You don't care what Dad wants. Or me. You only care about what you want."

The accusation stung. "I care very much about what you want and about what's good for you. The court granted me custody of you for a reason. Like it or not, I'm responsible for making decisions for you until you're eighteen."

Angry red crept up Cameron's cheeks. He looked away. "You can't make me do anything."

"Don't try me." She steered around another curve and, at the first sight of her childhood home, pumped the brakes lightly to slow the car. The familiar two-story ranch house sat on a knoll and looked out over the narrow valley through huge plate-glass windows. Snow covered the roof, and smoke curled from the chimney into the gray sky. Blankets of white coated nearby pine and aspen trees as well as the steep mountains behind the house. The scene looked warm and inviting, like something from a Christmas card.

"I'd almost forgotten how beautiful it is," she whispered, more to herself than Cameron.

"That's because we've been gone so long." Did she only imagine it, or did his voice sound a little less brittle?

Wanting desperately to believe it, she relented slightly. "As soon as we've unloaded the car, you can call your dad and let him know we're here."

"Gee, thanks." Cameron's lip curled and whatever softening she might have imagined disappeared.

Marti forced herself not to respond. When he got like this, nothing she could say made any difference. She accelerated slowly, pulled into the yard and stopped the car in front of the house. Almost immediately, her father opened the front door and stepped outside. He looked far older than she'd expected and smaller inside his coveralls than when she left Gunnison three years before, but a broad smile stretched his rugged face and warmed her heart.

Pulling the keys from the ignition, she glanced at Cameron. "Let's not talk about this right now. Grandpa doesn't need to hear us arguing before we even get inside the house."

Cameron climbed out of the car without responding and slammed the door between them. Marti watched him cross the yard toward his grandpa. For a moment, he looked happy again—young and eager and full of life the way he'd always been as a small boy, but she knew her son's mood wouldn't last more than a second after she joined them.

She climbed out of the car and followed slowly. When her father released Cameron from a bear hug, she stepped into his embrace. Leaning against his chest, she breathed in the familiar scents of burning wood and fresh air. She could have stayed that way forever, but Henry Maddock had never been comfortable with physical displays of emotion.

Releasing her quickly, he took a step backward and nodded toward the car. "You made it."

Marti smiled at his habit of stating the obvious, but Cameron's expression tightened. "Barely. Mom almost got us into an accident by the bridge."

She should have known he wouldn't honor her request to keep the incident between them.

Her father turned a concerned gaze on her. "By the

bridge? With who? Nobody should have been on that road."

"Rick Dennehy," Marti said. "But it wasn't any big deal. I just came around the curve too fast and skidded a little."

Cameron snorted in derision. "A little? He had to pull the car back onto the road."

Her father scowled. "You went off the road?"

"No," Marti said quickly. "We just slid sideways."

"Are you okay? Did anybody get hurt?"

Marti shook her head. "We're fine, and so is the car."

Henry studied her for a long moment, then turned to Cameron as if he thought the boy might tell him something different.

To her relief, Cameron shrugged. "We're okay."

Her father accepted Cameron's word, but refused to let the matter drop. "I knew the minute I heard Dennehy had come back that he'd cause trouble."

"He didn't cause anything, Dad." Marti touched his arm gently. "I'm the one who made the mistake. I've forgotten how to drive on the snow."

Henry shook his head and held out one hand. "Well, after that, you probably need to sit down for a spell. Give me your keys and go inside where it's warm. Cameron and I will unload the car."

Though Marti could have helped and made the job easier, she knew better than to argue. Henry Maddock had definite ideas about the roles of the sexes. Neither Marti nor her sister, Carol, had ever been able to change his mind and, at nearly seventy, he wasn't likely to suddenly become enlightened.

Dropping the keys into his hand, she walked back to

the car, pulled out her purse and laptop computer, then followed the narrow path through the snow to the front door.

The instant she stepped inside, she felt as if she'd never been away. She might have been ten years old again, looking at the fire blazing in the fireplace, the sturdy sofa facing it, the crocheted afghan lying across the sofa's back. She could almost see her brothers—Jed lounging in an armchair by the fire, Neal on the floor. She imagined her sister, Carol, doing homework on the heavy pine coffee table, and her mother knitting while she watched them all. But they weren't there, and a fine layer of dust and stacks of outdoors magazines scattered around the room reminded her that those days would never be again.

To her surprise, her father had done nothing to prepare for Christmas. The huge pine wreath wasn't hanging above the fireplace, the garlands weren't winding their way up the banister, the tree wasn't standing guard in the wide front window. Every year Marti's mother had decorated the house on the day after Thanksgiving. She'd covered everything with brass horns, red bows and her collection of carved wooden Santas. Marti had kept up the tradition until she moved away. Now, without everything in place, the house looked empty—only half-alive.

Sighing, Marti shrugged off her coat and hung it in the hall closet. She turned around just as Cameron stomped inside carrying both suitcases. Without a word, he brushed past her and started up the stairs.

She followed and made another effort to put their argument behind them. "Which room does Grandpa want you to take?"

Cameron dropped her suitcase at the top of the stairs and started down the back hallway with his own. "The little one up here," he said over his shoulder. "What else?"

Of all the empty bedrooms on the second floor, her dad had given Cameron the one farthest from her own. She supposed she shouldn't be surprised. Her father kept their childhood bedrooms empty, even when he knew no one would be coming to visit. Grandchildren and other visitors always stayed in the small upstairs bedroom or the guest room on the first floor.

As Marti picked up her suitcase, she told herself to be glad he'd put Cameron upstairs rather than alone on the first floor where he could sneak out without her hearing him.

She followed the main hallway to the front of the house and opened the door to her old room. Like downstairs, nothing had changed. Her narrow bed still stood where it always had, and the dresser and night tables held their time-honored positions. The blue flowered curtains and matching bedspread were the ones she'd had as a young girl, though the colors had faded a bit. She'd spent many happy hours in this room, sharing secrets with her best friend, Cherryl, whose mother, Greta, still ran the grocery store. Life had seemed so simple then, and suddenly she longed to hear Cherryl's voice again. Hopefully, they'd find time to get together during Marti's visit.

Slipping off her shoes, she resisted the impulse to lie on the bed even for a minute. A minute could easily stretch into an hour, and she knew Henry would want her to come back downstairs so they could visit before dinner.

A soft noise in the doorway pulled her around just as her father stepped into the room. He lowered her overnight case and duffel bag to the floor, placed a hand on his back and straightened again. "Well? How does it look?"

"It looks wonderful, Dad. Nothing's changed."

"Nope." He smiled, as she'd known he would, and gestured around the room as he stepped inside. "I give it a once-over every month or so. Your aunt Martha stopped by and put clean sheets on the beds yesterday."

"I'll call to thank her," she promised. "Next time, though, I can do that when we get here. There's no sense bothering Aunt Martha."

"She doesn't mind," her father said, crossing to the window that overlooked the front yard. "In fact, she's glad to help out when one of you kids decides to come home."

His implication wasn't lost on Marti. She knew she didn't come home often enough to please him. He'd been disappointed when Jed and Neal went away to college, one right after the other, and disheartened when they'd both chosen to pursue careers in other states after graduation.

But he'd been equally disappointed in his daughters. Carol had gone to college for a year, then dropped out to marry Bud Waverly. Henry hadn't approved of Bud at the time, and Bud hadn't been able to change her father's mind during the intervening fifteen years. After Carol's marriage, her father had focused his hopes on Marti—or, more accurately, on her marriage.

After she married Gil, her father had made no secret of his plans to leave the ranch to them. But her divorce had thrown everything into disarray again, and her father's belief that a woman alone couldn't handle the Lazy M had influenced her decision to leave Gunnison. She hadn't wanted to watch a stranger take over this land she loved.

With effort, she pushed aside an unwelcome surge of old resentment and picked up her duffel bag. "What do you want me to fix for dinner tonight?"

Her father glanced at her over his shoulder. "Martha left a casserole in the fridge. I figured we'd just heat that up tonight. There isn't much else in the kitchen."

Marti pulled several blouses on hangers from her bag and started toward the closet. "Does Martha fix many meals for you, or is this a special occasion?"

"She brings extras over once in a while," he admitted. "A couple of times a week, maybe."

Marti turned to ask something else, but when she noticed Cameron in the open doorway, she forgot what she'd been about to say.

The boy held himself rigid, his eyes flashed and his chin jutted out the way it always did before he started an argument. "I called Dad," he said. "He wasn't home, but I left a message telling him to pick me up tonight."

Marti glared at him. "Call him back and tell him not to come."

"No way. I told you I was going over there tonight."

"And I told you to stay here."

Henry turned away from the window and let his gaze travel from one to the other. "What's all this?"

Cameron put on an innocent expression and took a

step toward him. "I want to see my dad, but she won't let me."

"That's not true," Marti said. "I simply asked you to wait until tomorrow."

The teenager lifted his eyebrows at Henry, as if her response somehow proved his point.

Rubbing his chin, her father started toward her. "Well, now, I don't see any real harm in letting the boy see his father—"

"I never said he couldn't," Marti interrupted. "I just asked him to stay here tonight."

Her father put a hand on her shoulder. "I don't think it'll hurt anything if you let him go."

Marti had no intention of letting Cameron manipulate the situation. "I've given Cameron his answer, and I'm not going to change my mind." To her son, she said again, "Call your dad and leave another message."

Cameron's face reddened. "No."

"Do it," she insisted, "or I will."

"Fine," Cameron shouted. "Do it, then. I'm not going to." He pivoted away and stomped down the hall. His boots echoed on the hardwood floor and matched the sudden steady pounding in Marti's head. She bit back frustration and shoved a lock of hair from her face.

"Don't you think you're being a little hard on him?" Henry asked.

"No, I don't. You have no idea what's happened to bring us to this point."

"Maybe not," he said slowly, "but I know that boy, and I know he doesn't usually act that way."

She started to answer, but when she heard Cameron

go down the stairs, she abandoned the argument. She
didn't want him to run away—not now, not here, not
in the bitter cold miles from anywhere. She hurried
toward the door, but Henry stepped in front of her.

"Stay here," he ordered. "If you go after him now,
you'll just drive him away."

"Then *you* stop him. He'll run away. He always
does."

If she'd expected sympathy from her father, she'd
have been bitterly disappointed. He cocked an eyebrow
at her, and the expression in his eyes left no doubt he
thought she was the one at fault.

"One of us has to stop him," she insisted, and tried
to push past him.

"I'll talk to him." Henry turned away, motioning
her toward the bed. "You stay here."

Battling discouragement, she sank to the foot of the
bed. The flight, the long drive and the near accident
had taken their toll. She didn't have the energy for
another argument.

A second later, she jumped up again and trailed her
father as far as her bedroom door. Her father wouldn't
be able to change Cameron's mind. He had such a soft
spot for the boy, he'd probably let Cameron have his
own way. And that would undermine everything she'd
been trying to do. Cameron's counselors had warned
her that he would see compromise as weakness. Even
if she wanted to, she couldn't afford to relent, even for
an instant.

CAMERON HEARD his mom calling him as he walked
away, but he ignored her. He heard his grandpa move
down the hallway after him, but he didn't stop. If he

did, his mom would make him stay. She'd get right in his face and yell at him—well, not *yell* exactly, but she'd talk a lot. And she'd give him a hundred reasons why he should stay here tonight instead of going to see his dad.

Cameron didn't want to stay at his grandpa's house, not even for one night. He hadn't seen his dad in three years and now, with his dad less than ten miles away, he didn't want to wait even one day longer to spend time with him.

Right after the divorce, Cameron had believed his mom's stories about why he never got to see his dad. His dad had been busy that first summer after his mom made him move away. Cameron knew that. His dad was a busy man. But when Christmas came and went without a visit, and the next summer passed the same way, Cameron had started getting suspicious. Especially since every time his dad called, he promised to bring Cameron home for a visit. So lately, when his mom claimed that his dad couldn't work out a visit, Cameron knew who to blame. Somehow, his mom was screwing him over with his dad. He just knew it.

Moving faster now, he started down the stairs.

His grandpa picked up his pace and called him again. "Cameron, hold on there. Wait just a minute."

Yeah, sure. Wait just a minute so his mom could make up more excuses. Next thing Cameron knew, she'd claim his dad didn't want to see him this Christmas, either.

He stopped partway down the stairs and turned back. His mom stood just inside the door to her room. She'd put on that pathetic face she used sometimes to make him feel bad. But it didn't work. It hadn't worked in a long time. "I don't know why that stupid judge ever made me stay with you," he shouted at her. "I'll bet he didn't know what a bitch you are."

He could tell by the look on her face that the words hurt her. A little guilt wormed its way up his spine, but he didn't let it bug him. After all, she deserved it. She didn't care about him anymore. She only cared about the stupid articles she wrote for that stupid travel magazine, and taking him to counselors so people would think she cared.

He waited for a second, hoping he'd made her mad enough this time to show some emotion, to yell or something. But, as usual, she just stood there, clenching and unclenching her fists. Her face turned red, but she didn't say anything.

Anger coiled through him. He couldn't believe her. He'd just called her a bitch, and she didn't even say a word. Nothing. Before the divorce, he'd heard his dad say that she didn't have any feelings. The more Cameron thought about it, the more he decided his dad must be right. She probably didn't even have a heart anymore.

When his grandpa drew even with the top step, Cameron shot one last look at his mom and bolted down the stairs. He grabbed his coat and ran out the door. The cold sucked his breath away, but he didn't let it hold him up. He wouldn't stay there and listen to her lies. Not tonight.

He ran down the driveway to the dirt road, slipping on the ice several times before he turned toward the bridge. He had a plan—walk to the nearest house and ask to use their telephone to call his dad again. He knew what would happen when his dad got his messages. He'd be so glad to hear from Cameron, he'd rush right over to pick him up. That would show her. She'd realize Cameron was onto her lies, and maybe she'd stop telling them.

Before he'd gone even thirty feet, he changed his mind. He'd be stupid to follow the road to the bridge. She could see the road from her bedroom window and he didn't want her to know where he'd gone.

Changing direction suddenly, he plunged through the knee-high snowdrifts and made his way into the trees. Snow fell into the tops of his boots and wet the bottoms of his pant legs. The cold, dry air burned his lungs and hurt his nose and cheeks, but Cameron kept going. If she was watching, and he hoped she was, maybe she'd actually worry about him. He hoped so. At least she'd feel something.

RICK POSITIONED a log on the tree stump behind the main cabin, swung his ax in an arc, and split the log in two. After working in the frigid air for only twenty minutes, he'd already worked up a heavy sweat.

Pulling a bandanna from his pocket, he mopped his face and checked his progress. Not much. Certainly not enough to last more than overnight. At this rate, he'd never find time to fix the cabins—he'd be spending every minute of every day chopping wood.

Pushing one piece to the ground with the ax blade, he swung again. The muscles in his arms and back protested the unaccustomed exertion. Wincing, he tried to hold back a groan, but it escaped anyway. Once, he'd prided himself on staying fit. But the last two years behind a desk had left him in no better shape than the executives he'd once sneered at.

Lifting his gaze to check the clouds again, he glimpsed smoke curling into the slate-gray sky through the trees on Henry Maddock's side of the river. He wondered idly whether Marti Johansson had found time to settle in and whether that son of hers had stopped behaving like a spoiled brat.

Shaking his head a little, Rick lifted the half log onto the stump and swung the ax again. But exhaustion and sore muscles marred his aim. Instead of splitting the log in two, he only succeeded in chipping off a thin piece of wood and nearly struck his leg with the blade on the downswing.

He stepped back quickly and glared at the ax as if it were responsible. His breath puffed in thick clouds. The air bit through his jeans and reminded him he needed to finish before the temperature dropped even lower as night fell. He'd hoped—foolishly, he saw now—that he could make do with hand tools. But honesty forced him to admit that one seriously out-of-shape pencil pusher couldn't chop enough wood this way. He'd have to put out the money for a chain saw and log-splitter.

As he bent to pick up another log, an odd whisper of sound reached him. He sucked in his breath and listened. He'd never been nervous in these woods. In fact, when he and Jocelyn first bought the place, he'd discovered he liked the isolation and silence. But something about this particular noise made him uneasy.

The sound came again a few seconds later, and this time he realized it came from the wooded area behind him. Turning slowly, he scanned the forest and tried to convince himself it was only a small forest creature darting into some bush. But his heart beat a little faster, and for the space of a breath, he expected Jocelyn to step out of the woods and walk toward him.

As always, when he thought of her unexpectedly, a dull ache filled his heart. He tried to push it away. But her memory was harder to fight in these surroundings than it had been in Denver.

Swearing under his breath, he tossed the ax to the frozen ground a few feet away and picked up an armful of split logs. He'd work. Keep his mind occupied. Force away the need to have her back—if just for five minutes—so he could tell her everything he'd kept to himself when she was alive. No matter how much he wanted another chance to make things right, he wouldn't get one. Not now. Not ever.

He'd failed Jocelyn because he didn't know the right way to behave in a committed relationship. God knew, his parents hadn't been much of an example. Their entire marriage had been like his last night with Jocelyn. Rick had watched them volley insults and injuries and keep score of hits and misses as if arguing was a game to them. As a young man, he'd vowed never to let himself fall into that trap. But when Jocelyn hurt him, he'd turned into his father and extracted revenge by hurting her in return.

And now he'd have to live with regret for all the things he hadn't said, all the words he couldn't take back, all the wrongs he hadn't righted for the rest of his life. But at least he'd learned his lesson. He wouldn't let himself get caught in the trap again.

Pushing aside his thoughts, he crossed the clearing, stacked the logs against the back of the cabin and retraced his steps. As he started to gather more wood, the sound reached him again—louder this time.

Straightening, he glanced into the deepening shadows between the trees. This time, he saw something or someone duck behind a tree—someone tall and shadowy and very human. Not Jocelyn, of course, but someone else. Someone who didn't want him to know he was being watched.

He filled his arms and started back toward the house, keeping one eye on his visitor as he worked. The shadow didn't move again until Rick pretended to look away. Then it darted from the tree and hid behind another a few feet closer. Just before it disappeared again, the waning light revealed a lanky body and a long sheaf of blond hair.

Rick pushed to his feet and walked past the stump and the logs, straight toward Cameron's hiding place. "You might as well come out and tell me what you're doing."

No answer.

Rick stopped a few feet from the tree and tried again. "Come on out, Cameron. I know you're there. There's no sense hiding."

Hands on hips in a gesture he probably thought looked tough, Cameron stepped from behind the tree and glared at Rick. "I'm not hiding."

"All right. You're not hiding. What are you doing?"

"Taking a walk."

"In this weather?"

Cameron shifted his weight and glanced at the sky. *"This?"* He snorted a laugh. "This is nothing. It's not even cold."

"It could start snowing any second."

"So?"

"So, I'd hate for you to get lost out here."

"Lost?" Cameron's scowl deepened. "I was raised in these woods. I don't *get* lost."

"I see." With a shrug, Rick started to turn away. "My mistake."

"I need to use a telephone," the boy called after him. "Have you got one?"

Rick turned back again. "Yes."

"Can I use it?"

"Is it a local call?"

The boy nodded. "I've gotta call my dad."

Rick refrained from asking why he couldn't call from his grandfather's house. He simply nodded toward the back door and hoped he wasn't making a mistake by letting the boy inside alone. "There's a phone in the kitchen."

Cameron walked away, but when he reached the back step, he seemed to remember something. Turning, he shouted, "Thanks."

Oddly pleased that the boy had *some* manners, Rick nodded and bent again to his task. Despite his aching muscles, he forced himself to pick up another armful of wood.

Within minutes, the back door opened again and Cameron stepped outside. He still wore that dark scowl, but this time it looked more disappointed than sullen. He watched in silence for a few minutes, then shouted, "You're doing that the hard way, you know."

Rick lifted his head to look at him. "Doing what?"

Using his chin, Cameron pointed at the stump and the logs. "Cutting that wood. You're doing it the hard way."

Rick started to say he knew, but something in the boy's expression held him back. Frowning slightly, he glanced at the wood before meeting Cameron's gaze again. "Yeah? You mean I don't have to kill myself to do this?"

"If you had a chain saw," Cameron said, taking another step closer, "you could cut all those logs in a couple of hours."

"Well, then, I guess I'll have to get one."

Moving still closer, the kid stuffed his hands into the back pockets of his jeans. "Why are you opening the cabins again if you don't even know what you're doing?"

For some reason Rick couldn't explain, he didn't tell the kid the truth. Instead, he shrugged and said, "I guess I'll learn as I go."

Cameron rolled his eyes, then studied the smoke curling over the trees in the distance. "It sure looks different over here with all these cabins."

Rick stooped to pick up another log. "I guess it probably does."

"I used to play here all the time when I was a kid. Grandpa even let me build a clubhouse."

That must have been the ramshackle collection of boards Rick had cleared away when they'd started building the main cabin.

Rick pretended not to notice the wistful expression on the boy's face. "So, I take it you're pretty handy to have around. Your grandpa must be glad to have you on the ranch."

Cameron shrugged. "Not really. He doesn't do much anymore. Too old." He looked away for a second, then asked, "So, when are you opening the cabins again?"

"They're too rundown to rent right now," Rick said truthfully.

With a smirk Cameron glanced around the clearing at the smaller cabins. "You're right about that. So, what are you going to do, spend the rest of the winter fixing them up?"

"No. I have to be back in Denver in a month."

Cameron rubbed his hands together for warmth. "Then you'd better hire somebody to help you. You'll never get the cabins ready that soon."

Rick couldn't argue with that. The harsh winters had done more damage to the unused cabins than he'd imagined, even with Bix's warning. "You're probably right, but I'm on a tight budget. I can't afford to pay somebody."

Cameron shifted his weight and hooked his thumbs into his back pockets. "Maybe you could. I know somebody who needs a job, and he wouldn't charge you much."

"You do? Who is it?"

"Me."

"You?" Rick didn't even try to hide his surprise.

Cameron nodded. "I need to make some money so I can..." He paused, glanced uneasily at Rick, then finished in a rush. "I just need it, okay? Besides, I need *something* to do while my dad's at work."

"I take it your dad lives around here?"

Cameron nodded again. "Down in Gunnison. That's where we used to live until Mom screwed everything up." Some of the bitterness crept back into his voice.

"How'd she screw everything up?"

"She divorced him." The words came out sharp and angry.

Rick nodded slowly, remembering how angry he'd been when his parents divorced and the long months when he'd refused to speak to his father. "Divorce can be rough," he admitted, "but at least you can still see your dad."

"Only when I'm here, not when I'm in California."

Rick started across the clearing carrying an armful of wood. "I know. I've been through it, myself."

"You're divorced?"

"No, my wife passed away. But my parents were divorced." Rick stacked the logs and turned back to face Cameron.

"It sucks, doesn't it?"

"It's not pleasant, but—"

"It sucks." Cameron's face started to close down again.

Rick decided not to push. He wiped his forehead with the sleeve of his jacket. "What's your dad's name? Maybe I know him."

"Gil Johansson."

Rick nodded slowly. He'd met Gil once or twice when he and Jocelyn had first come to town. He hadn't been impressed, but he certainly wouldn't admit that to Cameron. He zipped his jacket and tried to lead the conversation to a more comfortable subject. "If I hired you, how much would you expect me to pay you?"

Cameron thought for a second or two, then named a figure.

Reasonable enough, Rick supposed, considering how much work he had ahead of him. Running his fingers through his hair, he studied the boy while he deliberated, but it didn't take long. The anticipation in the kid's eyes got the best of him. "Is this going to be all right with your mom?"

Cameron lifted both shoulders. "She doesn't care what I do."

Rick didn't believe that, but he didn't argue. He'd check with Marti himself. "What about your grandpa?"

"I can talk him into it."

Rick picked up a small piece of wood and tossed it to Cameron. "All right. You've got a deal. You can help me when you're not with your dad. As long as you're here now, you might as well work. I'd like to get all this firewood stacked against the main house before nightfall."

Cameron caught the wood easily, and grinned. Almost immediately, he wiped the smile away and tried to look as if he didn't care. "All right, I guess. If you say so." He turned away and picked up a few more logs.

Rick watched him for a minute before getting back to work himself. He might be making a mistake by giving the kid a job, but he *could* use the help. And days filled with physical labor might help Cameron burn off some of his hostility. And that might make some of the worry in Marti Johansson's eyes disappear.

The thought surprised him. Why should he care whether Marti worried or not? He didn't even know her. But for some reason he couldn't explain, the idea of making her pain disappear appealed to him.

CHAPTER THREE

MARTI SLIPPED into her coat and stepped outside onto the wide front porch. She'd been waiting for Cameron for nearly an hour, but he still hadn't come home. Her father didn't seem too worried. After telling her to relax, he'd closed himself inside his study. But he didn't understand. He didn't know Cameron these days.

The evening sun had already dropped below the western mountains, the sky had turned from winter-gray to charcoal, and she couldn't hide her concern any longer. Checking her watch for the umpteenth time, she called Cameron's name and watched the shadows for some sign of him. No one answered.

Something moist hit her cheek—first one flake, then another—and the panic she'd barely managed to keep at bay consumed her. Cameron was alone in the forest he hadn't seen in three years, and she had no idea where to find him.

Stepping off the porch, she followed his footsteps through the yard to the edge of the clearing. She could tell from the length of his stride, he'd been angry and probably walking fast. If he'd kept going in the same direction through the trees, he'd have ended up at the river. Maybe she'd find him there, sitting on a rock at the river's edge. If not...

She didn't let herself finish the thought. She wanted

to believe Cameron would come inside before the weather got worse. She and Gil, in a rare burst of unity, had tried to instill a healthy respect for nature into their son. But Cameron wasn't thinking clearly and he was at that frustrating age—certain he could control the situations in which he found himself.

She thought about searching for him on foot, but immediately changed her mind. If the storm worsened, not only might she never find him, but she could easily lose her own way. She'd be far wiser to use the car.

Turning back, she rushed to the house, raced up the stairs and grabbed her purse from her bed. Digging her keys from its depths, she hurried downstairs again and reached the bottom step just as her father strode through the door of the study and straight into her path.

He took in her coat, bag and frantic expression immediately. "What's wrong?"

"Cameron's not back yet, and it's starting to snow. I'm going to drive down to the bridge and see if I can find him."

"He's not back yet?" Her father's sudden frown made her feel a little better, but not much. "Where in the hell is he?"

"He could be anywhere, Dad. That's what I've been trying to tell you. He does things like this without thinking. For all I know, he's fallen into the river, or decided to walk into town."

"He wouldn't—"

"He might. You don't know what he's like these days."

Henry stepped around her to the closet and reached inside for his jacket. "You stay here. I'll go."

"No, Dad. *I* need to find him. He left because he was angry with me."

"Maybe," her father admitted. He glanced outside and scowled. "But a storm like this is no place for you, little girl. I know what I'm doing out there. The best thing you can do is stay here in case he comes back."

Frustration mixed with resentment and brought the flush of anger to her cheeks. "I'm not a little girl," she said, tugging open the door and stepping through. "I'm Cameron's mother."

"I know you are."

"I'm more than capable of driving through a little snow to find my son."

Her father sighed in exasperation. "We're not going to have that argument now, are we?"

"Not unless you want to," she snapped.

He looked past her to the storm. "You're too stubborn by half, girl."

If so, she'd learned at the feet of the master.

He sighed again. "All right. Go. I'll look around here a bit. But if you don't find him within half an hour, come on back. We'll call Gil and some others to help look."

Marti didn't want Gil involved, but she didn't argue. She'd find Cameron herself. She *had* to. She hurried from the porch to the car and drove slowly down the driveway. She let the car creep along the winding road toward the bridge and called for Cameron every few feet through her open window.

When she reached the bridge, still without any sign of him, she pulled to the side of the road, climbed out of the car and inched her way to the middle of the bridge. Glassy black ice covered the wooden planks and made her progress frustratingly slow. Thick snowflakes nearly obscured her vision. But she didn't give up.

Midway across the bridge, she stopped walking and clutched a two-by-four cross beam for support. Leaning slightly forward, she searched the gathering shadows, but the ever-increasing snowfall made it almost impossible to see.

Fighting panic, she checked the river and the brush along its banks then crossed to the opposite side of the bridge and looked downriver. Still no sign of him.

She tried desperately to calm herself, but she knew that if he'd walked even half a mile in either direction, she wouldn't be able to see him from here. Nor would she be able to see him from the highway—the forest was too dense.

The snow began to fall faster, thicker, rendering the world around her silent except for the too-rapid beating of her heart. She moved a few steps farther along the bridge, searching frantically and trying to decide what to do next.

Between the trees, a light flickered. Rick Dennehy's cabin. In her panic, she'd almost forgotten about her father's new neighbors. Maybe Rick or his wife had seen Cameron walking along the riverbank. Maybe they could help her decide where to look next.

Inching back to the car, she settled behind the wheel again and drove slowly across the bridge. Her windshield wipers slapped snow away, but thick, fresh flakes covered the glass again almost immediately. A few feet beyond the bridge, she turned into the tree-lined lane that led first to the main house, then to the other eight various-size and odd-shaped cabins that formed an open circle around a broad clearing.

She pulled in front of the main house and left the car running while she raced up the steps. Holding her breath, she knocked, waited a second, and knocked again. She told herself to remain calm. Nothing good would come of letting fear take over. But Cameron had been so angry when he stormed out of the house.

Muttering under her breath, she jerked open the heavy wood and mesh screen and pounded on the thick wooden door. "Come *on*. Open the damn door."

Just as she uttered the last four words, the door opened and she found herself staring up into Rick Dennehy's surprised face. He must have sensed her panic because the surprise vanished almost instantly and concern took its place. "Is something wrong?"

"My son is missing. Have you or your wife seen him? He might have been walking along the river, or crossing the bridge, or…"

Rick stepped back and gestured toward the room behind him. "Come on in."

"No." She shook her head quickly. "Thank you, but I don't have time. The snow is coming down fast, I'm afraid he'll become disoriented in the dark."

"He's here. In the house. He's been helping me stack firewood, and I just fixed him a cup of cocoa so he could warm up."

"Cameron's been helping you?"

Rick pulled open the door a few inches farther. "We're talking about the kid who was with you this afternoon, right?"

"Yes."

"That's the one. Come on in. You look like you could use something warm to drink, yourself."

Relief made her weak. She hesitated for a second and glanced over her shoulder at the beam from her headlights slicing through the snowfall. "I need to turn off the engine—"

"Let me do it." Rick took her keys and moved past her onto the porch, hunching his shoulders as he stepped into the storm. "Just go straight through to the kitchen. Cameron's in there."

Marti wiped her boots on the mat and walked through the living room into the cabin's small kitchen. Peeling off her gloves, she unbuttoned her coat and stared at Cameron who sat at the thick pine table, holding a mug of steaming cocoa in both hands. He didn't look up, but the surliness that had become so much a part of him had all but vanished.

She resisted the urge to rush across the room and hug him. "Cameron?"

At the sound of her voice, he glanced up and his expression went through a series of rapid changes and the hostility she'd grown to expect returned. "What?"

"What are you doing here?"

"Nothing."

He sounded so angry, her heart broke all over again, but she struggled to hide her reaction. One of the counselors had warned her that if Cameron knew how easily he could hurt her, he'd use it against her. "Mr. Dennehy said you'd been helping him stack firewood."

"Yeah? What of it?"

"Nothing. I just didn't expect to find you here. I've been worried."

Cameron glanced away and lowered his mug to the

table, but he clamped his lips together and didn't respond.

Marti's frustration doubled. But before she could do or say anything, Rick came through the doorway, shaking snow from his thick dark hair.

He filled the room with his presence. His shoulders stretched wide under his plaid wool shirt, and the scent of wood and fresh air—and something she couldn't identify—rushed her senses as he moved toward her and held out her keys. "It's snowing like the devil out there."

She took the keys, surprised by the warmth of his skin when their fingers brushed, and confused by her awareness of him.

He didn't seem to notice. He turned away and crossed to the stove in two strides. "Sit down and warm up. Do you want cocoa? Or should I put coffee on?"

"Nothing, thanks."

He glanced over his shoulder at her. "Sorry, that's not one of your options. You look half-frozen."

"Have something," Cameron snarled. "You don't have to make such a production out of everything."

Marti could feel the blood rushing to her face. But before she could respond, Rick turned to Cameron. He didn't say a word, just cocked one eyebrow in an expression of disapproval.

Marti expected Cameron's temper to flare, to hear him shout that this was none of Rick's business and stomp out of the house in a fit of anger. Instead, he merely shrugged and looked away.

Rick turned his gaze in her direction again and waited for her decision.

"Cocoa's fine," she muttered, and sat across the table from her son. "I'd like to thank you and your wife for seeing that Cameron is safe and warm."

Rick looked away quickly. "I'm here alone. My wife passed away two years ago."

"I'm sorry." Her words sounded weak and inadequate, but she didn't know what else to say.

"Thanks." He filled a mug and placed it on the table in front of her, then leaned one hip against the counter. "Cameron and I have been discussing business. He's offered to work for me for a few days."

"To work?" Marti looked from one to the other and tried not to sound stunned, but even she could hear the surprise in her voice.

Rick nodded. "The cabins are in horrible shape, and I've only got a month to get them fixed up." He looked as if he might say something else, then apparently thought better of it. "Cameron seems to know his way around, and I could use the help. But I don't want to accept his offer if you don't approve."

If she didn't *approve?* Marti wondered if she'd heard him right. She'd been trying for three years to interest Cameron in something—anything—besides his self-destructive friends. She studied Cameron's stony expression and tried to read the emotions there, but he'd closed himself off again. "When would you work?" she asked Cameron.

He lifted both shoulders in a lifeless shrug. "Whenever."

"I thought you wanted to spend time with your dad."

"I do. I won't work if I'm with Dad, but I'm not

going to sit around Grandpa's every day and stare at the walls just to make you happy."

His words pierced her, but again she tried not to show it. "I see. You want to avoid me."

Cameron didn't respond. He didn't need to—the smirk on his face said it all. His expression chilled her.

Vaguely aware of Rick moving closer, Marti pushed away the mug of cocoa with trembling hands.

"Maybe this isn't such a good idea," Rick said.

She shook her head and tried to smile, but her lips felt stiff and cold, and she could tell she had failed miserably. "No. If that's what he wants to do, I don't mind."

"Are you sure?"

"Of course." He kept his eyes riveted on hers for so long, she grew slightly uncomfortable. She managed a shaky laugh. "It's fine for Cameron to work for you. Really."

He smiled slowly, an infectious smile that drew an answering one from her. But when she turned toward Cameron, the icy look in his eyes made everything inside her grow numb. She could hear Rick's voice as he said something to Cameron, but she couldn't make out the words. Her hands trembled and her mind whirled. She watched Cameron respond to Rick and saw the hatred in the boy's eyes vanish for a moment. And she gave in to sudden, overwhelming despair.

All this time, she'd believed Cameron was angry with the world in general. But tonight, looking into his cold eyes and seeing how different he was around this stranger, she realized the truth for the first time. Her son hated *her*.

Somehow, she managed to pull herself together, to

keep her face from betraying her shock and heartache. When Cameron finished his cocoa, she stood and waited for him to get up. She couldn't be certain her legs would hold her, but she forced herself to lead him back through Rick's living room and out the door.

Still too shaken to speak, she drove slowly through the snow toward her father's house and darted frequent glances at Cameron across the front seat of the car. Shoulders tense, he stared out his window just as he'd been doing from the moment they'd driven away from Rick's cabin.

If she thought demands would get through to him, she'd create a list. If she believed for one moment that a motherly appeal would touch him, she'd beg. She was losing her son, and she felt powerless to stop it.

She turned through the gates to the Lazy M. Through the snowfall, she could see the dark outline of a vehicle that hadn't been there when she left earlier. A moment later, she recognized her ex-husband's Dodge truck and her heart dropped. Had her father called him to help look for Cameron?

She didn't want to see Gil right now. She didn't have the energy to explain the argument that had driven Cameron out into the storm. She didn't want Gil to know Cameron detested her.

Gil had been angry when the court awarded her custody of their only son, and livid when she'd decided to move away. In spite of his claims that he wanted Cameron to live with him, he'd presented one excuse after another to prevent Cameron from visiting that first summer. After that, Cameron had started getting into trouble and had spent most of each summer in make-up classes.

Cameron leapt from the car the second she pulled to a stop, and covered the distance to the house before she could get her own door open. Making an effort to hide her nervousness, she followed him across the snow and up the back steps into the kitchen.

She walked in just as Gil pulled Cameron into a quick hug, then held him at arm's length. "You've sprouted up, son. You look great."

Marti took in Gil's thick blond hair and rugged build, his hazel eyes and ready smile. She remembered when the sight of him had set her heart racing. But the two empty beer bottles and a third, half-empty on the table in front of him, brought back the other emotions she'd begun to feel shortly after their wedding.

He turned his gaze on her and whistled softly. "You look terrific, Marti. California must agree with you."

Forcing a smile, she unzipped her coat and shrugged it off. If Gil could be pleasant, so could she. For Cameron's sake. "I think it does." She paused and let her smile relax. "You look good, too."

Gil patted his stomach and grinned. "Yeah? I've lost a few pounds, I guess. I've been working hard."

Cameron plopped down in a chair beside Gil's and laced his fingers behind his head. "Are you going to stay for dinner?"

Gil glanced at Marti, obviously waiting for her to second the invitation. When she didn't, he looked back at their son. "Not tonight. I've got to get on home. I just stopped by to talk to your grandpa for a minute and to say hello to you and your mom."

The realization that her father hadn't called him brought Marti a measure of relief, which she hid.

Pushing away his beer bottle, Gil leaned back in his

seat. "Like I said, Henry, it seems to me there ought to be something you can do."

Marti poured a cup of coffee and held it between her hands, grateful for its warmth. "Do about what?"

Her father studied his fingernails, then glanced at Gil, as if he needed to check with him before he answered.

Gil didn't hesitate to tell her. "Your dad's worried about Dennehy opening those cabins again."

Marti glanced at Cameron for his reaction. He stared at her without blinking and she knew he didn't want her to tell his father and grandfather about the job he'd just accepted. She looked at Henry. "Why are you worried?" she asked.

"*Why?*" Her father stared at her incredulously. "Having people wandering all over the place will ruin the Lazy M, that's why."

"I don't think that will happen," Marti said.

Gil rolled his eyes, exactly the way Cameron always did when she said something he didn't like. "How do you know it won't?"

She lowered herself into the chair beside her father's. "How do you know it will?"

"He had them open for one summer before he left," Henry argued, "and I had nothing but trouble. I'll tell you, I thought I had trouble when those damn folks from Kansas City came through looking for a place to build their shop. But this—" He broke off and shook his head in despair. "This just might be worse."

"What folks?" Marti asked. "What shop?"

Gil waved her question away with one hand. "Don't change the subject. We're talking about Dennehy now."

Marti's cheeks flushed with embarrassment, but she did her best to ignore him. "Why don't you just talk to him, Dad? Tell him what your concerns are."

Gil covered one of her hands with his. "Marti, honey, why don't you leave this to your father and me? You can't be expected to understand."

She resented the endearment as much as she hated his condescending tone. "Why? Because I'm a woman?"

From across the table, Cameron sighed audibly.

Gil worked up a thin smile. "No, sweetheart. Because you've been away so long."

Henry snorted softly in agreement.

Marti didn't want Cameron to blame her for starting an argument, so she forced her voice to remain steady. "I haven't been gone that long."

"Things change," her father said slowly. "Times change. Three years is a long time to be away. You can't just step into a discussion as if you know what's going on."

She leaned an elbow on the table and rested her chin on her hand. "Then fill me in."

"Some other time, maybe," Gil said with a glance out the window. "I should go before the snow gets too deep. How about it, Cameron? Are you game for spending the weekend with me?"

Cameron's expression fell, but none of the hostility he reserved for Marti surfaced. "I was hoping I could go home with you tonight."

For half a second, Marti considered changing her mind and letting him go. Maybe that would make him a little less angry with her. But if she did, he'd find one excuse after another to stay with Gil, and she'd lose her only chance to mend things between them. "Not tonight, Cameron."

Gil frowned at her. "Why not?"

"Because I think he should stay here tonight. I've already told him no. Besides, you have to work tomorrow, don't you?"

Gil nodded reluctantly and scowled at Cameron. "Your mother already said no?"

Cameron nodded, but his eyes snapped with defiance. "Yeah, but it's stupid. She thinks Grandpa will feel bad. But he doesn't care if I go with you, do you, Grandpa?"

As she knew he would, her father shook his head. "No problem for me. I can see the boy later."

"That's not the point—"

But Gil cut Marti off. "If your mother already said no, son, then it's no. You'd better listen to her."

Marti couldn't believe what she'd just heard. Gil was actually supporting her.

Not surprisingly, Cameron's expression clouded. "But—"

"No buts." Gil clamped one hand on the boy's shoulder. "Your mother's right. I have to work all week. But I want you to spend the weekend with me—okay?"

"I don't mind being alone while you're working," Cameron argued. "I can find something to do."

Again Gil shook his head. "I don't think so, son. Let's do what your mother wants." Turning back to Marti, he lifted his eyebrows as if asking for her approval.

More than a little astonished, she smiled slowly.

Cameron sighed in disgust and pushed away from the table. "Fine."

Gil acted as if he hadn't heard the sarcasm in the boy's tone. He smiled, patted Cameron's shoulder once more and glanced again at Marti. "Do you mind stepping outside with me? I'd like to talk to you for a minute."

Marti hesitated for an instant. She'd always hated talking about Cameron when he could hear, but Gil had never before shown any concern about it. She wondered what he had to say tonight that he didn't want the others to hear, but he'd been acting so differently, it seemed only right to do as he asked.

Nodding quickly, she picked up her coat again. "Sure." She slipped into the coat, tugged on her gloves and walked toward the door. Before she could open it, Gil reached in front of her and held it while she stepped through into the cold.

Outside, she moved away from the door and turned to face him. "What is it?"

Gil stepped out of the glare of the porch light, which put him a little too close for comfort. Before she could insert any distance between them, he placed both hands on her shoulders. "You really look great."

This time, the compliment left her uneasy. "Thank you." She tried, again unsuccessfully, to step away from him. "What did you want to talk about?"

"I just wanted a minute alone with you. I've missed you."

Even in the dim light she could see his eyes darken. She'd seen that look often, and it left no doubt where he wanted to lead the conversation. She took a determined step back from him and started toward the door. "I need to get inside."

"I've missed you," Gil insisted. "More than I ever thought I would."

"We're divorced, Gil. I'm not interested."

"In what?" He used his innocent voice—the one he'd used so often over the years when he'd stayed late drinking at the Lucky Jack, or come home late for supper, or had forgotten something important to her. The one he'd used whenever she confronted him with the incessant rumors about other women that unfailingly made their way to her ears.

But his strategy didn't have the same effect on her it once had. "I know what you're trying to do," she said. "I'm not interested."

"I'm not trying to do anything," Gil asserted, and reached for her again. "I've missed you. Honest to God, I have."

"If that's true, then I'm sorry." She evaded his reach and moved closer to the door. "But I've never been happier."

"That's cruel."

"It's true."

Gil sighed heavily. "Marti, don't be like this. I still love you. I guess I always will."

Her pulse slowed and her mouth dried. Never in her wildest dreams had she anticipated having this conversation, and she did not want to have it now. "We're divorced, Gil," she repeated. "We have been for three years."

"That doesn't mean it's right. Look at Cameron. Look at the trouble he's been getting into. Obviously, the divorce hasn't done *him* any good. Or me."

"Don't do this," she warned.

But Gil didn't listen. "I want you back, Marti."

"No."

"Cameron needs us to get back together."

She glared at him. "*That's* cruel."

"It's also true. I'll bet you half the ranch he'd straighten up in a heartbeat if you came back home and we got married again."

Pushing his arms away, she yanked open the storm door. "It's not going to happen."

"Things would be different this time," he said. "I've got things going…" He let his voice trail away, but his lips curved into a smile.

"You always had things going," Marti reminded him. "You never were content with the way things were."

"There's nothing wrong with dreaming, Marti. Or with being ambitious."

"No, there isn't," she admitted. "But you were never prepared to work for anything. You weren't interested in going back to school or getting some training. You kept looking for an easy fortune around the next corner. Life doesn't work that way."

He held her arms again and spoke softly. "I know that now. I finally understand what you've been trying to tell me."

She stiffened automatically and met his gaze. "For your sake, Gil, I hope that's true. But it's too late for us."

"It doesn't have to be." He released her reluctantly and stepped off the porch into the snow. "Once you see how different I am, you'll change your mind."

Marti shook her head slowly and closed the door

between them, then crossed the room so he couldn't see her through the window. Thankfully, her father and Cameron were gone, so she sat at the kitchen table and buried her face in her hands.

She'd hoped to find peace and contentment here, but she'd been home less than four hours and already she'd found nothing but trouble. Gil's image floated before her for an instant, but in the next breath it changed. The hair and eyes darkened, and the smile grew friendly and genuine. Rick Dennehy? Why was she thinking of him at a time like this?

Because, she realized, he'd helped her out of bad situations twice during that same four hours. Without doing or saying anything that left her feeling inadequate, he'd come to her assistance. If Gil had ever offered help without leaving her feeling deficient, she couldn't remember.

She shivered in the cold air that had come inside with her and pushed Rick's image away. She had other things to think about. Important things. She didn't need distractions.

Uncovering her face, she stared around the empty room. Gunnison was home, and she wished more than anything that she could stay. Funny, but she'd left Colorado to find herself.

In the process, had she lost her son for good?

RICK ROLLED OVER in bed and squinted at the numbers on the alarm clock glowing red in the dim light of daybreak. He reached for the snooze button and groaned softly when the newly familiar ache of hard work tore through his muscles. Not only did he hurt everywhere, but Jocelyn had invaded his dreams for the first time in months and kept him from sleeping well.

After two solid days of working on the cabins with Cameron, they'd managed to fix the roof and do a few minor repairs on one of the cabins, but Rick still had a lot to do if he hoped to have everything ready to sell by the end of the month. No matter how tired he was, he couldn't afford to let even one day slip by without accomplishing something. But he *could* afford another five minutes' sleep.

As he turned his back on the alarm and closed his eyes again, his blanket rode up and exposed his backside to the chilly morning air. Muttering under his breath, he tugged the blanket into place once more. He'd certainly be more comfortable in the large bed he and Jocelyn had shared, but he'd avoided the master bedroom since his arrival.

Groaning, he tried to find a more comfortable position on the single mattress they'd found at a garage sale one weekend in Gunnison. No doubt about it, if he intended to sleep in this room he'd have to replace the mattress—soon.

Before he could relax again, his alarm buzzed for the second time. Forcing himself to sit on the edge of the bed, he stretched carefully to work the kinks from his back. After several minutes, he stood slowly and crossed to the window. But what he saw outside did nothing to lift his spirits.

A fresh blanket of white covered everything in sight, which meant he and Cameron would have to spend the first few hours of the morning plowing the access road and parking area and shoveling paths to the cabins before they could start any of the other jobs that begged for attention.

He started toward the bathroom, but when the bare floorboards sent icy fingers up his legs, he doubled back and stepped into his slippers. He hurried downstairs to stoke the fire, put on a pot of coffee, then climbed the stairs again and started the shower.

Stripping off the sweats he'd slept in, he stepped into the shower and let the hot spray take away the morning's chill and relax his tired muscles. Resolutely locking memories of Jocelyn away, he turned his thoughts to the present.

He wondered idly if Cameron was anywhere near as stiff as he was, or if the twenty-year difference in their ages meant the boy suffered less. And he wondered if the physical exertion had worked away a little of Cameron's hostility toward Marti. Hopefully so, for both their sakes.

Soaping himself liberally, he sighed with contentment, closed his eyes and turned to face the spray. But for some reason, a woman's image floated through his imagination as he stood there.

For half a second, he thought she was Jocelyn—until she turned to look at him and he saw the golden halo of hair and the clear blue of her eyes. Her lips curved into a slow, seductive smile, and Rick's heart began to beat a little too fast. Startled, he blinked his eyes open and stared at the tile wall in front of him. What was the matter with him? Why on earth would he conjure an image of Marti—especially one like that?

After shutting off the water, he stepped onto the bath mat, toweled himself dry and picked up his razor. But when he looked into the steamy mirror and gazed at his reflection with its stubble of black whiskers, he changed his mind. It didn't matter how he looked. He had no one to impress. He put away the razor, pulled on the ratty terry-cloth bathrobe Jocelyn had nagged him to throw away two years ago and hurried back to the bedroom.

There, he picked up his jeans from the chair where he'd dropped them the night before. But when the cold denim hit his legs, he dropped the jeans again. If he thought they were cold now, he could just imagine how miserable he'd be outside. He needed thermal underwear.

Tugging open the bottom drawer of the small dresser, he started to look for the thermals he knew he'd left here when he moved out. Almost immediately, he realized they wouldn't be in the spare room. He'd have to go into the master bedroom.

He told himself to forget about them. He didn't want to think about Jocelyn again. But common sense won out. Steeling himself, he hurried across the hallway and opened the thick pine door. Pale sunlight streamed through the eastern windows onto the bed still covered with the quilt Jocelyn's grandmother had made for their wedding.

Rick refused to look at it. He kept his mind focused on his task. Thermals. One pair. That's all he needed. Then he'd get out of this room and stay out until the memories and guilt had faded a bit more.

He opened the bottom dresser drawer and smiled grimly. There they were, just as he'd left them. He pulled out one pair, then realized he'd be far wiser to take all of them so he wouldn't have to come back later. He lifted two other folded sets from the drawer and started to straighten, but something at the bottom of the drawer caught his attention.

He didn't need to touch it to remember. He didn't have to pick it up to recall what Jocelyn had looked like wearing it. He could still remember the day he'd found it at that little shop south of Denver, his excitement when he'd placed the wrapped package under the tree, and the joy on her face when she'd opened it.

He lifted it carefully and slowly unfolded it. Black had always been her favorite color. Lighthouses had fascinated her. And the black sweater with the lighthouse pattern knit into it brought Jocelyn back to his memory so clearly she might have been standing beside him.

For the space of a heartbeat, he thought he could hear her voice chatting about her plans for the day. He closed his eyes and strained to make out her words, but the sound evaporated like morning mist in the sunlight. He tried to see her, but only a faint, shadowy figure formed in the recesses of his memory.

Blinking back the sting of tears, he lifted the sweater to his face and inhaled. Yes, there it was. The faintest suggestion of her scent still lingered on the wool. But like everything else, it would be gone soon.

He didn't know how long he sat there, savoring the feel of the soft wool against his stubbled cheek, before someone knocked on the door downstairs and jerked him back to reality.

Cameron. Just in time.

Grateful for the interruption, he lowered the sweater into the drawer. Wiping his eyes with the back of his hand, he hurried from the bedroom as the knock sounded again—louder this time.

He shut the door firmly, as if he could lock the past inside, and shouted down the stairs that he'd be there in a minute. He hurried into the spare bedroom, tossed the thermals onto his unmade bed and pulled on his jeans and his Denver Broncos sweatshirt.

Grabbing his shoes and a pair of socks, he ran down the stairs and told himself to keep his mind on the present. On leaky roofs and broken pipes and holes in walls.

Smiling grimly, he yanked open the front door and started to motion Cameron inside. Too late, he realized it wasn't Cameron standing there.

CHAPTER FOUR

"MARTI?" Rick's voice cracked a little, but he forced a smile. He knew he looked a mess—hair still wet from the shower, chin and cheeks dark with whiskers. So much for having no one to impress.

She took in his appearance slowly. "I'm sorry. I didn't mean to..." Her voice faltered. "Did I wake you?"

He glanced down at the socks and shoes in his hand and smiled back up at her. "No. Sorry. I thought you were Cameron."

She backed a step away. "I came by too early."

"No, you're fine. I'm just running late." He pushed open the door and stepped aside so she could enter. "Come on in."

She hesitated for an instant, then stepped through the door. "I've been meaning to stop by for the past couple of days to thank you for what you're doing for Cameron, but it hasn't been easy to find time."

Rick shrugged lightly and closed the door behind them. "There's no need to thank me. I need the help."

"Is it going well? I mean...is he working out all right?" She looked desperate for reassurance.

He tried to give it to her. "He's doing great. He's a good kid—you should be proud of him."

"It's been a long time since anyone said something

like that. Usually, I'm told how much trouble he is. I might suspect you of just saying what I want to hear, but I've seen how differently Cameron behaves around you.''

Rick motioned her toward the couch and sat on an overstuffed chair across from her. ''He does seem to have a little pent-up hostility.''

''A *little?*'' She let out a brittle laugh. ''It's more than a little when he's around me.''

Rick leaned forward and rested his elbows on his knees. ''I've noticed that. It must be rough on you.''

Her smile faded. ''It is at times. But I didn't come here to vent or whine, just to thank you and make sure Cameron is showing up on time and doing what he'd agreed to do.''

''He is,'' Rick assured her again. He laced his fingers together and sent her an uneasy smile. ''I'd like to say I understand what you're going through with him, but I'd be lying. Jocelyn and I didn't have any kids, so I can only imagine how tough it is.''

''Being a parent can be wonderful, too.''

He'd heard that platitude before. He didn't bother responding to it. ''How long have you been divorced?''

''Three years.''

''Maybe I'm wrong, but isn't that a long time for Cameron to still feel so bitter about it?''

''*I* think so,'' she said, ''but nobody else agrees with me.''

''Is there something other than the divorce bothering him?''

Marti hesitated, probably wondering about the wisdom of discussing her son with a relative stranger. When she finally spoke again, her voice sounded uncertain. "We moved to California right after the divorce. Cameron says he hates it there. He wants to live here."

"And he's mad at you because you won't let him."

"You guessed it." She sighed softly. "I don't know what's right and what's wrong anymore. After the divorce, I really couldn't see any other option. I couldn't stay here…" She let her voice trail away, then went on. But maybe I should have stayed for a while and let him adjust to the divorce first."

"Maybe," Rick said slowly. "It's hard to know. Hindsight's perfect, you know." Another platitude, he thought. Not knowing how to comfort her, he pushed to his feet and tried to steer the conversation in another direction. "I haven't had my morning coffee yet. Would you like a cup?"

Surprise darted across her face, but she stood to face him and shook her head quickly. "No. Thanks. I don't want to put you out."

"You won't be putting me out." He smiled gently and put a hand on her arm. "As a matter of fact, I'd like the company."

She looked as if she might protest again, but when her eyes met his, she seemed to change her mind. He wondered for a moment if she'd seen how much he wanted her to stay, but if she had, she gave no sign. "All right, then," she said with a smile. "I'd love some coffee."

Relieved, he took her arm. He realized his mistake immediately. Warmth curled in his stomach and spread through him slowly. He tried to ignore the sensation. He knew what it was—he hadn't been alone *that* long. But he didn't want to be attracted to Marti Johansson—

or to any woman, for that matter. Still, even after they reached the kitchen, he couldn't make himself withdraw his hand.

Determined to remain immune to her, he forced himself to speak. "How about breakfast? Will you join me?"

She shook her head, but she didn't look away. "I ate before I left home. But please, fix something for yourself."

Somehow, he managed to let go of her arm. He crossed the kitchen quickly to put some distance between them and pulled a frying pan from a low cupboard. "You're sure I can't talk you into sharing an omelette with me?"

"I'm sure." She sat at the table and gazed out the window. "You know," she said after a moment, "when I walked in here the other night and saw Cameron, I couldn't believe it. I haven't seen him looking so relaxed in a long time."

The obvious hurt in her voice touched something inside Rick. He tried to ignore it and took eggs, ham and cheese from the refrigerator. "He is a bit tense."

"A bit?" She laughed again. "You really are a master at understatement." Her smile faded slowly. "Actually, that was a horrible night for me. I finally had to admit that he hates me."

Rick's heart went out to her, but he didn't think she wanted sympathy. He pulled two mugs from a rack on the wall, rinsed them under the faucet and filled them with coffee. Crossing the room again, he handed one to her. "Hate's a strong word. He's angry, but I think he's angry with the situation, not you."

"I wish I could agree with you," Marti said. "Does he talk to you about it?"

"He doesn't really say much," Rick said, turning back to the counter and cracking eggs into a bowl. He tossed the shells into the sink and added, "But I do know he's upset about your divorce."

"Everyone's upset about the divorce."

"Who's everyone?"

"Cameron. My dad. My ex-husband."

Rick glanced quickly at her. "Gil Johansson."

She pulled back slightly, eyes wary, and lowered her mug to the table. "You know Gil?"

Rick shrugged casually, poured the eggs into a pan and turned on the burner. "Cameron told me who he is. I've seen him in town, but I don't really know him."

She seemed to relax again. "Cameron thinks I didn't try hard enough to make the marriage work," she admitted. "But he's conveniently forgotten how miserable we all were, how often Gil and I argued, and how much the fighting upset him."

"That's easy to do. People have a tendency to remember what they want to remember and forget the rest."

"I guess it's human nature. But I seem to be the only one who remembers how bad things were, and even I wonder sometimes if I made a mistake." She sighed and studied her mug for a moment. "Gil wants to patch things up between us."

Her candor surprised Rick. "Really?"

"Unfortunately."

"It isn't what you want?" He regretted the question immediately. It was none of his business.

To his surprise, Marti didn't seem to mind. "No, it

isn't. I might be confused about a lot of things, but I do know that much. But I do want Cameron to be happy again, and he needs his dad. And Gil *does* seem different.''

''Cameron may need his dad,'' Rick agreed, ''but it doesn't mean you have to marry him again...does it?''

''I suppose not,'' she said slowly, ''but I wonder whether Cameron will ever be happy again unless his family is back together.''

Rick sprinkled ham and cheese onto his omelette. ''If you were as unhappy as you say, even that won't make him happy. Nobody can make another person happy. Believe me, I know.''

She took another sip of coffee and brushed a stray lock of hair from her face. ''It would make Dad happy, too. He worries about me being alone, and he had such big dreams of leaving us the ranch, he's never quite gotten over his disappointment.''

Rick transferred his omelette from the pan to a plate, carried it to the table and sat across from her. ''What does the divorce have to do with the ranch?''

''I've wanted to run the Lazy M since I was a little girl,'' she said softly. ''But Dad won't leave it to me because I'm a woman. God forbid a *girl* should run a ranch.''

Rick couldn't believe he'd heard right. Henry Maddock sounded positively medieval. ''So, if you want the ranch, you have to marry Gil again?''

Marti worked up a grim smile. ''I don't know if he'd insist on that, but I do know he won't turn it over to me as long as I'm alone. He's old-fashioned—just like so many men of his generation. He thinks the ranch would be too much for me to handle on my own.''

"But if it's what you love—"

"It is. But it's not going to happen. I suppose I should just accept it, but it's not easy." She picked up her mug and let her gaze travel toward the window. "You have a great view. I always thought there should be a house here."

Rick could tell from the set of her shoulders and the look in her eye that she wanted to change the subject.

He leaned forward to look out the window with her. "Yeah. It's a great place."

"Your wife must have loved it here."

Everything inside froze. He could feel his expression shift. He didn't want to discuss Jocelyn and their life in Gunnison, but he didn't feel right about shutting Marti out when she'd just been so honest with him. "Not exactly," he admitted. Before he could decide what else to say, he caught a glimpse of Cameron's jacket through the trees as he crossed the bridge. He nodded toward the window. "Here comes Cameron."

Not surprisingly, Marti lowered her mug to the table and stood. "I'd better go."

After two days in Cameron's company, Rick suspected the kid might actually welcome his mother's interest. Just as Rick would have welcomed interest from his father—if the old man had ever shown any. "Why don't you stay?" he suggested.

"Because I don't want him to find me here."

"Why not?"

"Because this is the one good thing Cameron's done in three years, and seeing me here will only ruin it for him." Her voice came out sharp. Brittle.

Rick trailed her back into the living room and stood by while she put on her coat and tugged open the front door. For Cameron's sake, he wished she'd change her mind and stay. But it wasn't his place to tell her that. After all, he barely knew her.

"Thanks for the coffee," she said, stepping onto the porch. "I'll see you around."

After checking to make sure Cameron hadn't rounded the bend yet, she ran down the steps and hurried toward the far corner of the cabin. Rick watched until she turned the corner, then stepped back inside and closed the door. Which disappointed him more? he wondered. Her sudden departure or her unwillingness to talk to her son? He couldn't say.

MARTI STIRRED her homemade spaghetti sauce one last time before pulling the pan from the burner. Behind her at the table, her father and Cameron were deep in conversation. She loved listening to Cameron when he sounded like this—animated, happy, and more like himself than he'd been in a long time. But she didn't let herself relax. She didn't want to do or say anything to ruin his mood.

She poured the sauce into a bowl and carried it to the table. Her father looked up as she approached and passed one knobby hand over his thinning hair. "Sounds like Cameron's got tomorrow planned. What will you be doing?"

"I don't have any set plans," she admitted. "I'd like to call Cherryl. I still haven't been able to reach her."

"I'm not surprised. She's working at the Wagon Wheel now, you know. Even Greta doesn't see much of her daughter these days," Henry said.

"The last letter I got from her said she and Jess have

been busy since they took over the place. Have you been in there lately?''

Her father shook his head. ''I haven't been out much since winter hit.''

Marti pushed aside a pang of anxiety. She couldn't remember her father avoiding driving before, even in bad weather. But she tried not to act overly concerned. Henry had never taken pampering well. ''I'll probably look for Mom's Christmas things and decorate the house.''

His expression softened as it always did when someone mentioned her mother. ''That would be nice. If you have a minute, maybe you should call your aunt Martha, too.''

''Yes, of course, I will.''

He nodded approval and patted the chair beside him. ''Sit down here. I've got some news I want to share with both of you.''

Cameron stopped shoveling salad onto his plate. Curiosity brightened his eyes, but when Marti smiled at him they clouded again.

She hated knowing that a simple smile from her could ruin his mood so thoroughly. But she sat beside her father and made an effort to keep her voice light. ''What news?''

''I heard today that Dennehy's fixing to sell out. What would you think if I bought that land back from him?''

His question caught her by surprise. ''Can you afford to do that?'' she asked, passing him the bowl of sauce.

''You don't need to worry about that, girl. I've been thinking that it's time for me to start doing something with this place. I've let it sit for too long.''

Cameron pursed his mouth so that he looked exactly like Gil when something surprised him. "What would you do?"

"Oh, I don't know." Henry ladled sauce onto his pasta and shrugged at the same time. "It'll depend on what kind of help I can get. I'm too old to do much by myself."

Marti didn't know how he planned to hire help and buy Rick's property on his limited budget, but she didn't ask. "Are you thinking of anything in particular?"

Henry shrugged again. "I've got a plan...*if* I can find someone to take over the reins for me when the time comes."

His choice of words made Marti's internal warning bells sound. He'd used that phrase often in the past when talking about Gil, and she had a sinking feeling that's who he had in mind now.

Cameron tore a piece of garlic bread from the loaf and leaned forward in his seat. "I can help you, Grandpa."

"You could," her father said, "but you'll be going back to California soon. I need someone permanent."

With growing uneasiness, Marti took the bowl from him. She knew exactly how Cameron would respond. She could feel it in the air and see it in Cameron's eyes.

"Well, that's the thing, Grandpa. I'm not going back to California, so I *will* be here all the time."

Marti forced herself not to overreact. She'd been expecting Cameron to try something like this—just not so soon. And she hadn't expected her father to open the door for him.

Looking disappointed, Henry patted Cameron's hand. "I don't want you to go back, either, son. But that's up to your mother."

"You both know I love it here as much as you do, but we can't stay," Marti said. "We have to go back after Christmas."

Cameron's eyes snapped, his jaw tightened and his face reddened. "Why?"

"Because that's where we live."

"You don't have to live there," her father reminded her.

Marti clenched her fists and lowered them to her lap so neither of them could see how much effort it required to hold herself together. "I'd like to stay—"

"Don't lie," Cameron snarled. "You don't want to stay, but I do. I'm not going back."

She was silent for a few seconds, trying to steady herself. It didn't help. Her entire relationship with Cameron hinged on this one issue, and she could see him drawing further away with every word she spoke. "Cameron, please try to understand—"

"I understand, all right." He shoved his plate away. "You won't be content until you've totally screwed up my life."

"I don't want to screw up your life—"

"No? Well, you're sure as hell doing a great job of it."

The accusation made her lose the slim hold she'd kept on her temper so far. "If you want to see who's screwing up your life," she said, "take a look at the things *you're* doing."

Her father tugged Cameron back into his seat and frowned at her. "Enough of that. There's no need for this kind of talk.'' He patted her arm soothingly, but each time his hand touched her, she grew more irritated.

She jerked away.

Henry's frown deepened. ''Just calm down, sweetheart. There's no need to get all riled up.''

''I'm not riled up,'' she snapped, but even she could hear the lie in her words. She pushed a lock of hair from her face with an unsteady hand and tried to calm herself.

Her father sighed heavily. ''I know the idea of staying in Gunnison upsets you, but maybe Gil's right. Maybe you should give some thought to patching things up between you.''

Marti struggled to keep her voice level and her words rational. She knew better than to get angry. She'd just be reinforcing her father's opinion of women and their emotional behavior. ''Gil and I *don't* belong together—''

Cameron blew out a burst of air and leaned back in his seat. ''Well, *I* belong with him.''

''Of course, he'll always be your father—''

''Not if you have anything to say about it.'' Cameron pushed to his feet again. This time, he knocked over his chair as he stood. ''I'm *not* leaving here again, Mom, so get used to it. If you want to go back to California, you can go by yourself.''

Without waiting for her response, he rushed from the room. Marti held her breath, praying he wouldn't go outside in the cold.

To her immense relief, she heard his footsteps thundering up the stairs. She let out her breath slowly and met her father's gaze. ''Thanks a lot, Dad.''

"What did *I* do?"

She shook her head and waved away the question. It might be easy to blame him for suggesting that she reconcile with Gil, but her problems with Cameron weren't his fault. "I don't want Cameron getting ideas about staying here. I don't want him to think I'll get back with Gil again."

"But Gil's good for you, girl. He takes care of you. I'm not going to be around forever, and you're the only one of my children who's not settled."

"I am settled," she insisted. "I'm doing very well on my own."

Her father sent her a pitying glance and jerked his head toward the door, which was still swinging from Cameron's exit. "You call *that* doing well?"

Not by any stretch of her imagination, but she wouldn't admit it aloud. "I'll work things out with Cameron. That's why I'm here."

"He needs a steadying influence," Henry said. "He needs his father."

"You don't honestly believe Gil's a steadying influence?" Marti might have laughed if the idea hadn't been so unbelievable. "He spent most of our marriage drunk."

"I know he likes to have a beer now and then—"

"Now and then? He spent more time at the Lucky Jack than he did at home." Marti's voice rose with every word, but she couldn't seem to control it. "He was never there when I needed him. He was too busy chasing around with other women."

"Maybe he flirted on occasion," Henry said carefully, "but what man doesn't?"

"What man doesn't?" She turned away. "I can't believe you said that."

"Don't get upset with me," her father protested. "I'm just saying there's no proof Gil actually did anything wrong."

She laughed bitterly and stood. "Why do you always stick up for him? Gil did a whole lot more than flirt with other women."

"You don't know that, Marti. You heard a few rumors."

"Rumors that had their basis in fact."

"Even if he slipped up once—"

"Don't defend him, Dad. You're saying every man fools around on his wife. So does that mean you did, too?" Surely he'd realize how ridiculous his argument sounded if she put it that way.

"Did I what?"

"Did you chase around with other women when you were married to Mom?"

Her father leaned back in his seat, but she could tell by the way his lips thinned she'd asked him something he didn't want to answer.

Her pulse slowed ominously. *"Did* you?"

He met her gaze, again slowly. "Your mother and I had our problems," he said. "But she didn't go running off somewhere on her own and drag you kids with her. She stayed here. She forgave me. And she made the best life she could for her children."

Bile rose in her throat. Her stomach clenched painfully. "You cheated on Mom?"

Now he refused to meet her gaze. "We had our problems."

Her hands trembled and her throat tightened painfully. She clutched the table to keep herself upright. She couldn't believe it. No... She didn't *want* to believe it. She'd always thought her parents had a wonderful marriage, and she'd wondered what she'd done to fall short of their example. Now, it seemed, she'd lived up to it better than she'd ever imagined.

Bitterness and anger welled up inside her. "Do the others know?"

"There's nothing *to* know."

"You just said—"

"What happened between your mother and me was our business. We worked out our differences and made a home for you kids. And you all turned out just fine. Jed and Neal are doing well. Carol's happily married. So, you tell me whether we did the right thing. And tell me honestly whether you'd have turned out the way you did if your mother had gotten her feelings hurt and run off on me."

Gotten her feelings hurt? Marti stared at her father for a long moment, unable to make a sound. The clock on the stove marked time as the seconds passed. Her thoughts raced, but she didn't trust herself to speak or move.

She searched her memory, trying desperately to remember if her mother had ever betrayed heartache. But if she had, Marti hadn't seen it.

"Your mother and I owed it to you kids to stay together," he said. "And you owe Cameron the same thing. You owe him a family. You owe him stability." Her father leaned toward her again and touched her hand. His skin felt paper-dry. Thin. Old. She didn't feel the usual warmth in his touch. In fact, she felt nothing but revulsion.

She snatched her hand away and shook her head. He was wrong. *Wrong*. Marriage to Gil would give Cameron nothing but misery. But she still couldn't speak.

Her father softened his voice and tried to make her look at him again. "Why do you think Cameron's having such problems out there in California?"

"That's not fair." The words squeaked out of her tight throat. She sounded weak. Childish. Uncertain.

"Gil loves you, girl. Just like I loved your mother." He scooted his chair closer and touched her arm again. "So his head turned once or twice. You don't know he actually cheated on you. You've judged him and found him guilty without proof."

Her stomach knotted. "He was never there when I needed him, Dad. You know that. You remember—"

"Maybe he was there the best he could be. Gil's a good man. He tries hard." He gestured toward the upper floor and looked deep into her eyes. "And he's a good father to that boy up there. You can't deny that."

"He's *no* father to Cameron. He hasn't seen him in three years."

"That's not all his fault, and you know it. You took the boy clear across the country so he *couldn't* see him."

Marti looked away, but he used his free hand to tilt her face back toward his.

"I'd better warn you about something else, girl. Gil's going to be helping me out on the weekends, so you'll be seeing a lot more of him."

She jerked her chin away from his touch. "Why?"

"Because I'm too damn old to do it all myself. I need the help."

"I'll help you. Cameron will help. You know how much I love this place."

Not surprisingly, her father shook his head. "You're not here all the time. Besides, this place is too much for a lady. I need a man. Someone I can rely on."

"And you think you can rely on Gil?"

Her father fixed her with a stern gaze. "I know I can. Gil's changed. He's steady now. He knows what he did wrong, and he wants a chance to make it up to you. Your trouble is, you won't let go of the past. Somebody makes a mistake, you worry on it forever, like a dog with a bone."

The accusation hit her like a blow to the stomach. She stood and took two steps backward to put herself out of his reach. "There are some things that are impossible to forgive."

"Well, you've gotta try, girl, for your own sake. If you don't, they'll eat you up."

She *had* tried. Over and over again, she'd tried to put what Gil had done out of her mind. Not for his sake, but because she couldn't bear thinking about it. Even after all this time, the memories were too raw. Gil had shrugged it off and gone back to the Lucky Jack two days later, as if nothing had happened. As if their entire world hadn't fallen down around them. But Marti hadn't. She couldn't.

She lifted one shaky hand to her forehead, as if she could stop the sudden, incessant pounding. "Maybe Cameron and I should leave. I can't stay here if Gil's going to be around all the time."

"I'm just giving him a chance to see Cameron."

"He doesn't have to work here to see Cameron."

"That's not the way he tells it."

Pain shot through her temples and settled behind her eyes. "How *does* he tell it?"

Henry sighed heavily and crossed one ankle on his knee. "He hasn't even seen the boy in three years. Now you're back, but the boy's spending all his time with Dennehy. Gil's afraid he's losing his son."

"Gil can see him whenever he wants," she told him. "But Rick's been good for Cameron."

"Rick?" Her father cocked an eyebrow at her. "That sounds pretty darned familiar to me, girl. What's going on with you? Have you been seeing him on the sly?"

"No. But I do talk to him when I run into him."

"Well, don't get too friendly with him. He's already taken half my property, I don't want him interfering in your marriage, too."

"You *sold* him half your property, he didn't steal it. And there's no marriage to interfere *with.*"

"All I'm saying is, he took advantage of me when I was down. I wouldn't put it past him to do the same to you."

"That's ridiculous. You put the property up for sale."

"Only because I had to. After you left, I didn't have the help I needed to keep this place running." He pushed to his feet, crossed to the swinging door and held it open with one hand. "Things have been rough on all of us since you divorced Gil and moved away. Don't get so wrapped up in what you want, that you don't take the time to look around you. Gil's unhappy, Cameron's miserable and I've lost half of what's rightfully mine because you can't find it within yourself to forgive your husband."

He pushed through the door into the living room. It swung shut behind him, and each *whoosh* of the door against the frame found an answering echo in Marti's heart. She didn't want to believe what she'd just heard, but a small kernel of uncertainty teased her. Was she responsible for everyone's unhappiness? Had she been too quick to end her marriage to Gil? Was she responsible for Cameron's surliness?

Lowering her head, she held back tears of frustration. She'd come home to find peace; instead, she'd found turmoil. She'd come back hoping to salvage her relationship with Cameron; instead, it seemed to be growing worse every day. Maybe she *had* brought this heartache upon herself and everyone else. If so, only she could fix it.

She crossed to the counter and gripped it with both hands to steady herself. She didn't want to believe it, but honesty forced her to question whether her inability to forget that one horrible night had kept her from trying to work things out.

Maybe Gil had changed. If she didn't at least give him a chance to prove himself, she'd never know. And by stubbornly refusing, she ran the risk of making Cameron so angry, she'd lose him forever. Whatever else she might have to tolerate, she couldn't endure that.

CHAPTER FIVE

CAMERON LAY on his bed, staring up at the ceiling and wondering what was wrong with his mom, anyway. Why did she have to be so mad at his dad? Why did she have to be so angry with everyone all the time? How could he fix things if his mom didn't even listen?

She hadn't always been this way. She used to smile a lot. Laugh, even. They used to do stuff together—fun stuff. Now, every time they spent more than five minutes in a room together, they had a fight.

She *said* she was tired of fighting with him, but she sure didn't act like it. It seemed to Cameron that she enjoyed the arguments. She sure started enough of them.

When a soft knock sounded on the door of his bedroom, he raised onto his elbows and glanced at it. He wondered for a second whether he'd only imagined it. But the sound came a second time, still just as soft.

It had to be his mom. He could hear the TV playing in his grandpa's study.

"Yeah?" He used his toughest voice, to make sure she didn't think she'd hurt him.

"Cameron?" Her voice came through the door. "Do you mind if I come in?"

He wanted to say yes, but he knew she wouldn't give up. Instead, he dropped back on the bed and covered his eyes with one arm so she wouldn't see that he'd been crying. "I guess so."

The door creaked open and he heard her footsteps halt just inside the door. "I brought your dinner up for you."

Yeah? Good. He was so hungry, his stomach hurt. But he didn't want her to know that. He grunted and hoped she'd leave so he could eat.

Her footsteps moved closer. He could feel her standing over the bed staring down at him. He stiffened his arm, hoping she wouldn't try to pull it away from his eyes.

"I've been doing a lot of thinking since you left the table." She sounded kind of sad, but Cameron resisted the urge to peek at her face. She might be faking it. She'd done that before. "You really want to stay here, don't you?"

He grunted again.

She sighed softly. "Cameron? Look at me, okay? This is hard enough to say without having to say it to your arm."

He shifted his arm a little and peered at her over the top of it. "What?"

"I've been thinking that maybe you're right. Maybe I should give it another chance."

His heart jumped, but he didn't let himself get excited. Not yet. He didn't trust her. "Give what another chance?"

She waved her arm around the room. "This. Gunnison. Staying here."

Was she serious? He squinted to see her face better. She *looked* serious. His heart gave another skip. "We're going to move back?"

"I'll think about it."

It should have been enough for him, but he needed to know if she meant it. He decided to push, just to see what she'd do. If she got mad again, he'd know she was lying. "What about Dad?"

She shifted her position, her shoulders slumped, and she frowned. But she didn't get red in the face, and she didn't start yelling. "I'll think about him, too."

Cameron sat up, forgetting all about keeping his eyes covered until he saw the look on her face. It was too late to cover them again, but if she meant what she said, maybe it didn't matter so much anymore. "You'll think about getting back together with him?"

She almost smiled. "I'll think about it."

He tried not to smile back, but he couldn't stop himself. "You're serious?"

"I'm serious."

He flopped back on the bed and tried to wipe the silly grin from his face. "Okay." He didn't say anything more. He didn't want her to think she'd gotten to him or anything.

But she knew. He could see it in her eyes. She stood there for a few more seconds, looking at him as if she expected him to say something else. When he didn't, she turned away and crossed to the door again. There, she glanced back over her shoulder and motioned toward the plate she'd left on his dresser. "Eat your dinner before it gets cold, okay?"

"Yeah. Sure." He sat up on the edge of the bed so she'd stop worrying about it. "I will."

This time, she *did* smile right before she closed the door and left him alone. He lay back on the bed and let his own smile spread across his face. She'd think about it. It wasn't much, but it was enough.

Cameron knew—he just *knew*—that if she gave his dad half a chance, she'd eventually be able to forgive him. And if she could forgive his dad, maybe some day she'd be able to forgive Cameron, too.

It wasn't as if he'd made a *little* mistake or anything. This whole stupid mess was his fault. And he knew he'd be lucky if she ever forgave him.

But for the first time since he was a little boy, since the night he'd shown everyone just how stupid he really was, he felt a little hope that maybe he could actually make up for what he'd done.

RICK SAT on the floor in front of the fireplace and held his hands toward the blaze. One dim lamp burned near the window, but most of the light in the room came from the fire. If he hadn't been alone, the mood would have been cozy, even romantic. But he was alone. And he knew better than to think the situation would—or should—change.

Leaning his head back against the couch, he closed his eyes. Working in the dry wind and snow all day had left his face red and raw. The cold had worked it way deep into his bones. The physical exertion left his muscles stiff and sore. He could almost hear his bed beckoning him. But he didn't move until the telephone startled him a few seconds later.

He stood quickly, hurried into the kitchen and snagged the receiver from the wall phone.

"Rick?" a woman's voice demanded when he answered. "Did I wake you?"

The voice sounded so much like Jocelyn's, his heart

skipped a beat. In the next second, he realized it was her sister. "Lynette. No, you didn't wake me. I was just sitting in front of the fire." How had she found him? No one knew where he'd gone.

"I tried to reach you at work to talk about plans for Christmas. Your assistant told me you'd taken the month off."

"That's right," he admitted slowly. "But I didn't tell her where I'd be."

"Well, she figured it out. Apparently, your Realtor called with your new number after the phone company assigned it. You'd already gone, so she made a note of it in case she needed to reach you...I talked her into giving it to me."

He made a mental note to have a chat with Noreen when he got back to the office and tried to hide his irritation. "Is that why you're calling? About Christmas?"

"Yes, of course. What are you doing at the cabins?"

"Fixing them up so I can sell them."

"Oh, Rick." She sounded disappointed. "You're going to get rid of them?"

"I am."

"Is that wise? I mean, you and Jocelyn were so happy there."

No, they hadn't been happy. But Rick hadn't admitted the truth to Lynette in two years, and he didn't intend to start now. Nor did he intend to give her a chance to talk him out of his decision. "So, what did you need?"

She hesitated so long before answering, he worried she might argue with him anyway. To his relief, she didn't. "Tom and I would like to get together with you over the holidays."

Rick didn't want to spend the holidays with Lynette's family. He'd spent part of the previous Christmas with them, and it had been an emotional disaster. Lynette still hadn't fully accepted Jocelyn's death, and she'd wanted to spend every waking hour talking about her. Their younger brother, Ryan, had worked equally hard to avoid talking about Jocelyn, and Rick had been caught in the middle. He didn't want a repeat this year.

He made an effort to keep his voice sounding normal. "Well, I guess that's out of the question since I'm not in town."

"Not necessarily."

"I can't come back. I have too much to do around here."

"You don't need to come back," she said. "Tom's got a long holiday, and we've decided to bring Christmas to you."

He shook his head, slowly at first, then faster. "No. That's impossible."

"It's not impossible," Lynette insisted. "It's only a day's drive. We'll be there the day after the girls get out of school for the holidays."

He thought frantically, trying to find some excuse to keep them away. "The cabins are in horrible shape," he warned. "There's no place for you to stay."

She laughed softly. "Jocelyn told me they were rustic, but you know us. We don't need anything fancy. In fact, we'd love a chance to see the cabins."

"They're worse than rustic," he told her. "They're dilapidated."

Another laugh, this one slightly harsher than the last.

"We don't care. Honestly, we don't. We just want the family together for Christmas. In fact, I'm going to call Ryan and Anne after we're through talking."

Rick took a bracing sip of coffee and tried a different argument. "I'm not planning to celebrate Christmas this year—"

"Oh, but you *have* to. Jocelyn loved Christmas."

Rick didn't need the reminder. "I'll be too busy to celebrate. I'll be working all the time."

"You can't work all the time," Lynette argued. "And if we're there, Tom can help you. Ryan might even be willing to help out."

Ryan wouldn't help. And Tom hated manual labor as much as Rick loved it. Rick could just imagine how he'd react to Lynette volunteering him. Strike that. He knew how Tom would react. He'd hate every minute of it, but he'd give in. Tom loved his wife, but he knew—as Rick did—that arguing with Lynette never accomplished anything.

"I wouldn't let Tom work—"

"He'd love to help," Lynette said, cutting him off. "Now, no excuses. I know how hard this Christmas will be for you. Personally, I think you should have waited until after the holidays to go back, but since you're there—" She broke off as if he could fill in the rest himself.

And he could. Since he was here where Jocelyn had died…since the anniversary of her death was only a couple of weeks away…since Lynette hadn't fully accepted the reality of her sister's death. He took a deep, steadying breath. "I don't want company for the holidays."

"Maybe not," Lynette conceded, "but you need it. Besides, think about the girls. They miss you."

Rick closed his eyes and leaned his forehead against the wall. He wouldn't hurt Ashley and Kendra for anything in the world. If they wanted to spend Christmas with him, he couldn't say no. He couldn't help resenting Lynette for using them to get the results she wanted.

He took another steadying breath and let it out again slowly. "All right."

"Wonderful. The girls are through with school on Wednesday. We can be there Thursday—" She broke off again and listened to something Tom said in the background. "Tom says not to count on us before Saturday."

That left only five days. Five short days to put one of the large cabins in order and to get used to the idea of having Jocelyn's family around. Making an effort to keep the edge out of his voice, he gave Lynette directions and hung up the phone, then walked back into the living room.

Trying to put Lynette's call out of his mind, he stretched and groaned aloud, then dropped to the floor again and extended his legs toward the fire.

Although the day's work had left him exhausted, he couldn't completely ignore the sense of satisfaction that teased the edges of his consciousness. But that kind of thinking wouldn't do him any good, either. He couldn't stay here. He'd never be able to live with the guilt if he did.

As he reached for the cup of coffee on the floor beside him, the muscles in his back twinged. He closed his eyes for a moment, reopened them slowly and took a long sip. No, he couldn't stay here. He'd come to escape Christmas and all its irritating trappings, and to get the cabins ready to sell. He had no business entertaining second thoughts.

He was just about to take another sip when a knock sounded on the front door. Now what? He lowered his mug to the floor and pushed to his feet. Only two people would stop by this time of night—Cameron or Marti.

Telling himself to ignore the flicker of hope that it would be Marti, he crossed the room and turned on the porch light. He steeled himself for the rush of frigid night air and opened the front door.

She stood in the glow of the light, smiling uneasily and holding the collar of her coat close to her neck with one hand. She'd tucked her hair under a knit cap that fit snugly over her ears. The wind had whipped color into her cheeks that made her even more beautiful.

He tried to ignore the sudden, rapid beating of his heart. "Looking for Cameron again?"

She shook her head. "No. Actually, I was out walking and saw your light on. I hope I'm not disturbing you."

"Not at all." He pushed open the door a little farther. "Come on in, it's freezing out there." He waited until he'd closed the door to ask, "Is there a problem?"

"No…" Smiling nervously, she released the choke-hold on her collar and tugged off the cap. Her hair tumbled to her shoulders and caught the glow of the fire. She ran her fingers through it, but when she met his gaze, he saw something unsettled lurking in her eyes. "Yes, I guess there is a problem. But not with Cameron. Not really."

She looked so vulnerable Rick's heart went out to her. "You need to talk?"

Letting out a whisper of a sigh, she nodded uneasily. "If you have a few minutes. I need some perspective."

Perspective? From him? Boy, had she come to the wrong place. "I'll do my best," he promised. "Sit down." He gestured toward the couch and trailed her into the room. "Can I get you something to drink?"

Her lips curved into a ghost of a smile. "Do you have wine?"

The request surprised him, but he didn't let her see that. He nodded and scooped up his coffee mug from the floor. "White or red?"

"Red, please."

"Red it is. Make yourself comfortable. I'll be right back." He hurried into the kitchen and left his mug on the counter. He pulled two stemmed glasses from the top cupboard, uncorked a new bottle and poured some wine into each glass.

When he carried the glasses back into the living room, he found Marti perched uncomfortably on one end of the couch. She looked incredibly sad. And extraordinarily desirable.

That realization left him uncomfortable. Pushing aside the thought, he told himself that if she hadn't been sitting in a dimly lit room silhouetted against the fire's glow, he'd never have had such an idea. He considered turning on another lamp, then decided against it. He was an adult, for hell's sake. He could control the way his mind worked long enough to have a conversation with a neighbor.

She accepted a glass and met his gaze steadily. Again, something disturbing danced across her expression. "Thank you."

He gulped a mouthful of wine from his own glass and sat on a chair across the room from her. The wine warmed him from the inside, something the coffee hadn't been able to do. "So, what's on your mind?"

That earned a weak smile. She sighed again and studied the wine in her glass for a few seconds. "I had an argument with my father tonight. I needed to get out of the house, but I was too upset to drive anywhere."

Rick winced inwardly and reminded himself she didn't know what a nerve that comment touched. "It's dangerous to drive anywhere when the roads are icy, especially when you're upset."

He'd tried to sound normal, but she must have heard the strain in his voice. She lowered her glass to one knee and studied him for so long, his heart began to thud in his chest. A log on the fire popped and sizzled. A branch from a tree outside brushed against the side of the cabin.

"Yes," she said at last. "It is."

A nervous laugh escaped him. He kneaded his forehead with one hand and averted his gaze. "I'm a little touchy on that subject. Tell me what's on your mind."

She studied the fire while another long silence fell into the space between them. "I don't even know where to begin."

"You had an argument with your father…"

"Yes." She inhaled deeply and went on. "It's strange. The evening started out fine. Cameron was even in a good mood. Before I knew what was happening, Cameron was refusing to go back to California with me, and my dad was telling me that I need to reconcile with Gil.''

Rick shifted position in his chair and propped both elbows on his knees. ''Do you think Gil's been talking to your dad?''

She darted a glance at him. ''About us getting back together? Maybe. Probably. He suggested it to me the night we got here.'' She stood quickly, paced to the fireplace and sat on the hearth.

''When you were here the other day, you said you didn't want to get back together with him,'' Rick said. ''Have you changed your mind?''

''I don't know. Not really, but maybe I'm being self-ish. Maybe Dad's right and I'm letting stubborn pride get in my way. I know I'm not putting Cameron's needs first.'' She sent him another uneasy glance. ''Anyway, I promised Cameron I'd think about it.'' She broke off and looked away again.

Rick could understand her confusion. She'd made a promise she didn't know if she could keep—just as Jocelyn had when she agreed to move to Gunnison with him. But as he watched Marti and realized how deeply the promise affected her, he wondered whether Jocelyn had agonized over hers. Had she feared what it would do to their relationship if she told him, as Marti was doing?

Marti stood again and started to turn away from the fireplace, but the framed picture of Jocelyn he hadn't been able to put away caught her eye. Rick readied himself for the inevitable questions. He'd certainly been asked them often enough in the past two years.

But she didn't ask anything. She said only, "Your wife was very beautiful."

"Yes," he said softly. "Yes, she was."

Marti sipped her wine and glanced around the room. "This is such a lovely cabin, she must have loved it here."

Rick lowered his glass to the table beside him. "Actually, she wanted to move back to Denver." His willingness to discuss Jocelyn aloud surprised him, but not nearly so much as the admission. He'd never told anyone that, not even Jocelyn's family.

"Really?" Marti's eyes widened. "So you were planning to leave here at the time your wife died?"

This time, Rick braced himself with wine before he answered. "No. I told her I didn't want to leave. She…she told me that she'd go back without me, but she wouldn't stay here any longer. I got angry and said things I never should have said." The memory left him cold in spite of the wine. "Never."

Marti smiled. "So, you're in the same boat I am. You blame yourself."

Rick stared at her. How could she compare the two situations? "She left here angry with me. Before she reached the valley, she went off the road—"

Marti took a couple of hesitant steps toward him and touched his shoulder gently. "You can't blame yourself for her death. Ultimately, it was her decision to get into the car and drive when she was angry."

He knew he should pull away, but her hand seared his skin even through the thick fabric of his shirt. Her words soothed something inside him, even though he couldn't let himself believe them. He'd lived with the responsibility for that horrible night for two years, and he'd live with it the rest of his life. But just now, here in this warm cabin with the fire blazing and the wine affecting his reason, they were exactly what he needed to hear.

As if his hand belonged to someone else, Rick lifted it and placed it on top of hers. The world seemed to shift beneath him, and the sudden, urgent need for her woman's touch consumed him.

She didn't draw her hand away. Instead, she looked deep into his eyes. He saw a need that mirrored his own. Without allowing himself time to think, he pulled her closer. She didn't fight him, but leaned toward him until their faces were close. Too close.

He told himself to stop, but he couldn't. Need raged within him. Leaning up, he touched his lips gently to hers. Her mouth felt soft beneath his. So soft. So warm. So giving.

Groaning deep in his throat, he wrapped his free arm around her waist and drew her against him. She hesitated for less than the space of a breath, then lowered herself onto his knee and melted into him. He could taste the wine on her lips and smell the wind in her hair.

She touched the back of his neck with one warm, soft hand, and his need doubled. He deepened the kiss, drawing strength from her just as she drew from him. But in the next instant, when she parted her lips slightly, reason returned and he pulled away. What was he doing? What in the hell was he thinking? He couldn't do this—not to her, not to himself, not to Jocelyn's memory.

Marti's eyes opened slowly, and he watched the yearning die and realization dawn as it had for him.

She stood quickly, brushing her pant legs with her hands.

"I'm sorry," he said, but the apology sounded weak.

"It wasn't your fault," she said. "I shouldn't have come."

"I don't know what came over me," he said. But it wasn't true. He did know. He'd responded to the firelight and the wine, to his frustration over Lynette's impending visit, but mostly to Marti's openness and candor.

Cursing himself silently, he tried to see into her eyes again.

But she worked hard to avoid his gaze. "I'd better go." Without giving him a chance to stop her, she grabbed her coat, opened the door and stepped onto the porch. Words rose to Rick's lips, but they died there. He had no right to say anything. Without looking back at him, she shut the door between them.

She'd come looking for a friend, but Rick had let his own needs come first, just as he always did. Everything inside screamed for him to stop her. To explain. To beg for her forgiveness. But he didn't. He let her walk away, just as he had with Jocelyn. And the helplessness he felt now almost matched what he'd felt that night.

CHAPTER SIX

RICK WIPED sweat from his forehead, lowered his pipe wrench to the floor in front of the sink and glanced up at the loft overhead. "I'm finished down here. How are you coming with that window?"

"Almost done." Cameron crawled to the loft railing and peered over at him. "Just give me a couple more minutes."

Rick tried, as he'd been doing for the past four days, not to notice how much the kid looked like Marti, but whenever he looked at Cameron the resemblance jolted him. He hadn't seen Marti since he'd let her walk away from him, but he hadn't been able to wipe the memory of that kiss from his mind.

He forced a smile at Cameron and turned away. "Good. Three cabins down, five more to go. You know, kid, with your help, I'm beginning to think I might make it." He leaned back on his haunches and started putting the tools back into his toolbox.

"You'll make it," Cameron said, but he grunted with effort, and a second later, something banged to the floor overhead.

"Do you need some help up there?"

"Nope. I got it." As if to prove it, he reappeared in front of the railing, this time on his feet. He wiped his forehead with his sleeve and started down the ladder.

At the bottom, he checked his watch and slanted a glance at Rick. "So, are we through for the day, or what?"

Rick cocked an eyebrow at him. "It's only two o'clock."

"I know, but my dad'll be at Grandpa's pretty soon."

"Is he coming to pick you up for the weekend?"

"No." Cameron handed him a screwdriver and socket wrench. "He's working with my grandpa on the weekends."

"You guys are fixing up things over there, too?"

Cameron's gaze shifted slightly. "Yeah. Sort of." He stuffed his hands into his pockets and leaned one shoulder against the wall. "Him and my mom are probably going to get back together again, so he's helping Grandpa out."

"Really?" Rick forced away a shaft of disappointment and concentrated on putting the tools away.

"Yeah." Cameron shrugged casually. "They never shoulda gotten divorced in the first place, and I think Mom's finally starting to realize it. He's been having dinner with us almost every night, and they're getting along great."

Rick told himself the concern that streaked through him was for Marti's sake, not his own and that only discomfort over discussing Marti behind her back caused his sudden uneasiness.

Whatever the reason, he didn't want to talk about Marti anymore. He closed the toolbox and stood. "All right, then. We'll call it a day."

Unfortunately, Cameron *did* want to talk about her.

"Dad says that if things keep going this well, he's gonna buy her a diamond for Christmas."

Earrings? Necklace? No, Rick couldn't misunderstand that, even if he'd wanted to. Gil planned to give Marti an engagement ring. He slanted a glance at Cameron. "Does your mom know?"

"Nope. Dad's gonna surprise her."

Some surprise. He wondered how Marti would handle that. Would she accept Gil's proposal to please Cameron? Or had she decided that's what she wanted, as well?

Cameron flashed him a hint of a smile so like Marti's that Rick's stomach knotted. "Cool, huh?"

"Cool."

Cameron must not have heard the sarcasm in Rick's voice. He pulled his hands from his pockets and looked as if he might say something more. But before he could speak again, a car horn blared in the stillness.

Irrational hope that Marti had come to pick up Cameron filled Rick. He glanced out the window, but he couldn't see the driveway from this vantage point. He picked up the toolbox and started toward the door.

Cameron followed, whistling softly. The boy's contentment grated on Rick's nerves. He tugged open the front door and stepped onto the broad covered porch, squinting when the sun's glare on the snow hit his eyes.

"Rick?" A woman's voice. For half a second, he let himself believe it was Marti. But when she called his name again, hope died. Lynette. A full day early.

She bounded into view a second later, followed by her husband, Tom. With her dark hair and eyes, her elfin face, and tiny figure, she looked far too much like Jocelyn. She pulled him into a quick embrace and released him. "This place is *great*. Now I see why you've kept it all these years."

He forced a smile. "I'm glad you like it.

"It's perfect. Absolutely perfect." Lynette brushed past Cameron, climbed onto the porch of the cabin they'd just finished and peered in through one of the windows. "Oh, I like this, Tom. I really do. It's so quaint."

Obviously embarrassed, Tom shook Rick's hand. "Hope we're not intruding."

"No," Rick lied. "Of course not."

Lynette tried the cabin door, squealed with delight when it opened and disappeared inside.

Watching her, Tom stuffed his hands into the pockets of his khaki pants. "Look, Rick, I know what a spot this puts you in. Believe me, I tried to talk her out of it, but she's convinced you need company for the holidays. She really means well."

Rick waved away his explanation. "The cabins aren't in great shape," he warned. "Like I told Lynette, I'm here just to fix them up. I wasn't even planning to celebrate Christmas."

"This one looks great," Lynette said. Her voice so close to his ear startled him. He hadn't heard her come back outside.

Tom shrugged as if the situation was beyond his control. Cameron stared from one to the other, and Rick thanked him silently for not mentioning the other cabins they'd finished.

Before he could say anything else, he heard another shout from somewhere near the house.

"Uncle Rick!" His nieces, Ashley and Kendra, raced into view a second later.

Kendra threw herself at him and wrapped her arms around his neck. Her fourteen-year-old cheeks glowed pink with excitement. "This is the greatest place in the world."

Ashley followed more slowly. She'd always been more sedate than her younger sister, but her eyes glittered with an enthusiasm Rick hadn't seen in her before and her smile wiped away the remainder of his objections.

Lynette tugged Kendra toward the cabin. "Come and look inside. This is perfect for us. It's rustic and so quaint. And you know what would be great? A sleigh ride. Isn't this the perfect place for one?"

Still watching in confused silence, Cameron stepped out of their way. Lynette didn't spare him a second glance, but Kendra did. She smiled shyly as they passed, and two bright red patches flamed to life on the boy's cheeks.

Well, well, well, Rick thought. Look at that. The kid obviously recognized Kendra's charms. And why not? She was a beautiful girl.

Holding back a grin, he introduced Cameron to the girls, then added, "You'll be neighbors for the holidays. He's staying with his grandpa on the property across the river. And he's been helping me fix up the cabins."

Lynette acknowledged the introduction and gave Cameron a slow once-over. Her eyes hardened a bit more with every feature she looked in—his hair, the smudges of dirt on his face, his clothes—but she kept a strained smile on her lips. "Well, now you don't have to ruin your Christmas," she said to Cameron. "My husband can help Rick from now on."

The splotches on Cameron's cheeks darkened with embarrassment, and resentment rose like bile in Rick's throat. "Cameron and I are a team," he said, and took a step closer to the kid. "Of course, if Tom wants to help, he's welcome to join us."

Tom didn't look thrilled by the suggestion, but he didn't argue. Lynette's eyes narrowed. Kendra's smile widened. Ashley ducked her head.

Rick met the challenge in Lynette's gaze without faltering. She didn't like being contradicted, but Rick didn't care. He might let her barge in without an invitation. He'd even let her ruin his non-Christmas holiday. But he wouldn't let her get away with insulting Cameron.

The force of his anger surprised him. Sure, he knew he liked the kid, but he hadn't realized until this moment just how much he cared about him. The realization left him slightly uncomfortable. Somehow, without him even knowing it, Marti and her son had managed to make a chink in the walls he'd constructed around his heart.

RICK PULLED two bottles of beer from the refrigerator in the main house, handed one to Tom and opened the other for himself. Lynette and the girls were making beds and setting up house in the guest cabin. Rick took a long drink and rubbed his neck with his free hand.

Sinking into one of the chairs at the kitchen table, Tom let out a heavy groan. "Cameron and I could kill ourselves helping you cut the wood. I never thought I'd say this, but maybe you should hire someone to cut the rest of the firewood we're going to need. It might be worth the few extra dollars."

Rick laughed and sat on the chair across from him. "It's worth the extra money as long is it's coming from my pocket, you mean."

Tom grinned. "Of course."

"I'll drive into town in the morning and rent a log-splitter," Rick promised. "That should make the rest of the job go a little faster."

Tom groaned again and palmed his graying hair.

"You don't have to help," Rick reminded him. "You're a guest."

To Rick's surprise, Tom laughed. "I'm not going to sit around on my butt while you do all the work."

Rick smiled. He'd always liked Tom, and one of his favorite things about the man was his ability to look honestly at himself. He took another drink and groaned with pleasure as the cold liquid traced a path down his throat.

Tom leaned both elbows on the table and wrapped his hands around his bottle. "This is a great place. Are you sorry you left?"

Rick looked around the small kitchen and shrugged. He didn't want to acknowledge the growing regret—even to himself. "Not really."

"You know, you could have made a go of this place. You're in a great location."

"I know." He leaned back in his chair. "But there are a lot of memories here."

Tom followed his gaze around the room as if Rick's memories might be visible. "It's been hard coming back, hasn't it?"

"A little." It was an understatement, and Rick suspected Tom recognized it, but he didn't say so.

"It's going to be hard on Lynette, too."

Rick knew that was probably true. Lynette and Jocelyn had always been close. "Lynette took Jocelyn's death harder than anyone else, I think."

"Anyone but you," Tom amended.

"Yes, I guess so. If coming here bothers Lynette so much, why are you here?"

Tom picked at the label on his bottle. "Because she's so damn determined to keep everything the way it was, it's almost spooky at times." He leaned back in his seat and fixed Rick with a steady gaze. "Tell me honestly, does it bother you to have us here?"

He didn't want to cause any hurt feelings, so he said, "Not really. Why should it?"

Tom shrugged. "No reason, I guess." He pulled a long piece of the label away. "Just that...well, you know. With Jocelyn gone, I thought it might bother you to have your old in-laws hanging around all the time."

"You don't hang around all the time," Rick protested. He might have left it at that, but he couldn't ignore the tiny flicker of guilt at being dishonest with Tom. He smiled and added, "I just know that it's time for me to get on with my life. That's one of the reasons I came back."

He nodded thoughtfully and sent Rick a lopsided smile as he lifted his bottle. "Enough maudlin talk. I've been meaning to ask you where the best place will be for us to run the snowmobiles once they get here."

"Snowmobiles?" Rick didn't try to hide his surprise. "Who's bringing snowmobiles?"

Tom let out an annoyed sigh. "Lynette didn't tell you?"

"She never mentioned them."

"Great." Tom shoved his beer bottle a few inches away. "I *told* her to check with you about them."

"Well, she didn't."

"We made arrangements to rent some in town," Tom said. "Lynette's thinking maybe we can run them in that big field across the river."

Rick shook his head quickly. "Can't do it. I told you, it's not my property."

"Yeah, I know. But maybe we can get permission from the owner to use it."

"Maybe," Rick said, "but I doubt it."

"We can ask, can't we?"

Rick supposed they could, but he could think of half a dozen things he'd rather do than approach Maddock with the question. If he had to ask, he'd rather talk to Marti about it first. That thought brought a slow smile to his lips. "I could talk to his daughter, I guess. She might be able to get him to agree."

"Well, then?" Tom leaned back in his seat and smiled with satisfaction, as if the problem had been solved.

A tingle of anticipation at the thought of seeing Marti again worked up Rick's spine. "I'll talk to her tomorrow."

"Great." Tom drained the last of his beer and pushed to his feet. "You want another one?"

Rick shook his head. "No, I'd better keep a clear head if I'm going to be swinging an ax again in the morning."

Tom chuckled. "Not me. If I'm going to haul fire-wood around all day, I'd rather be numb."

"If you have too many," Rick warned, "you won't be numb. You'll be hungover."

Tom crossed to the refrigerator and pulled out another bottle. "One more, then I'll head back to our cabin. You know, of course, that if Lynette accuses me of getting drunk, I'll be forced to blame you for making me drink it."

"Yeah." Rick grinned at his brother-in-law. "I'm sure she'll believe you."

"She might."

"And she might not."

With an elaborate sigh, Tom opened the refrigerator again. "Fine. I'll put it back. Some pal *you* are," he joked. "Won't even take the blame for what I do."

Rick laughed. "I'm not an idiot. I know what Lynette's like when she gets upset." The instant the words left his mouth, his smile faded. Lynette's temperament was the same as Jocelyn's, and he couldn't help remembering how he used to tiptoe around her when she was angry—until the night she died.

Tom didn't seem to notice the change in his mood. He closed the refrigerator, crossed the room and clapped one hand on Rick's shoulder. "I'd better get back before she comes looking for me. Thanks for agreeing to ask if we can use the field. Even if the guy says no, at least Lynette can't claim I didn't ask."

"You aren't asking," Rick reminded him. "I am."

Tom worked up an expression of surprised hurt. "I asked *you.*"

Rick laughed again. "So you did." He stood and followed Tom through the living room to the front door. When he was alone again, he sank into one of the armchairs in front of the fire and leaned his head against the chair's back.

Visions of Jocelyn danced through his head, but they

weren't pleasant images. He didn't like remembering that Jocelyn had been very much like Lynette.

She'd made demands like a child. He'd placated her like an anxious parent—like Marti did with Cameron—but he'd resented having to do so. And then, he'd felt guilty about the resentment. He saw the same pattern replayed between Tom and Lynette. Lynette demanded. Tom placated. He just hoped Tom wouldn't let things build up inside the way he, himself, had.

His anger and resentment had driven Jocelyn away. And guilt had been his constant companion since her death.

MARTI PRESSED the save key on her computer, leaned back in her chair and glanced out the living-room window. Afternoon sun glittered on the icy snow. Deepening shadows lengthened across the front yard and stretched toward the forest and the river beyond. Melting icicles dripped steadily from the side of the house onto the ground.

Outside, she could hear voices—her father's deep baritone, Gil's slightly higher, and Cameron's deep enough now to match his father's. Gil said something she couldn't make out, but her father and Cameron laughed aloud. They sounded happy working together, and Cameron seemed like a different person with Gil around. Only Marti had reservations about the arrangement.

Her father and Cameron made no effort to hide their hopes for a reconciliation, but Gil hadn't pushed her—at least not very hard. He'd been friendly, talkative, amusing, entertaining and even sensitive. She suspected him of wearing his "courting" face and worried it wouldn't last long—just as it hadn't the first time.

She wondered whether all men put on such a show when they were trying to win a woman, and whether they all changed so completely once the vows had been exchanged. Take Rick, for instance. He seemed to be all the things Gil pretended to be. But she couldn't help wondering if Rick had listened to Jocelyn with the same intense interest he showed around her, or if he'd changed once he became a husband.

Holding back a sigh, she scrolled to the top of her article and began to reread it. Since she'd been back in Gunnison, she'd let family concerns and Rick take over her thoughts for too long. See? Here she was again, daydreaming and speculating, instead of working. She needed to put Gil, her father, Cameron and Rick out of her mind. Surely she could make herself concentrate long enough to finish this article and mail it to her editor.

Making a few minor edits as she worked, she read the article once more and then sent it to print. Later, after dinner, when her mind was fresh and Gil had gone home, and her father and Cameron were busy watching television, she'd read the hard copy. But for now, she needed to do something else. She could try again to call Cherryl, or she could get out of the house. Take a walk in the fresh air. Maybe stroll down by the bridge and see if she could glimpse Rick working outside.

Great idea, she thought with a laugh. Her relationship with Gil was still unsettled, Cameron had barely started speaking civilly to her again, and here she was, daydreaming about the neighbor. She turned off her computer, pushed away from the desk and stood. Instead of Rick, she should be thinking about Christmas. It was only ten days away. Instead of sneaking down to the bridge for a peek at Rick, she ought to carry in the boxes of her mother's decorations from the barn and make some concession to the holidays.

She dialed Cherryl's number, but after eight rings, she hung up. She pulled on her jacket, gloves and hat and stepped onto the wide front porch. But when she realized the men had gone into the barn, she changed her mind. There'd be plenty of time to decorate tomorrow.

She hopped off the porch, walked the trail of packed ice to the driveway and hurried toward the road. The weather had turned slightly warmer, and the air felt so refreshing, she decided to trust herself with a short walk. Toward the bridge.

She walked slowly and watched the sky turn a deep inky blue as the sun dropped ever lower. She'd almost reached the bridge when the sound of voices caught her attention. She stopped walking and listened. They were close, obviously on this side of the river.

With her heart in her throat, she listened more intently, hoping to hear Rick's deep voice among them. Before she realized they were moving, a young girl of about fourteen burst from the trees holding a mound of snow in both hands. A second later, an older girl— maybe seventeen—came through the trees after her.

As the first girl's gaze swept over Marti, she ground to a halt. The older girl quickly followed suit and smiled. "Hi. You caught us."

Marti glanced over her shoulder, expecting to see her father barreling along the road toward them. To her relief, she didn't see him—yet. "It looks as if you're having fun."

The older girl nodded. "We're having a snowball fight." She took a step toward her sister. "I'm Ashley Waverly, and this is my sister, Kendra. My uncle owns the cabins over there." She pointed across the river, and glanced back quickly. Tufts of dark hair peeked out from beneath her knit cap and her pretty face clouded, as if she expected trouble.

"We've wandered over the line, haven't we?" Kendra asked.

Marti couldn't help but smile. "Actually, you did when you crossed the bridge."

Ashley's face reddened and she jabbed Kendra with her elbow. "I *told* you." To Marti, she added, "Uncle Rick told us not to come over here, but it's so pretty, we couldn't resist."

Kendra's face clouded. She shared her sister's dark hair, but the nearly perfect features made her look almost exactly like the picture of Jocelyn she'd seen on Rick's mantel. "So, are we in trouble for being over here?"

Marti hooked her thumbs in the back pockets of her jeans. "I don't mind, but it's my father's property, and he gets pretty upset when people trespass." Loyalty kept her from adding that he only really cared if the people were connected to Rick. That sounded too petty.

Kendra's eyes widened. "Are you Cameron's mom?"

"Yes, but you can call me Marti. I take it you've met Cameron?"

Ashley nodded, but she didn't look nearly as impressed as Kendra did. "Yeah. When he was working with Uncle Rick and my dad."

"He's going to find someone to take us on a sleigh ride when it gets closer to Christmas," Kendra said.

"Cameron is?" Marti didn't try to disguise her surprise. It had been a long time since he'd offered to do anything for someone else. "That's great."

Kendra looked as if she might say something else, then stopped and frowned slightly at the road behind Marti. A second later, Marti heard the sound of an engine coming their way. It had to be her father or Gil. Or both. Her smile faded.

Ashley's expression sobered instantly. She grabbed Kendra's arm and started toward the bridge, but before they could make it, Gil's truck loomed around the last curve in the road.

He braked, skidded a little and came to a stop not far from where Marti stood. Throwing open the door, he jumped to the ground and crossed to stand beside Marti. "What's going on here?"

Marti frowned at him, more than a little resentful of the possessiveness in his voice. The Lazy M wasn't his yet, and she certainly didn't owe him any explanations. "I'm talking to Dad's neighbors."

Gil parked his fists on his hips and turned his scowl on the girls. "Don't you know this is private property?"

Ashley nodded and sidled closer to her sister. "Yes."

"Well, then?" Gil took a step toward them.

Marti's cheeks burned and her chest tightened with anger. "Leave them alone, Gil. I called them over here."

Ashley stared at her for a second, then looked away quickly. Marti prayed Gil hadn't noticed the surprise on the girl's face.

His expression shifted subtly. "Your father wouldn't like that," he warned. "You know how he feels about trespassers."

"Yes, I do," she admitted. "But that doesn't mean I think he's right." She struggled to control her temper. After all, Gil was only trying to respect her father's wishes. "Anyway, there's no harm done. We were just talking."

Gil dipped his head in a curt nod. "That's fine," he said, turning back to Ashley and Kendra. "But you'd best get back on your own side of the river before it becomes a problem."

They didn't need to be told twice. Spinning away, Ashley pulled Kendra after her. She reached the bridge, then turned with a wary smile. "It was nice to meet you," she called to Marti.

Marti smiled back. "It was nice to meet you, too."

Gil waited until the girls had crossed the bridge, then scowled at Marti. "Get in the truck. I'll give you a ride back home."

She shook her head and stepped back. "I'll walk. It's nice out. Besides, you're obviously on your way home."

"Oh, for hell's sake, Marti. I'm not going to bite you. Besides, we need to talk about where Cameron's going to be for Christmas."

She hesitated for a second, then nodded. She supposed she couldn't avoid the conversation, and she'd rather have it when she and Gil were alone. "I guess you're right," she said and tried to soften her expression.

To her surprise, her efforts had an immediate effect. The tension faded from Gil's expression and something like relief took its place. "Henry thinks we should all spend Christmas together, but I told him that's up to you."

Her step faltered, but she tried not to show the new, sudden panic that filled her. She could refuse, of course, but then she'd just be handing Cameron another reason to resent her.

She forced a smile. "I guess that would make Cameron happy."

"Yes, it would."

"Then, I guess that's what we should do."

Gil put his arm around her shoulders and started toward the truck. "I'm glad you think so."

Marti forced herself not to pull away from him. She told herself it would get easier with time. But his arm felt like lead on her shoulders and she couldn't rid herself of the strange empty feeling in the pit of her stomach.

And she wondered, for just one moment, if she could honestly give him a second chance, or if her feelings for him had been dead too long even to try. She didn't want to sit beneath the Christmas tree with Gil or look at him over their holiday dinner. But Cameron did. And Marti wanted Cameron to be happy. More than anything in the world, she wanted her son to love her again.

CHAPTER SEVEN

EARLY THE NEXT MORNING, Marti closed the front door of her father's house behind her and walked across the snowy parking area toward her car. Weak winter sunlight peeked out from behind pale gray clouds and a light breeze teased her as she walked. Shivering slightly, she tucked her shopping list into the pocket of her jacket and pulled her keys from her purse.

At least it wasn't snowing. She could easily make the drive into Gunnison, visit her aunt Martha for a few minutes and try once again to make contact with Cherryl. She could pick up the groceries she needed, and come back in time to make lunch. She sighed and worked her keys into the car-door lock. At times, when she let herself think about it, the ease with which she'd fallen into her mother's role in her father's house amazed her.

She didn't mind doing things for Henry. She'd always enjoyed cooking, though cleaning house was another story entirely. But she still had to work at putting aside the resentment that arose each time she looked across the table and saw Gil sitting there.

From the moment she'd agreed to give him another chance, he'd become a regular fixture around the house. Only the delight on Cameron's face kept her feelings in check.

Smiling ruefully, she unlocked the car. But before she could get inside, Cameron called her. She stopped and looked back toward the house. He hadn't willingly sought her company in so long, her heart raced. And when he hurried from the house to the car and actually *smiled* at her, she had to blink rapidly to hold back the grateful tears.

"Are you leaving now?" he asked.

"I was planning to."

He opened the passenger-side door and slid inside. "Then, can you drop me off at Rick's on your way?"

"Of course." The thought of seeing Rick again sent apprehension rushing through her, but she tried to match Cameron's casual mood. She worked up a determined smile and settled behind the steering wheel. "How are things going on the job?"

Cameron shrugged. "Okay, I guess."

Marti didn't want to push her luck. She let silence lapse between them and maneuvered the car carefully over patches of ice dotting the road where the trees blocked the sun.

"I talked to Dad last night," Cameron said after a long moment. "He says you're going to let him spend Christmas with us."

No wonder Cameron seemed so pleasant this morning. Marti worked up another smile. "Yes, if you want him there."

He looked faintly irritated. "Of course I want him there. Don't you?"

"I wouldn't have agreed to let him join us if I didn't." She hoped he didn't notice the lack of enthusiasm in her voice.

Apparently satisfied, Cameron leaned back in his

seat and tapped his knee in rhythm to a song only he could hear. "Good. You won't be sorry. He's changed."

Marti didn't know if she believed that, but she didn't argue. This tentative channel of communication between them was too precious to destroy. "I hope so."

Cameron frowned at her. "All you have to do is give him another chance."

"I'm doing that, Cam."

He nodded slowly and changed rhythm on his knee. "What are you going to give him for Christmas?"

Marti tried to hide her dismay. She hadn't even thought about buying Gil a gift. "I haven't thought that far ahead."

"He's already got your present."

Wonderful. Now she'd have to buy him something or look bad in front of Cameron. "Has he?"

"Yeah. It was expensive, too. But I can't tell you what it is."

Great. An expensive gift. Marti forced a weak smile. "What are you going to give him?"

"I'm not sure yet." Cameron slid down on his tailbone. "I don't know what he wants."

"Well, you'll have your own money. I suppose you'll be able to buy him whatever you want."

"Yeah." A cloud crossed Cameron's expression, but it disappeared so quickly she wondered if she'd really seen it. "Yeah," he said again.

"What are you going to do with the rest of your money?"

He shrugged casually. Too casually. "I don't know yet."

All-too-familiar concern stirred inside her, but she

refused to make it real. Instead, she turned into Rick's driveway and changed the subject again. "Where do you want me to drop you?"

Cameron sat up a little straighter and nodded toward the house. "Just out front. Rick's probably still home."

Marti pulled in beside Rick's truck and shifted into Park. "You won't be late, will you?"

Cameron climbed out of the car and looked back inside at her with a lopsided grin. "Not if I can help it."

Marti's heart soared. "Do you want me to pick you up after work?"

"Sure," he said with another shrug. "If you want to."

When he closed the door between them and walked away from the car, Marti nearly laughed aloud. *If she wanted to?* She'd move heaven and earth to win another smile like that from Cameron or to spend another ten minutes in his company without fighting.

She put the car into reverse and checked the rear window before backing out. But someone stood behind her car and blocked her path. She could only see the bottom of his jacket and the top of his jeans, but she knew immediately it was Rick.

Her heart gave a lurch and her hands grew clammy inside her gloves. While she watched, he came out from behind the car and approached her window. He waited until she rolled down the window, then propped both hands on the car door and smiled down at her. "Good morning." Simple words, but his smile and the deep timbre of his voice shook her to the core. He held her gaze, and the look in his eyes felt almost intimate.

She tried to smile back, but her lips felt stiff. She

tried to ignore the masculine scent that drifted through the open window, but it brought back the memory of their kiss in a rush. She managed to respond, but her voice sounded weak and shaky. "Good morning."

"You're up and about awfully early."

"I am. I've got to go into Gunnison. I've put off grocery shopping long enough."

He dragged his gaze away and checked his watch. "You'll have quite a wait. The store doesn't open until nine o'clock."

"I know. I'm going to visit my aunt first."

Rick nodded toward the house. "I was just going to make a fresh pot of coffee. Do you want to join me?"

Every instinct urged her to accept. Logic warned her to say no—especially with Cameron watching every move she made. "I'd like to," she said honestly, "but my aunt is expecting me, and she's already a little upset with me for not stopping by sooner."

He looked so disappointed, her heart gave another skip. "Another time, then."

"Yes," she said softly. "Another time." Why not? she thought. She enjoyed his company. She didn't want to avoid him. After all, her decision to give Gil another chance didn't mean she couldn't have friends of her own.

But when Rick touched her arm and the familiar tightening of desire curled in her stomach, she knew she was making a mistake. And when the surge of heat crawled up her arm from the place where his gloved hand touched her jacket, she knew she'd have to work very hard to avoid this man in the future. If she didn't, she'd undermine everything she was trying to do with Cameron.

SOMETHING CAMERON didn't like filled him as he watched Rick talking to his mom. Her face turned all red and that goofy-looking smile stretched across her face, and made Cameron feel kind of sick.

What in the hell did she think she was doing? Flirting? She wasn't supposed to be flirting with Rick. She was *supposed* to be getting back together with his dad. She probably thought Cameron couldn't tell what she was doing. She thought he was too stupid to know. But he knew. Anybody with two eyes would know.

As he watched, his mom laughed at something Rick said, and the anger tightened like a fist in his gut. Oh, yeah, she complained all the time about he way his dad had flirted with other women while they were married—but look at *her.* She was doing exactly the same thing. What did she have to complain about?

She said something Cameron couldn't hear. Rick's face looked kind of odd, and for a minute Cameron thought his mom would get out of the car. Thank God, she didn't. But her smile turned all funny, and Cameron felt his own face heat with embarrassment.

Didn't she know she was making a fool of herself? Rick didn't want her here. He was just being polite. Couldn't she tell that?

Obviously not.

A rush of sympathy for his dad tore through him. How was Cameron supposed to fix the mess he'd made if she was going to do stuff like this? How could he undo everything and get his mom and dad back together again?

Suddenly angry, Cameron crossed the snowy yard back to the car and leaned against it. He sent his mom

a look she *had* to understand. There. Her smile faded.
Good. She knew he was on to her.

Rick dragged his eyes away and smiled at Cameron.
"So, are you ready to hit it again today?"

Cameron nodded. Rick might try to look upset by
the interruption, but Cameron could tell he appreciated
the rescue. "Sure. What are we doing?"

Rick stepped away from the car. His mom tried smiling at him, but Cameron didn't smile back. Her smile
slipped and she looked away again, working the car
into reverse as she did. For some reason, Rick put his
hand on the window again and leaned down to look at
her. "I'll talk to you later, okay? There's something
important I need to ask you."

Cameron scowled. He didn't like the sound of that
at all. Rick made it sound as if he *wanted* to see her
again.

His mom nodded. "Yes, of course." She tilted her
head to see Cameron better. "Maybe when I pick up
Cameron after work."

Not if Cameron's life depended on it. He brushed
hair from his eyes and glared at her. "You don't need
to pick me up. I'll walk home."

Her smile died on her lips, and Cameron felt a surge
of satisfaction.

Rick frowned at him, but he didn't say anything until
after she'd backed the car around and driven away.
"Why don't you want your mom to pick you up? Are
you having problems again?"

He sounded as if he felt *sorry* for her. Cameron
shook his head. "No."

"It would mean a lot to her if you'd let her pick you
up. She wants things to get better between you."

Cameron shrugged without answering. Things wouldn't get better if she went around flirting with other men. Acting as though she wasn't going to get married to his dad again. Giving guys like Rick the wrong impression. "Why do you care?"

Rick's eyes widened for a second, and Cameron could tell the question surprised him. Good. Maybe Rick needed to think about what he was doing, too.

Rick's eyes narrowed again. "I care because I like you both. Your mom's a friend."

"Yeah? Well, don't worry about it." Cameron started away, then turned back to look at Rick again. Maybe he didn't know what he was doing. His mom probably hadn't told him that she was getting married again. And maybe Kendra and her family showing up early had made him forget what Cameron had told him about the diamond ring his dad had bought.

Rick was an okay guy and Cameron was pretty sure that if he knew about Cameron's mom and dad, he wouldn't let her flirt like that with him.

He tried not to look angry. "We're not having any trouble," he said. "In fact, everything's great."

"Really?" One of Rick's eyebrows shot up. "I'm glad to hear it."

"Yeah." Cameron worked his hands into his pockets. "Did she tell you the news?"

"What news?"

"She and my dad are getting married again."

Rick's face froze. Cameron was right. He hadn't known. He must be embarrassed as hell. Or mad at her for flirting around with him when she was about to marry somebody else.

"No," Rick said slowly. "She didn't tell me."

"Yeah. Well. They are. In fact, we're all spending Christmas together. Great, huh?"

A weird expression crossed Rick's face. "Yeah. Great."

Cameron felt better now. Much better. He'd get the situation with his mom and dad worked out. He had to.

ADJUSTING HIS SUNGLASSES against the glare of the sun, Rick slowed his truck and pulled into the parking lot of Greta's Groceries.

He was glad to escape the wood splitting for a few minutes to pick up chips and soda to go with the lunch Lynette had volunteered to fix. He'd been plagued with thoughts of Marti since she drove away the day before—since Cameron had dropped his bombshell. He'd been thinking about her all morning, since well before sunrise, and he needed to do something to take his mind off her. Chopping and stacking firewood certainly hadn't worked.

He parked to one side of the small building and climbed down from the cab of his truck. Just as he started across the parking lot, the sound of another vehicle approaching made him look back at the road.

Marti waved when she saw him, but he could tell even before she reached him across the parking lot that something had upset her.

He didn't ask what. If she wanted him to know, she'd tell him. Instead, he nodded a greeting and hooked his thumbs in the front pockets of his jeans. "We meet again."

"Yes." She tucked a lock of hair behind one ear. "Did Cameron make it to work on time this morning?"

"He did, and he's still there chopping firewood until I get back." An expression of such relief flashed across her face, Rick wanted to say something that might set her mind at ease. "He's doing a good job, you know. I'm lucky to have him helping me."

She smiled again and looked down at the toes of her boots. "You probably think I'm a horribly overprotective mother."

"Not at all. I think you're a very worried woman— and not without reason."

She sighed softly, but lifted her gaze again. "Thank you."

"For nothing." He touched one hand to the small of her back, intending only to urge her inside out of the cold. But when she looked into his eyes in that second before she started walking, anticipation curled through him. He knew he should pull his hand away, but he didn't. He liked having her beside him.

When they reached the steps to the porch, he removed his hand reluctantly and followed her up the stairs. The soft curve of her hips in her jeans caught his eye and stirred the same need he'd given in to the night he'd kissed her.

Without warning, she glanced back at him and he could tell from the look in her eye she'd caught him ogling her. He forced a smile. "You're just the woman I wanted to see this morning. I think we're going to have a problem, and I'm hoping you can help me come up with a solution."

"With Cameron?"

"No. Actually, it's with my family."

She cocked her head to one side and eyed him curiously.

"My brother-in-law is planning to rent some snow-mobiles," he said. "They want to run them in that big field of your dad's."

She groaned aloud and pressed the heel of one hand to her forehead. "Oh, please, no."

"You don't think he'll go for that?"

She let out a brittle laugh. "No. Not exactly."

"Well, then, I'll just have to do my best to keep them on my side of the river."

"Even that probably won't be good enough," she said. "Dad'll have a fit when he hears them, even if they don't cross onto Lazy M property."

He turned slightly to move out of the sun's glare. "Great."

She didn't miss his sarcasm, but she smiled slightly. "Great isn't the word."

"I don't suppose there's any way you could convince him not to let them bother him…"

She shook her head quickly and made a face. "I don't think so. He's too stubborn. I've never been successful at convincing him of anything. He's sure your cabins are going to ruin the Lazy M."

"I'm not keeping them," Rick told her. "In fact, my Realtor called with an offer this morning."

She flicked a glance at him. Could that be disappointment he saw in her eyes? "Was it a good offer?"

"No," he said with a shake of his head. In fact, the offer had been a lucrative one made by a company interested in building a small factory on his property. In spite of the money, Rick hadn't accepted. Somehow, being here again made him appreciate the serenity of the place all over again. If he sold—*when* he sold—he wanted buyers who loved the land as much as he did.

Marti glanced at him again and smiled slowly. "This is selfish of me, I know, but I hope you find good people to take your place. Dad thinks it's my fault he had to sell the property to you."

"Your fault?" Another strike against Henry Maddock in Rick's book. "Why?"

Because of the divorce. Without Gil to help him, he couldn't manage the whole thing on his own. I think that's why he's so determined to see me reconcile with Gil."

Rick tried not to look overly interested. "And are you going to?"

She shrugged lifelessly. "Cameron still hates me. It's no secret that he believes I've screwed up everybody's lives. I told him I'd give his dad a second chance—not a reconciliation, exactly, but a chance to prove that he's changed. So, Gil's at the house all the time, and he acts as if he's changed, but I have trouble believing that he really has."

Cameron had sounded so certain that Marti was planning to marry Gil again, Rick couldn't help the surge of relief that swept through him. He battled the urge to pull her into his arms and make everything all right for her. It wasn't in his power to make anything all right. "And here I am, making it all worse by asking you about snowmobiles."

She waved his words away with one hand. "You're not doing anything."

He liked hearing her say that, but he wasn't at all certain it was true. "I'd be glad to come over and talk to your dad about using his field if you think it would help."

"I don't think it would. The only person Dad's listening to these days is Gil."

Rick had no intention of talking to Gil. He climbed the steps to stand beside her. "I'll talk to your dad." He paused, smiled halfheartedly and tugged open the door. "One of these days."

She laughed softly and stepped into the store. Inside, the scent of coffee and cinnamon rolls filled the air.

Greta looked up when they entered. She'd decked herself out in Christmas garb—a red Santa sweatshirt, candy-cane earrings, bells at her wrists and on her neck. In spite of his usual aversion to the holidays, Rick smiled.

She hurried out from behind the counter and wrapped Marti in a huge hug. "How are you, sweetheart?"

Immediately, the distress in Marti's face lessened. She looked young, worry-free, and more beautiful than ever. Rick suddenly wanted very much to find some way of keeping that expression on her face.

"I'm fine," she said. "Fine."

Greta held her at arm's length and looked her up and down until the candy canes danced on the older woman's ears. "Well, you look wonderful. But Cherryl tells me you and she still haven't gotten together."

"Not yet," Marti admitted. "I've left her a couple of messages, but I haven't heard back from her."

"Well, you know that daughter of mine," Greta said. "She's been busy with the restaurant and the kids and Christmas. Even I have trouble catching up with her. But keep trying. She'll never forgive you if you leave without seeing her."

Rick hesitated for a moment, torn between the desire

to finish his conversation with Marti and the dawning realization that she'd moved on. He turned toward the potato-chip aisle and made a selection quickly, then walked to the back of the store and the refrigerator that held the soda.

Dimly aware of the bell over the door tinkling when someone new came in, he pulled out a six-pack of cola and started to turn around. But when he remembered that Lynette refused to drink anything with caffeine, he replaced the cola in the cooler. Just as he reached for an acceptable choice, someone's hand brushed his shoulder.

He turned quickly and came face-to-face with Marti. Her smile reached all the way to her eyes, and they looked so clear, so bright, so inviting, he couldn't tear his gaze away.

"I'm sorry. I didn't mean to ignore you like that. Greta is my best friend's mom, and she's always been like a second mother to me."

"It's all right. No harm done." Her hand lingered on his shoulder. Her scent enveloped him. Her eyes refused to let his go. And he realized suddenly that, no matter how hard he might try, how much smarter he'd be to walk away from her, or how wrong he'd be to bring even more trouble into her life, he couldn't change the way he felt around her.

By some miracle, and only because they weren't alone, he resisted the urge to wrap his arms around her and kiss her. He could feel Greta watching them from behind the cash register. *He* didn't care—not at the moment, anyway—but he didn't want to make Marti the object of speculation among her neighbors.

With effort, he ignored the tempting fullness of

Marti's lips, the swell of her breasts beneath her jacket and the luscious curve of her hips. But he wasn't ready to leave her. Not yet.

"I've just had a great idea." His voice came out gruff with longing. He pretended not to notice and so, thank God, did Marti. "Why don't you follow me home and join us for lunch? It will give you a chance to spend time with Cameron when he's on his best behavior. Unless you have other plans?"

If possible, her smile grew brighter. "I'd love to."

He felt the silly grin creep across his face again, but this time he didn't even try to get rid of it. He pulled two packs of soda from the cooler, adjusted everything in one hand so he could rest his other one on her back and followed her to the front of the store.

She stopped once to pull a can of coffee from the shelf, once more for non-dairy creamer and sugar, then took her purchases to the cash register.

Greta kept her face a perfect mask, but Rick could see the approval in her eyes when she looked at him. To his surprise, he wanted this woman who obviously cared deeply for Marti to approve. After all, she might be the only person around who did approve of their silent decision to explore the attraction between them. Marti's family certainly wouldn't like it, and neither, he thought sadly, would Jocelyn's.

MARTI PLUGGED a tape into the cassette player in the rental car and followed Rick down the mountain. She didn't let herself question her reasons for agreeing to have lunch with him. She'd seen the look in his eyes. She'd seen the smile that matched her own whenever she was near him.

She'd had enough of surly attitudes, hostility and thinly veiled threats to last a lifetime. She'd met someone who enjoyed her company and who didn't talk to her as if she were a child. She wouldn't let anyone make her feel guilty for seeking his company—not even herself.

Pulling off the highway, she followed him into the parking area in front of the cabins. He hopped from the truck and hurried across the ice to her car. As she watched him walk—his legs long and lean, his shoulders broad and strong—a splinter of desire knifed through her. She'd tried for nearly a week to forget his kiss, to stop thinking about the way his arms felt around her and the muscles in his legs supported her when she sat on his lap. She'd even managed to convince herself she'd been successful. But now honesty forced her to admit she'd failed miserably. She hadn't forgotten, nor did she want to.

He stopped beside her car and opened the door. A little embarrassed by the direction her thoughts had taken, she left her groceries in the car and hooked her bag over her shoulder.

As he had at the store, he put one hand on the small of her back as they walked. She liked the way it felt there. Strong. Sure. Confident. But as they neared the house and Cameron, she had to work harder to relax. Would Cameron really be on his best behavior, or would he embarrass them both in front of Rick's family?

Rick's smile faded. "Is something wrong?"

She started to shake her head, then stopped and said honestly, "I'm just a little nervous about Cameron."

He looked relieved for some reason. "It'll be okay.

You'll see.'' He opened the front door and waited until she stepped inside, then came in behind her. He stood close enough for her to feel the heat emanating from his body. His fingers brushed her shoulders when he helped her with her jacket, and she melted into his touch for a second.

But before she could even look at him again, one of his nieces—the younger one—bounded into the room. She skidded to a stop on the hardwood floor when she saw Marti. "Oh. Hi."

Marti smiled, but heat flooded her face and she wondered if the girl had noticed the way she'd leaned against Rick. "Hi."

"This is my niece, Kendra," Rick said. "Ken, I'd like you to meet—"

"Mrs. Johansson." Kendra finished for him and grinned again. "Yeah. We've met."

"You have?" His eyes widened slightly, but he smiled easily and motioned for Marti to step into the living room.

"Yes. Briefly." Marti tucked a lock of hair behind one ear and tugged on the hem of her sweater, both nervous habits she usually managed to keep under control. "I ran into the girls while I was taking a walk the other day."

"Oh." He grinned as if it were the best news he'd heard all year and turned to Kendra. "Is lunch ready?"

"Almost." The girl glanced over her shoulder as if she needed to confirm her answer, then grinned back at them. "Should I get Cameron and Dad?"

Rick nodded. "Sure."

Marti watched the girl scamper to the front door.

Almost as an afterthought, Kendra pulled her coat from its hook and slipped into it. "Back in a minute."

She looked so eager, Marti wondered if she always acted that way or if maybe she had a crush on Cameron. She hoped for the latter. It might make Cameron more reluctant to behave badly during lunch.

Rick touched her again, the merest brush of his hand against her back, but it made her breath catch. "Do you want to join the others in the kitchen, or wait here?"

She wanted more than anything to spend a few more minutes alone with him, but she didn't say so. "We can join the others."

He led her into the kitchen and put the soda and chips on the counter by Lynette, who was already surrounded by an open loaf of bread, three empty tuna cans, a head of lettuce and a half-empty jar of mayonnaise. "I brought company for lunch," he said. "Marti Johansson...Lynette Waverly."

Lynette sliced a sandwich in half and placed it on top of the others she'd already stacked on a plate. She glanced at Marti and smiled. "Yes. You're Cameron's mother." In the next instant, she saw Rick's hand on Marti's shoulder and her smile slipped.

The change in attitude surprised Marti, but she tried not to let it bother her. "Can I help you with anything?"

"It's all ready." Lynette focused on another sandwich, but her lips pursed in a tight frown.

Marti looked at Rick to see if he'd noticed. He hadn't. Smiling easily, he pulled out a chair for Marti and nodded toward the six-pack on the counter. "I hope I got the right kind of soda."

Lynette glanced briefly at the cans. "It's fine."

Rick crossed to the cupboard and pulled out a large bowl. Still oblivious to the tension radiating from Lynette, he opened the bag of chips, poured them into the bowl and carried it to the table.

But Marti couldn't ignore Lynette. She wondered if life with Cameron had made her overly sensitive to it, or if she was misreading Lynette's suddenly sharp movements, but she didn't think so.

Rick started to sit beside her, but the telephone rang and stopped him halfway into his chair. He stood again quickly, obviously surprised. "I wonder who that could be? Everyone I know is right here."

Lynette wiped her hands on a towel. "I'll get it. I left a message for Ryan to call."

"You're busy," Rick said, and started toward the door. "I'll get it in the other room."

When he left the room, Lynette ignored Marti for several long seconds, then flicked a glance at her that made her even more uncomfortable. "Are you and Rick good friends?"

"I guess so," Marti said. She tried to smile at the other woman, but her lips felt stiff and unwieldy. "We haven't known each other long."

A near smile lifted Lynette's mouth but it held no warmth. "I see."

Desperate to remove whatever barrier Lynette imagined between them, Marti asked, "How are you related to Rick? Are you his sister?"

"Sister-in-law." Lynette lifted her gaze. This time Marti saw a challenge there. "Jocelyn was my sister."

Closing her eyes for a second, Marti took a deep

breath. Wonderful. That would certainly explain the animosity.

But Jocelyn had been dead for two years. Surely even her family couldn't expect Rick to grieve forever.

"I've seen her picture," Marti said. "She was very beautiful."

"Yes, she was."

"Rick loved her very much."

Lynette stared at her for a long moment. "He still does, you know."

Marti's heart skipped a beat, but she tried not to let Lynette see her uncertainty. "Of course he does. I'm sure he always will."

Lynette's smile changed subtly. She looked... satisfied. "They were a perfect couple. Rick hasn't ever recovered from her death."

Marti remembered the flash of pain on his face when she'd looked at Jocelyn's picture, and wondered why she hadn't realized before how much he still hurt. "No. Of course he hasn't."

"That's why he asked us to come for Christmas," Lynette said with another challenging glance. "It's a way for him to keep her memory close and stay a part of the family."

Marti hadn't realized Rick had asked Jocelyn's family to come, but now that she knew she felt foolish. Had she really seen desire in his eyes, or had she only wanted to see it there? Was she so desperate to feel loved and desired that she'd deluded herself?

No. She'd seen the way he looked at her. She hadn't imagined it. But desire didn't mean caring. It didn't mean he loved her.

Physical need. Was that all Rick felt? Marti didn't

want that. Getting involved in a brief but passionate affair would only make her feel worse about herself and her life than she already did.

She stood quickly and picked up her bag. "Will you apologize to Rick for me? I've just remembered that I promised to take my dad into Gunnison this afternoon. He's probably waiting for me right now."

Lynette lifted both eyebrows in silent question, but she looked almost triumphant.

CHAPTER EIGHT

WITH HIS HEADLIGHTS slicing through the early evening shadows, Rick drove his truck slowly across the bridge toward the Lazy M. Wind buffeted the truck and leaked into the cab. He turned the heater a little higher and swerved to miss a chunk of ice on the side of the road.

He still didn't understand why Marti had left so quickly before lunch. According to Lynette, they'd been having a pleasant conversation when Marti suddenly grabbed her things, offered a lame excuse and ran out of the house. But that didn't make sense.

Surely, if Marti really had to take Henry somewhere, she would have mentioned it when they were talking about him outside Greta's. No doubt, she'd gotten cold feet about facing Cameron. But if she'd seen the disappointment on her son's face, she'd have realized her mistake.

Well, Rick didn't intend to let it slide. After he talked to Henry about using his field for the snowmobiles, he'd try to catch Marti alone. And he'd try to make her understand how much running away had upset Cameron.

He slowed the truck outside the Lazy M's gates, but he didn't turn in immediately. Ridiculous, he told himself. He had no reason to be nervous about approaching her. Gritting his teeth, he wrenched the wheel and accelerated up the gentle slope.

He parked in front of Marti's rental car. Hopping from the truck, he walked to the front porch and knocked on the door.

She answered almost immediately. She'd pulled her hair into a ponytail and changed into an oversize forest green sweater and knit pants to match. She looked as if she belonged in these mountains—something Jocelyn had never managed to do.

When she saw him standing there, her eyes widened slightly. "Rick? Is something wrong?"

"No. I came to talk to your father about letting us use his field for the snowmobiles."

Her eyes clouded. "Oh, I don't..." She stopped, darted another quick glance behind her and tried to work up a smile. "He's in his office."

And she obviously didn't intend to disturb him. She stepped onto the porch and pulled the door nearly closed behind her. When a gust of wind tossed snow against the windows, she shivered but she still made no move to invite him inside.

"All right, then. I'll talk to you."

Even in the dusk, he could see the heightened color in her cheeks. "I can't give permission for you to run the snowmobiles in that field."

"That's not what I want to talk about." He took a step closer. "Can we get inside out of this wind? I'm freezing, and you don't even have a coat on."

She hesitated for a moment, then nodded. "Of course." She pushed open the door and led him into the huge living room. Immediately, the welcome heat rushed at him. A fire blazed in the broad fireplace and a log popped, sending a shower of sparks up the chimney. She turned to him. "Let me take your coat."

Rick slipped out of his jacket. She hung it in the closet then nodded toward a door at the back of the room. "We can talk in the kitchen."

He followed her, taking in the open boxes of Christmas decorations against one wall as they walked. An artificial pine wreath lay on the floor beside the couch next to a stack of red velvet bows. A variety of Santas and two brass horns stood in a cluster on the coffee table. He probably should apologize for interrupting her, but he didn't want to give her a chance to send him away.

Without warning, another thought intruded. Jocelyn. Familiar guilt and regret began to inch its way up his spine, but Rick forced it away. Jocelyn had no part in this conversation.

His step faltered. The thought surprised and even disturbed him, but it unlatched a part of his heart he didn't remember having, and he felt curiously free. As if Jocelyn had somehow stepped aside to let him get on with his life.

Marti waited to speak again until the kitchen door swung shut behind her. "Is it Cameron?"

"Cameron's fine. It's you I'm worried about."

She pulled back ever so slightly. "Why?"

"You tell me. Why did you leave the house today?"

"Like I told Lynette—"

"No," he interrupted, then made an effort to temper the sharpness of his voice. "If you'd had plans with your father, you would have remembered them up at Greta's. Something else happened, and I'd like to know what it was."

She glanced away quickly. Too quickly. "Nothing happened." Her voice came out little more than a whisper, and any lingering doubts Rick might have had disappeared.

He took her shoulders gently and turned her to face him. "You were afraid to see Cameron."

"No."

"Then what?"

She shook her head slowly, but she didn't speak.

He grew suddenly, quickly frustrated. "Lynette is as confused as I am," he began, but when her shoulders stiffened noticeably beneath his fingers, he stopped speaking and studied her face. "Does this have something to do with Lynette? Did she say something to offend you?"

Marti shook her head again. "No. She didn't say anything wrong."

"What *did* she say?"

"She didn't say anything wrong."

"But she did say something."

Marti nodded.

"What was it? What were you talking about?"

Marti looked deep into his eyes, as if she needed to find something there before she could answer. When she spoke again, her voice sounded a little stronger. "Jocelyn."

"Jocelyn?" Rick took a quick step backward and narrowed his eyes. "What about her?"

"She was a beautiful woman, and I know you're still grieving for her. I don't want to do anything to get in the way of that."

"You aren't."

She unfolded her hands and touched his arm. "I know you still love her—"

Yes, dammit, he probably always would love her in a way. But Jocelyn wasn't here. Jocelyn couldn't touch him, couldn't listen to him, couldn't make his heart beat faster. And she'd never been able to understand what went on inside him the way Marti did.

Without taking time to think about it, he reached for Marti again and pulled her into his arms. "Jocelyn's gone," he said. "You're here."

He lowered his lips to hers, but she turned and he only managed to graze the side of her mouth with his.

"Please, don't." She put both hands on his chest and pushed him away. "I don't want that."

"You don't want what?"

"This." She gestured at the space between them, little as it was. "I don't want…" She hesitated, as if she didn't know how to explain.

But Rick needed an explanation. He closed the distance between them again, determined to pull the truth from her one way or another. "Jocelyn's been gone for two years, Marti. She's not an issue between us." That he was able to say it aloud surprised him. That he meant it surprised him even more.

A light flickered in her eyes, but died away quickly. "I think she is. I've seen her in your eyes, and I know she's still in your heart. I don't want to be a third party in your life."

Rick clenched his teeth and tried not to show how much her response affected him. "You aren't."

"Yes, I am."

"Is that what Lynette said?"

She shook her head, but without conviction. "She

didn't have to. I've seen the way your face changes when someone mentions Jocelyn's name. It's obvious how much you love her still. Maybe you're not even aware of it, but I am, and I don't want to be a substitute for her.''

Rick wanted to argue, but he couldn't form the words. He wanted to deny the accusation, but doubt kept him from speaking. He could feel Marti watching him, waiting for a response, but the suggestion that he might be looking for someone to take Jocelyn's place staggered him.

He shook his head slowly. ''I don't want a substitute for Jocelyn,'' he managed to say at last.

Sadness darkened her eyes. ''You're not ready for anything else.''

Maybe she was right. Maybe he hadn't gotten over Jocelyn yet. He still avoided their bedroom, still couldn't make himself visit her grave, still dreamed about her most nights. If that were true, he had no right to seek comfort in Marti's arms.

As if his silence gave her an answer, Marti took another step away. ''I think you'd better go.''

''Maybe I should.'' Rick pivoted and pushed through the swinging door. He could hear her following as he crossed the living room and yanked his coat from the closet. He could feel her watching as he shoved his arms into the sleeves and wrenched open the door.

He made the mistake of looking at her once more before he stepped outside. What he saw in her expression made him hesitate, but he refused to let himself respond to it. He ignored the deep sadness in her eyes, the slight frown on her lips and the way she'd folded her arms and held on to her sweater as if she needed something to support her.

He closed the door firmly behind him and crossed the snow to the truck. Grinding the engine to life, he reversed and drove away. He forced himself to concentrate on the driving and tried to put Marti out of his mind, tried to forget the pain in her eyes and the sweet taste of her mouth.

When the headlights from an oncoming vehicle hit his windshield, he pulled as far as he could to the side of the road. Driving slowly, he began to pass the other truck. But when his lights hit the cab and he recognized Gil Johansson as the driver, his hands froze on the wheel and his stomach knotted.

There could be only one reason for Gil Johansson to be driving this road at this time—he was on his way to see Marti. Nausea welled in Rick's stomach. Anger churned with it. He knew how greatly Marti feared losing Cameron, how guilty Cameron and Gil made her feel about the divorce, and how much she wanted to run the Lazy M when her father couldn't do it any longer. Only one person could give her what she wanted most, and Rick wasn't that person.

Rick stopped his truck and watched in his rearview mirror as Gil turned off the road onto the Lazy M. There was someone between them, he thought bitterly—someone far more real than the specter of Jocelyn's memory.

In spite of everything, Marti was too trusting. Too vulnerable. And that jackal Johansson wouldn't hesitate to use those traits against her. Already, she believed he held the key to her happiness.

But Rick hated to see her reconcile with him if she

didn't love him. No, he *wouldn't* let that happen. He cared about her too much to sit back silently while Gil played on Marti's uncertainty.

He thought about turning the truck around and following Gil to the Lazy M, but confronting Gil in front of her would only make things worse. Marti didn't need him to erase trouble for her, she needed him to help her see how she could solve her problems on her own. She didn't need Gil or her father—or even Rick— to take care of her. She needed to believe in herself again. Then she'd be able to take charge of her relationship with Cameron. She'd find the strength to stand up to her father. And, hopefully, she'd believe that Rick was interested in her, not just looking for a substitute for Jocelyn.

RICK'S IRRITATION hadn't lessened by the time he reached his own place. He pulled up in front of the house and climbed out of the truck. Wind lifted bits of old snow from the ground and flung them against the truck and into his face. High overhead, it whistled through the trees, accentuating the hush of the night.

Shivering, Rick readjusted his Broncos cap and started toward the house. He stomped his feet on the welcome mat and put the key into the lock, but before he could open the door Lynette called out from the inky shadows.

"Rick?"

He pivoted toward the sound and searched for her. "Yes?"

She materialized in front of the toolshed. The wind teased her dark hair away from her face, and in the

him, but the exchange brought a sudden, vivid picture into his mind of Jocelyn doing exactly the same thing the night she died. *Call him,* she'd insisted. *Call Daddy and ask him if we can buy the house on Beekman Street, but don't tell him I'm the one who told you about it or he'll think I'm trying to manipulate him.*

Rick closed his eyes and tried to force away the sound of her voice, the feel of her hands on his shoulders and the whisper of her breath on his neck while she'd tried to listen to the conversation. He tried to forget the anger, frustration and betrayal that had consumed him during that final argument.

A chill rushed through him and turned his fingers to stone. As if in a nightmare, he listened to the phone ring. Lynette stood close, just as Jocelyn had, and in spite of his best efforts to forget, he remembered.

He tried to swallow, but his throat had grown dry. He tried to draw one breath after another, but his heart raced and his lungs labored as if he'd run for miles. His hands grew so clammy the receiver nearly slipped from his grasp, and he could hear Jocelyn's parting words to him.

"If you weren't so selfish, I wouldn't have to do this," she'd shouted from the doorway with her suitcase clutched in one hand. *"If you cared even a little bit about our marriage, we could work this out."*

"Get out," he'd roared. *"Go back to Denver and make yourself happy. I don't care what you do."*

"If I leave, I won't come back," she'd warned.

He'd glared at her. *"You think I care?"* he'd shouted, though he'd cared so deeply he thought the pain would shred his heart. *"Well, I don't. I don't need you. I can make it on my own."*

Behind him, Lynette made a noise and pulled him back to the moment. Blinking rapidly, he tried to get her into focus again, but tears stung his eyes as his final words to Jocelyn echoed repeatedly in his ears. *I don't need you. I don't need you.*

He hadn't meant it, and he'd regretted the words the second they left his mouth. But anger had kept him from calling them back. Pride had held his feet still when his heart had urged him to go after her. Jocelyn had been dead within twenty minutes, and he'd spent the past two years knowing he could have saved her life if only he hadn't let foolish pride stand in his way.

He tried once more to pull himself together, but it was no good. He couldn't talk to Ryan—not until he could get his emotions under control again. Not until he could lock away his accountability for the death of the man's sister in a safe place again, just as he'd done for the past two years.

He replaced the receiver and pushed past Lynette to the door of the kitchen. Without looking at her, he said, "I'll call him in the morning. Let yourself out." And without giving her a chance to stop him, he hurried up the stairs to the spare room and shut himself inside.

MARTI STOOD in front of the darkened window where she'd watched Rick drive away. She'd been so certain about everything a few minutes ago, but he'd looked so devastated when he left she wondered now if she'd been wrong.

No, she told herself firmly, she hadn't been wrong. He might want her physically, but his heart still belonged to Jocelyn. From everything she'd heard, Jocelyn had been the perfect wife. The perfect companion for Rick. Even if Marti wanted to, she could never hope to compete with that kind of memory. She'd be a fool to try. Besides, she had Cameron to consider. And her promise to give Gil another chance. If she followed her heart, she would lose everything.

Sighing softly, she turned away from the window and started to draw the blind. But when a truck turned from the access road onto the Lazy M's driveway, her hand stilled, her breath caught and her heart raced. Rick had come back. Maybe she'd been wrong, after all.

Dropping the cord, she smoothed her hair and tugged the hem of her sweater over her hips, then hurried to the door. She pulled it open just as the truck drew up in front of the house. Immediately, she recognized Gil's truck. Her excitement died and everything inside her grew cold.

She couldn't face Gil. Not now. Not with these stupid tears threatening to spill over onto her cheeks any second. Not with her heart and mind suddenly numb with disappointment.

Before she could turn away, Gil jumped from the truck and hurried up the steps toward her. He pulled her into a quick embrace and pressed a kiss to her cheek near her mouth. She wanted to withdraw, but she was too numb to resist.

He jerked one thumb toward the road. "Was that Rick Dennehy I saw driving away just now?"

She nodded, but she didn't trust her voice to speak.

Gil stepped inside the house and shrugged out of his jacket, then looked back at her with eyes narrowed in suspicion. "What in the hell did he want?"

She shrugged and tried to look casual, but her mind raced to come up with an explanation he would accept.

Before she could say a word, her father opened the door to his study and peered out at them. "Gil? Is that you?"

"Yeah." Gil palmed his hair. "What in the hell was Dennehy doing here?"

Her father shot a confused look at her. "Dennehy? When?"

"Just now." Gil nodded toward the road again. "I just passed him leaving."

Henry cocked one eyebrow and his face turned blotchy red. "Dennehy was here, and you didn't tell me?"

As always, his temper made Marti feel powerless. Her knees threatened to buckle, but this time she wouldn't let him see the effect he had on her. She crossed to one of the overstuffed chairs flanking the fireplace and sank into it. "I didn't see any need to tell you."

Gil's eyes widened. He shot a look at Henry, then glared at her again. "No need? What do you mean by that?"

Marti flashed him a look of irritation. "I mean, you were busy, and anyway he wanted to talk to me."

"He wanted to see you? Why?"

"We're friends."

Gil snorted in derision. "*Friends.* I'll bet he'd like to be more than that. He's after the rest of your property, Henry."

"He doesn't want the rest of your property," Marti said. "You know that. He's fixing his cabins so he can sell them."

Henry looked confused. "Then what does he want?"

"He probably thinks Marti will inherit this place after you die," Gil mumbled.

Marti glared at him. "He knows I won't inherit the Lazy M. I've told him."

Gil nodded knowingly. "Then the subject *has* come up between you."

Marti started to explain, then changed her mind. She knew this side of Gil only too well. He'd take her words and twist them to fit his own beliefs.

"This is ridiculous," she said. "I can't believe what you're insinuating."

"I'm not insinuating anything," Gil snapped. "It's obvious what he wants—to everyone but you."

"You're wrong."

"Am I?" Gil closed the distance between them and put one hand on her shoulder. "Are you sure?"

"Yes." She shrugged his hand away and leaned away from him. "Yes," she said again. "I'm sure."

Gil barked a mocking laugh, but he turned his attention to her father. "Don't worry too much, Henry. Once Marti and I are back together again, Dennehy won't ever get his hands on the Lazy M. *I'll* see to that."

Marti glared at him again. "Once we're back together? Aren't you taking a lot of things for granted?"

Gil let out a deep sigh. He sent a frustrated look in her father's direction, but spoke to her. "Come on, Marti. Why do you keep playing this game with me? You know as well as I do the best thing for Cameron is for us to be together."

"I don't know that." She willed her hands to stop trembling, but without success.

"Are you trying to tell me you haven't seen a difference in him the past few days?" Gil demanded.

Henry nodded thoughtfully. "I've seen a difference. He's acting like a different boy. A different boy, altogether."

"Yes," Marti admitted. "Because I've given him what he wants. But that doesn't mean it's good for him. Or for me."

"You never have known what was good for you," Gil insisted. "Why do you think your dad's so keen to have someone around to take care of you?"

Marti tightened her fists and met his gaze steadily. "I don't need someone to take care of me."

Her father put a hand on Gil's shoulder and sent Marti a disappointed smile. "Somebody needs to take over the Lazy M when I'm too old. Carol doesn't want it, and neither do your brothers. That leaves you. But I can't leave it to you unless I know you have someone like Gil to help you with it."

"Why won't you let me take over—without Gil?" It was an empty question. She already knew the answer. She could have recited it verbatim as he spoke.

"Because this place is too much for a woman to handle alone."

She stood for a moment, facing both of them and wishing she could think of an argument that would persuade her father how wrong he was. But nothing she'd ever said had made a difference, and he'd grown so much more pigheaded since her mother's death, she couldn't imagine being able to get through to him now.

Bone-deep sadness worked its way through her. She looked around the room at her mother's things—the furniture, the afghans, the Christmas decorations—and wished that her mother was still alive. Naomi Maddock had always been able to help her husband understand when he was being unreasonable. Marti had never known how she did it, but more than once her mother had managed to persuade her dad to change his mind about something one of the kids wanted. To be fair, Naomi had also helped the kids understand when they were asking too much.

Marti could have used her steadying influence now. Because as far as she could see, the bottom line was, she could do one of two things: marry Gil again or lose Cameron—and the Lazy M—for good. Either way, it didn't seem like much of a choice.

CHAPTER NINE

MARTI PUT the last of the dinner dishes into the cupboard while she watched Gil and Cameron playing cards on the kitchen table. After her encounter with Gil, she'd wanted nothing more than some time alone and maybe a nice, long chat with Cherryl. Instead, she'd had to spend the evening listening to Gil insinuate himself further into her father's life.

Worse, she'd had to fix dinner for him again and sit across the table from him while they ate, as if they were still family. Thankfully, they'd managed to get through the meal without discussing Rick again and without any talk of a reconciliation. Even Cameron had been surprisingly non-hostile. Still, it had taken her some time to relax.

She turned the volume on her portable CD player a little higher, hoping the Christmas music she'd put on earlier would help keep the mood light. Maybe later she'd call Cherryl. She frowned, thinking about how difficult it was to catch up with her friend. Even if Greta was right, and Cherryl was busy with family, the restaurant and the holidays, surely she could have found time to call.

Gil looked up from his hand and caught her looking at them. He winked slowly and grinned at her as he dropped his cards onto the table. ''Two pair, Jacks high.'' He turned his grin on Cameron. ''Read 'em and weep.''

Cameron folded his cards. ''One more hand.'' When he looked at his father, his eyes sparkled and his lips curved into a smile. He swept his gaze over Marti. To her surprise, he didn't sneer or glare at her. Her reward, she supposed, for making the effort to be pleasant to Gil during dinner.

She ventured a tiny smile at him. He didn't respond, but at least he didn't go out of his way to avoid her gaze.

Gil shook his head and pushed from the table. ''Can't, son. I've got to work in the morning.''

''Come on,'' Cameron pressed. ''One more. Give me a chance to win back a few of my matchsticks.''

Standing, Gil clapped one hand on Cameron's shoulder. ''Another night. Besides, I need to talk to your mother for a few minutes. Alone.'' He followed the last word with a conspiratorial wink.

Marti's relaxed mood vanished. The muscles in her neck tensed and her shoulders tightened. ''Why?''

With a glare in her direction, Cameron stood and began to gather the cards. ''Can't you just *talk* to him without getting bitchy?''

Marti glared at him. ''Of course I can.''

''Yeah,'' Cameron muttered. ''Right.'' He put the deck of cards into its plastic case and snapped it shut.

Gil's easy smile didn't falter, but the expression in his eyes grew slightly harder. ''We might be divorced, Marti, but I am still Cameron's father, and we're always going to have to discuss things that concern him. Just give me a few minutes, okay?''

She nodded, but she didn't relax. ''Fine. We'll talk.''

"Good. Cameron tells me he wants to stay in Gunnison."

Her heart slowed and her mouth grew dry. She flicked a glance at Cameron who sat back in his chair and folded his arms across his narrow chest. "He's mentioned it."

"He wants to live with me, and I think we should seriously consider it."

"No." The word popped out of her mouth before he even finished the sentence.

"No?" Gil looked stunned. "Just like that? No discussing it?"

She didn't want to discuss it—especially in front of Cameron. "I thought we were going to talk alone."

"It's about *me*," Cameron said, and the surliness took over completely. "I should be able to stay."

"I'd rather talk to your dad alone."

She could have predicted Cameron's response. He tossed the deck of cards across the kitchen so hard the plastic case cracked. "Why?"

Before she could answer, Gil motioned for Cameron to leave the room. Cameron didn't look happy, but he obeyed. Just like that. All Gil had to do was lift a finger and Cameron pushed through the swinging door and left them alone.

"Marti—" Gil took a step closer and clamped his hands on her shoulders.

She shrugged them off and took a step away. "He's not going to stay here with you."

"Don't you think we should at least discuss it? Cameron wants to stay. *I* want him to stay."

Her throat constricted, but she tried not to show the

fear that rolled through her with every dull thud of her heart. "You're both forgetting that I have custody—"

"I'm not forgetting anything, Marti. But you're misunderstanding what I'm trying to say." He smiled slowly, but the smile didn't reach his eyes. They still looked cold. "We belong together—all three of us. We're a family."

"No," she insisted, "we're not."

"Yes." He took her by the shoulders again. This time his fingers dug into the tender skin beneath her shoulder blades. "And I thought you were reconsidering. Are you so taken with Dennehy that you're just lying to make Cameron happy?"

She knew she should admit the truth, but she couldn't. Fear clogged her throat and kept her from speaking.

Gil sighed, as if what came next caused him pain. "I've talked to Brian Douglas about this. He thinks there's a good chance of getting the divorce decree altered."

"You've been to an attorney?" Her voice sounded faraway, eclipsed by the thudding of her heart and the roaring in her ears. The instrumental version of "Silver Bells" on the CD player seemed to grow louder, taunting her.

"I just asked him a few questions." Gil's grip tightened slightly. His eyes bored into hers. "I'm concerned about all the trouble Cameron's been in since you took him away from home. And only a fool could miss seeing how upset he gets when you're around."

She hated him for trying to make this her fault. And she knew he'd gladly pay Brian Douglas to convince the judge it was all her fault. If he could do that, he'd take Cameron away from her. He hadn't changed at all. She'd been a fool to believe he had.

"Obviously," Gil said, pulling her a little closer, "I don't want to take this to court. But I know how stubborn you can be, and I'm worried that you'll let your pride keep you from doing what's best for Cameron—for *all* of us. If you won't see reason, if you won't help me put the family back together the way it should be, then you leave me no other choice."

Marti's lungs refused to draw breath and her knees threatened to give way. She balled her hands into fists so tightly her fingernails dug into her palms. "You can't take Cameron away from me."

"I've told you what Cameron wants. I've told you how I feel. You know what your father thinks. This doesn't have to end up in court, and I certainly don't want it to. But it will if you insist on making things difficult." Gil loosened his grip on her shoulders and brushed the back of his fingers along her cheek.

Once, the gesture had sent delicious chills through her. But not tonight. Tonight, the shivers were revulsion.

"I still want you," Gil whispered into her ear. "I still love you. And I'm willing to forget everything if we can just put the family back together again." He brushed his lips against her cheek. "The choice is yours, Marti."

The choice *wasn't* hers. Not by a long shot. She couldn't lose Cameron. She wouldn't survive if she did.

The memories of that horrible night that had sealed the fate of their marriage came rolling back. The pain. The hospital. The loneliness. She could almost hear the doctor's horrible words as he'd explained that her daughter had died in her womb. She remembered crying for Gil—wishing that he cared enough to be with her instead of at the Lucky Jack. But he hadn't come until later.

She'd never been able to put aside the pain or forget the loneliness. But she'd already lost one child. She wouldn't lose another. No matter what it took.

Gil must have sensed her hesitation. His lips curved, and the smile transformed his face just as it always had. But it didn't have the same effect on her it had had in the past. When he lowered his mouth to hers, she felt none of the desire that had once overwhelmed her at his touch. Instead, Rick's image formed in her mind and the memory of his kiss swept through her.

Pulling away quickly, she held Gil at arm's length. "Don't. Please."

Gil's smile grew. "You know what you need to do, sweetheart. I can see it in your eyes. I'll be content with that for now." He retrieved his straw cowboy hat from the counter and slipped on his jacket, then turned at the door to let his gaze travel over her once more. "We were always good together, babe. You can't deny that."

"We were once," she admitted.

"And we will be again. Trust me." And with that, he disappeared into the night, closing the door softly behind him.

Marti sank onto a chair and clasped her hands over her mouth to prevent her hysteria from escaping. *Trust?* How could he talk about trust when he was blackmailing her into a reconciliation? How could he speak of love in the same breath he threatened to take her son away?

She stood suddenly and crossed the room to the CD player. She stopped the music and stared at the portable stereo for a long moment. She might have to marry Gil again to keep Cameron, but she'd never trust him again. Nor would she love him.

Something inside warned her that she couldn't make Cameron happy this way. But it didn't matter. Happiness wasn't the issue any longer—for either of them.

CLUTCHING A SMALL bouquet of silk flowers, Rick picked his way across the snowy cemetery toward Jocelyn's grave. Part of him didn't want to be here—after all, he'd managed to avoid coming for the past two years. But his more rational side knew that he had to come. He'd put it off for too long. The experience in the kitchen had convinced him that hiding his emotions had done nothing to diminish them. He had to tell Jocelyn how sorry he was for the argument they'd had, how responsible he felt for her death, how very much he'd loved her. And what better time than on the anniversary of her death?

Slowly he started down the row toward Jocelyn's grave. Too soon, he reached the gray headstone with roses chiseled into marble beside Jocelyn's name. He'd chosen to bury her in Gunnison because, at the time, he'd believed he'd stay forever. But it had taken less than a month for him to change his mind, pack up everything he owned and move back to Denver.

He pulled off his cap and stared at the engraved marble: Jocelyn Bennett Dennehy, Beloved Wife and Daughter. Yes, she had been both. She'd died knowing how much her parents and siblings loved her. But in her final moments, she'd doubted Rick's love.

Giving himself a mental shake, he hunkered down in front of the headstone and put the flowers on the ground. He pushed to his feet slowly. Tears blurred his vision and a lump blocked his throat. Like a shaft of lightning, pain tore through him and the echoes of it reverberated until the next shaft came.

Maybe Marti was right. Maybe his feelings for Jocelyn ran too deep to overlook. Maybe he'd mistaken loneliness for genuine affection, and friendship for something deeper.

Pushing to his feet, he put his cap back on his head and started away from the grave site. When a biting gust of wind hit him in the face, he turned his head slightly and caught sight of someone standing in front of another grave several rows away. A second later, he recognized Marti and his step faltered.

He told himself to look away and keep walking, but something about her rigid posture and brittle movements held his attention.

Without giving himself time to think, he changed direction and walked toward her. Twice before he reached her, he thought about changing his mind, but he kept walking. Marti looked as if she could use a friend. And Rick could do friendship. In fact, he made a pretty good friend. He just wouldn't let this friendship develop into anything more complex.

By the time he drew up beside her, he felt a little stronger. She'd placed a large bunch of flowers on the grave before her, and a few matching carnations on top of a tiny headstone beside it. For a split second as she met his gaze, she looked shocked to see him there. A second later, surprise gave way to a pleased smile.

"Rick? What are you doing here?"

He gestured vaguely toward Jocelyn's grave. "Just paying a visit. And you?"

An expression he couldn't read crossed her face. She flushed slightly and looked at the headstone in front of her. "Talking to my mother. Unfortunately, she's not giving me much help."

"Help with what?"

She rolled her eyes in exasperation. "My dad. Cameron. Gil. My job." A shy smile teased the corners of her mouth. "Pick one."

The smile lifted some of the heaviness from his heart. He even managed to smile back at her. "Gil."

"What?"

"You said to pick one. I pick Gil. Tell me what's bothering you about him."

She looked confused for a second longer, then smiled again. "You don't want to know."

"Sure I do." He realized he meant it. He really did want to hear what bothered her about her ex-husband. But when she tilted her head to look at him and her smile grew into one that seemed to hold the missing sunshine in it, an unexpected twinge of desire tweaked him. And Rick had to ask himself just why he wanted to hear about Gil's failings.

She sighed softly and glanced away. "You know that I've been trying to do what Cameron wants. I've been trying to give my relationship with Gil another chance—at least to see if there's anything left between us to build on."

Rick's smile froze in place, but he tried not to let

her see that. "And? Is there anything left between you?"

"I wasn't sure at first. I told myself that maybe my dad was right. Maybe I did overreact to...to what happened when we were married. But now—" She shook her head slowly. "Gil stopped by the other night after you left."

"I know," Rick said carefully. "I passed him on my way home."

She glanced up at him so quickly, he wondered if his voice had given something away. "Dad is willing to sign the Lazy M over to me, but he wants me to get married again first. And he thinks I'm foolish to turn up my nose at Gil."

That was nothing short of emotional blackmail, but Rick didn't say so aloud. He tried to look impartial.

Marti laughed bitterly and looked down at her gloved hands. "Running the Lazy M is what I've always wanted to do," she said softly.

And now you can, he thought. Well, good. At least she'd be happy.

She lifted her eyes to meet Rick's again. "I realized that I don't want the Lazy M," she said. "Not at that price."

Overwhelming relief flooded through him. He tried to ignore the sensation and reminded himself they were friends. Just friends.

"I think you made a wise decision," he said at last.

"Cameron will hate me again."

"Not forever."

"I hope not." She shivered in a sudden blast of cold air and pulled the collar of her jacket up over her ears. "But I don't know what to think anymore. Maybe I should just let him live with Gil for a while. Maybe I'm wrong to fight them both so hard. After all, Gil hurt me terribly when we were married, but he didn't hurt Cameron—not directly, anyway.''

"Would you feel safe leaving him with Gil?"

She shrugged, but the gesture seemed almost lifeless. "Safe? Yes, I guess so. The worst that can happen is that Cameron will grow up to be just like his dad." She smiled sadly. "Gil's not the kind of man I want Cameron to be, but if he stays with me, he may turn out even worse. He's already been in trouble with the law and with his school. The way he's been going, he'll be in jail within five years."

Rick's heart went out to her. "It's not because of you. You know that, don't you?"

"I hope not." Her eyes clouded and her lips quivered. "I've done my best, but I'm at the end of my rope."

Another gust of wind whipped past them. She shivered, and Rick realized the temperature had dropped suddenly. But he didn't want to leave her yet, and he certainly didn't want to make her go back home alone.

"I don't know about you, but I'm getting cold. How about letting me buy you a cup of coffee at the Wagon Wheel before we go our separate ways?"

She hesitated, and for a moment he thought she'd turn down his offer. But she smiled. "Thanks. I'd like that."

Rick felt his own smile grow.

"Great. Shall we go together? Or should I meet you there?"

"I'll follow you."

"Great," he said again. He took her arm and guided

her across the uneven ground. He tried not to think about the step he'd just let his heart take. But he knew that if he ever again told himself he wanted nothing more than friendship from Marti, he'd be lying.

MARTI SCOOTED into the booth in front of the plate-glass window that looked out over Main Street and waited while Rick slid onto the bench across from her. The aroma of something wonderful and spicy filled the restaurant. Christmas music played softly in the background. Painted snowmen and reindeer decorated the huge front window. And a tiny artificial tree with white lights and red ornaments near the cash register reminded her how few days remained until Christmas.

She scanned the large room, hoping to see Cherryl or her husband somewhere, but she couldn't see anyone she knew well. She'd just have to leave a message with one of the employees.

She slipped out of her coat and settled herself comfortably on the seat, trying not to worry about being here with Rick. After all, one of Gil's friends might see her and tell him. Marti didn't have to let her imagination work very hard to know how he'd react.

Not that she cared, exactly. Except that when she had that confrontation with Gil, she wanted the timing to be of her own choosing, not his. But Rick had appeared just when she needed company the most—and she hadn't been able to resist his offer.

She watched Rick unzip his jacket and turn over both of their coffee cups on their saucers. Sighing contentedly, he rubbed his hands together as if for warmth. "Do you want something else with the coffee? Soup? Salad? Pie?"

Marti started to shake her head, then thought better of it. "I'd love some of their chicken noodle soup if they still have any this late in the day."

"Ah." He leaned back in his seat with a grin. "I see you're a connoisseur."

"Of chicken noodle soup, yes." She returned his smile and felt herself relaxing slightly.

He pushed the silverware rolled in a napkin to one side of the table and glanced out the window. Tiny white lights trailed the buildings across the street and illuminated trees and wire reindeer in the huge concrete planter boxes that dotted the sidewalk.

He scowled slightly. "Can you believe it's the eighteenth already?"

"It's unbelievable. I haven't even had time to really think about Christmas yet."

"I've had time to think about it," he said with a wry grin, "but I haven't done anything about it."

"I guess that means you haven't finished your Christmas shopping yet?"

She'd meant the question to sound lighthearted, but his smile faded suddenly and he lowered his gaze to the cup in front of him. "I don't like Christmas much," he said. "I've put off thinking about it as long as humanly possible the last couple of years."

She didn't know how to respond to that, so she didn't say anything.

To her surprise, he glanced up at her and made an effort to smile again. "Jocelyn used to love it, though."

Marti's heart twisted painfully. She told herself not to be foolish. She knew how much he still loved Jocelyn, she should expect him to talk about her. She forced herself to return his smile and managed to say, "Oh."

His eyes narrowed slightly, as if he heard something revealing in the word. He turned the coffee mug around on the table for several long seconds.

When he looked up at her again, his eyes were full of anguish. "She died a week before Christmas." He hesitated, then added softly, "Two years ago today."

Guilt immediately took the place of Marti's misplaced resentment. "Oh, Rick. I'm sorry. I had no idea. No wonder you hate it."

"Yeah. Well." He shrugged and tried to smile, but the effort fell flat. "To tell the truth, I didn't like the holiday all that much before she died, either. But the music, the lights, the decorations... They always bring everything back as if it happened yesterday."

She clutched her own coffee cup, but she didn't speak.

He broke the silence after a few seconds. "I try not to think about it, though. Life goes on, doesn't it? After two years, you'd think I could put some of it behind me."

"Why?" The word escaped before she had a chance to consider its impact.

His eyes flashed to her face again. "What?"

She regretted the impulsive question, but now that she'd asked it she couldn't very well pretend she hadn't. "Why should you be able to put it behind you? You loved her. You still do."

"It's been a long time."

"I see. And there's some law I don't know about that says you can only grieve for a certain number of months?"

His lips curved into a smile. "No."

"Okay, then. If you're still grieving, for heaven's sake, let yourself do it."

He fell silent again and studied his cup, his fingers, even the rolled silverware. The song on the loudspeaker changed, and a chorus of bells pealed into the room. Rick remained silent for so long, Marti kicked herself mentally for saying the wrong thing. But when he met her gaze again, she saw something different in his eyes.

"It's not that I'm still grieving," he said softly. "It's more like—" But before he could finish the thought, he broke off and smiled up at a waitress who materialized out of nowhere beside their table. "Two cups of coffee," he said, "and two bowls of your chicken noodle soup."

Marti struggled to be patient while he ordered and willed the waitress to hurry so he could finish what he'd been about to say. Instead, the waitress seemed to take forever to write the order on her notepad. Marti could feel the woman's eyes on her. Some friend of Gil's, no doubt, taking stock of the situation so she could tell him all about it.

With a scowl, she looked up at the woman. But instead of censure, she saw a sparkle in the woman's blue eyes, and the familiar broad smile of her childhood friend. "Cherryl? Is that you?"

Cherryl dropped onto the seat beside Marti and wrapped her in a warm hug. "It's about time you came in. I've been worried that you'd leave town again before we had a chance to even see each other."

"So have I." Marti returned her friend's embrace and caught Rick's curious gaze. "Do you know Rick?"

Cherryl shook her head and offered him her hand. "Rick Dennehy? I've seen you around."

"Cherryl's been my best friend since we were young," Marti explained. "She and her husband own this place now."

Rick smiled and shook Cherryl's hand. "So you're the one responsible for the world-famous chicken soup."

"World-famous?" Cherryl said with a laugh. "Hardly. Besides, it's my mother-in-law's recipe."

Marti worked up a mock scowl and said playfully, "Don't encourage her, Rick. This place already keeps her far too busy."

"You think I'm busy?" Cherryl protested. "Why haven't you returned my calls?"

"Don't try to pin the blame on me. You're the one who hasn't returned *my* phone calls."

Cherryl released her and pulled back a little. "But I have. Didn't Gil give you my messages?"

Marti stared at her. "You talked to Gil? When?"

Cherryl frowned. "I've called a couple of times but, just my luck, Gil answered both times. He said the two of you are getting back together. Is that true?"

Marti shook her head quickly. "No," she said firmly. "No, we're not."

Relief flashed across Cherryl's face. "I have to admit, I'm glad to hear it. I've been worried about you. I remember how miserable you were before the divorce." She checked the room for new customers and settled more comfortably in her seat. "I guess I shouldn't be surprised he didn't tell you I'd called. He never did like us hanging out together."

No, he hadn't. For some reason, their friendship had threatened him. And this was one more piece of evidence that he hadn't changed at all. Everything he'd said and done since she came back had been a lie. But why? What did he want? To get Cameron back? He hadn't shown much interest in the boy to date. Why now?

When the front door opened, Cherryl glanced at the man who came inside, and relaxed slightly when he chose a seat at the counter. "If you're not getting back together, why is he at your place all the time?"

Marti glanced quickly at Rick before she answered. "He's helping Dad. Dad's decided he needs to do something with the place again, but I'm not sure I understand why."

"Maybe it's because of that ski-equipment company that's been trying to buy property in the area. They're talking about building a plant here. After they made Henry that offer—"

"Offer?" Marti's voice came out sharp and a little too loud. She tempered it and asked again. "What offer?"

Cherryl looked confused. "Your dad didn't tell you about it?"

"No. He hasn't said a word."

Cherryl glanced at Rick, who shifted uncomfortably in his seat.

"Do you know about this?" Marti asked him.

"Not about an offer to your dad," he said. "But they made me an offer last week."

"Are you selling to them?" The thought made her ill.

He shook his head quickly. "No. I turned them down."

"So did your dad," Cherryl said. "In spite of Gil."

"Gil?" Marti reared back in her seat. "What does Gil have to do with it?"

Cherryl averted her gaze for a second. "Some of us think he plans to get his hands on the Lazy M and sell it to them."

Marti didn't want to believe it—not even about Gil. But suddenly everything fell into place.

Rick leaned back in his seat and ran one hand along his chin. "That would certainly put my cabins out of business."

"Yes," Marti admitted. "It would." Bile rose in her throat when she remembered the conversation she'd interrupted between her dad and Gil about doing just that. She tried to force away the sick feeling along with the niggling sense of guilt that accompanied it. She wasn't responsible for Gil. She had to stop thinking she was. "Who else knows about this?"

Cherryl shrugged. "Just everybody, I guess. Except you."

"And Dad," Marti whispered. "He can't know about it, or he wouldn't even consider letting Gil have the ranch. He cares more about keeping the area natural than anyone I know."

"I think you're right," Cherryl said with a nod. "I don't think he knows. After all, he turned down their original offer."

She sighed again. "Maybe I should have said something in my letters, but I figured your dad had told you about the factory, and I didn't hear anything about Gil's plans until a couple of weeks ago."

She started to say something else, but the door opened again and a large group came inside. She groaned aloud and slid out of the booth. "I wish I could stay, but I've got to get back to work. But promise me we'll get together before you leave.''

"We will,'' Marti vowed. Nothing would stop her from keeping her word.

Cherryl touched Marti's shoulder with a gentle hand. "Are you going to be okay?''

Marti nodded. She'd be fine. But she was furious. Furious with Gil and very concerned about her dad. Gil had been playing him for a fool. He'd probably spent the past three years convincing Henry his children had deserted him. If her father believed Gil was the only one who truly cared about him, no wonder he was so determined to get Gil back into the family.

The one thing she didn't understand was how marrying her fit into Gil's plans. Surely he knew she'd resist selling the Lazy M. Wouldn't it have been better to let her go back to California after Christmas?

Like a bolt of lightning, another realization hit her. Gil didn't care about her, and he didn't really want to marry her again. Otherwise why hadn't he made some effort to win her back while she was still in California? He'd only started courting her again after she came back to town. Maybe her father had given Gil some indication that he intended to give the ranch to them after they were married. Did Gil really believe that even if she remarried him she'd agree to part with the ranch?

The idea disgusted her, but worse, the realization that she'd come so close to going along with his plan, angered her. She put one hand to her forehead and gulped air in an attempt to calm her rolling stomach.

As if he'd read her thoughts, Rick reached across the

table and touched her arm. "You didn't know," he said softly.

"No," she admitted, "but I should have."

"Just be glad you know now."

"I am, but—"

"And now that you know, you can do something about it."

The knot in her stomach loosened a little and her heart stopped thumping so wildly in her chest. "Yes," she said, "I can, can't I?"

"Will you tell your dad?"

She shook her head. "Not right away. I think I'll hear what Gil has to say first."

"Do you think he'll tell you?"

She laughed bitterly. "Gil? You don't know him very well, do you? My only worry is what this will do to Cameron and Dad. I don't want them hurt."

"They'll be more hurt if Gil gets his way," Rick said.

He was right, of course. She met his gaze steadily. "He won't get his way. Not now that I know the truth. But I don't want to ruin Christmas for everyone by telling them what Gil's been up to. I'll just have to think of some way to convince him to back off."

Rick smiled slowly and covered her hand with one of his. "Do you have any idea how beautiful you are when you look like that?"

His words caught her off guard. She ducked her head and flushed. "Like what?"

"Determined. Strong." He traced the curve of her cheek with one finger. "Ready to stand up for yourself and do battle."

Her heart raced again, but for a different reason entirely this time. "Gil wouldn't think so. He doesn't like women who stand up for themselves."

Rick shrugged. "I guess the weak ones don't. They're afraid a strong woman will somehow diminish them."

Marti could only stare at him. She'd never considered Gil a weak man before. In fact, his bluster and bravado had always made her think just the opposite. But the idea freed something inside her. And for the first time in more years than she could remember, she felt a measure of control.

CHAPTER TEN

RICK WATCHED the smile cross Marti's face and the light in her eyes grow. Yes, he thought with satisfaction. This was how he'd always imagined she should look. Strong and fierce. Confident and capable. And ready to kick her ex-husband's sneaking, conniving butt.

He glanced away quickly, suddenly aware of his unexpected physical reaction to her. Why here? Why now? And why did a man's desire have to be so damn obvious to everyone around?

He tried thinking of something else—car engines, chopping wood—anything but Marti. But her scent drifted toward him across the table. Her leg brushed his when she moved. And her voice... She might only be asking for cream for the coffee, but it felt like a caress to him.

"How about you, Rick?" Cherryl was back and leaning in front of him to fill his cup. "Do you take cream?"

He shook his head and met her gaze, but his face burned with embarrassment. To his relief, embarrassment worked as car engines and woodpiles hadn't. He let out a sigh and allowed himself one tiny peek at Marti. He couldn't help wishing that women displayed their desire as obviously as men did. It would let him know whether he was just chasing rainbows.

With a farewell grin, Cherryl took the coffeepot and disappeared. Marti sighed and looked through the painted window at the stores across the street. "I guess I should at least try to do some shopping before I go home again, but I really have no idea what to get Cameron or my dad."

"Cameron's good with his hands and he seems to like the work he's been doing on the cabins. Maybe a tool belt with a few tools to put in it—unless he already has one in California."

She shook her head. "No, he doesn't. I've never..." She glanced away again. "I haven't exactly encouraged him to work with his hands. I've told him he has to get his grades up before I'll let him take woodshop again."

"Does he have a hard time in school?"

She sighed softly. "Yes, but I don't know why. He's a smart kid, but he's so incredibly stubborn. Sometimes I think he lets his grades in the important things go just to spite me."

Rick laced his fingers around the mug. "The important things? What would those be?"

"Math, English, science, history. The basics."

Rick knew he should keep his mouth shut and his nose out of her business, but he couldn't stop himself. "Did he get good grades when he lived here?"

"No, but they've gotten much worse over the past few years."

"Have you ever thought that those subjects may be difficult for him?"

"He's a bright kid, Rick. And he's fifteen years old.

If he doesn't shape up soon, he won't get into a good college and he'll wind up working at menial jobs the rest of his life.''

His father's words, so achingly similar, echoed in his mind. Rick had worked hard to please his father, but he'd never measured up to the old man's expectations. Even his job at the court hadn't been good enough. The old man had died wishing Rick had gone further, climbed higher, done better.

"Does he want to go to college?"

She shook her head. "He says he doesn't, but—"

"But you want him to go."

"I want him to do well."

"Isn't it more important that he be happy?" He knew the instant he asked the question he'd gone too far.

Marti's eyes clouded and her cheeks flushed. "Of course I want him to be happy. That's why I'm pushing him to do well in school. How happy can he be working minimum-wage jobs or doing something—"

"Menial?" he finished for her, then added more softly, "Like his father?"

Her eyes widened, then narrowed immediately and she pulled back as if he'd slapped her.

"Do him a favor," he said as gently as he could. "Don't judge him by his father."

"I don't."

"And don't judge his success by your own yardstick. Not everyone enjoys school. Not everyone does well in the basic subjects. The way the schools are set up, you're considered a failure unless you have one of a very few talents. Believe me, I know. But Cameron has a real talent for working with his hands. Maybe if you let him spend some time doing what he likes, he won't resent having to spend time working on things he doesn't like quite so much.''

Her lips thinned and her eyes narrowed even further. ''Is it wrong for me to want my son to succeed?''

The words pricked him, but he didn't let her see that. Nor did he tell her how many times in his own life his success had been measured by that same yardstick. ''No, but it just might be wrong to expect him to live up to someone else's definition of success.''

She shook her head quickly, and for a moment he thought she'd say something more. Instead, she pushed away her coffee mug, gathered her coat and purse, and slid out of the booth. ''Thanks for the coffee, Rick, but I think I'd better go.''

He'd gone too far. ''Maybe I shouldn't have said anything—''

''You're entitled to your opinion,'' she said. ''But I don't have to share it.'' Pivoting away, she hurried across the restaurant and out the door.

WELL, Rick told himself with a bitter laugh, you certainly screwed that up. He wouldn't have to worry about taking their relationship too far any longer. In fact, he'd probably just destroyed their friendship.

He watched through the window as she crossed the street and ducked inside Morrison's Department Store. Then he pulled out his wallet, tossed enough to cover the bill and a tip onto the table, and followed her outside. He told himself to walk straight to his truck and drive away. But his heart didn't want to listen to his head, and his feet wouldn't listen, either.

Arguing with himself the entire way, he dashed

across the street and followed her into Morrison's. He had no idea what he'd say if he found her, or whether he could even convince her to listen to him. He only knew he had to try.

A small crowd of shoppers outside Morrison's blocked his path for a few seconds. He battled frustration and kept a smile pasted on his face while he made his way through the glass doors.

He could see almost to the back of the store's first floor, but so many shoppers filled the aisles, he doubted he'd ever find her. Mannheim Steamroller's version of "Joy to the World" blared from a speaker near his ear. Somewhere nearby, a bell jingled with annoying regularity. And the voices of excited shoppers rose and fell, at times nearly drowning out the music.

He searched the crowd for a glimpse of Marti's honey-colored hair or the deep blue of her jacket, and found her near the back of the store standing beside a rack of mens' sweaters.

Without giving himself a chance to change his mind, he worked his way around dozens of shoppers and giant plywood candy canes at the end of several aisles to reach her. He tried not to let frustration take over as he lost sight of her in the crowd. He kept going until he finally reached the mens' department. To his relief, she hadn't moved. She pulled a forest green sweater from the rack and held it up for inspection, tilting her head to one side as she studied it.

With his heart thundering in his ears, he made his way through the last few shoppers and came to a stop behind her. "That would look great on Cameron."

She whirled to face him. A hesitant smile flickered

across her lips before it disappeared and a slight frown took its place. "Do you think so?"

"Absolutely." Apprehension blocked Rick's next breath, but he refused to let it stop him. "Marti," he said softly, and took a step closer. "I'm sorry about what happened back there. I shouldn't have said anything about Cameron."

It seemed like an eternity before she lifted her gaze to meet his again. "I shouldn't have gotten so angry." She spoke so quietly, he had trouble hearing her over the din.

He had so much else he wanted to say, but he didn't want to say it here where he'd have to shout to make himself heard. He glanced over his shoulder toward the door. "Can we talk for a minute outside?"

She put the sweater back on the rack and nodded slowly. "All right."

He took her arm and held her close to his side as they pushed through the crowd to the front of the store. Once on the street, he guided her a few feet away from the busy entrance to a bench on the curb. She sat so close, her thigh brushed his and the breeze carried her scent across the space between them.

But now that he had her alone again, he had difficulty getting the words out. He watched a couple of cars pass while he searched for the best way to explain.

She waited in silence, giving him the time and space he needed.

"When I was a kid," he managed to say at last, "I was just like Cameron. I was always in trouble, and I didn't do well at all in school. For most of my teenage years, I was the bane of my parents' existence."

Her lips curved in a soft smile, and he could tell she didn't believe him.

But he had to make her understand what her expectations might do to Cameron. "I almost flunked out of high school. None of the subjects they taught there came easy to me. In fact, school was so hard, I eventually gave up."

Her eyes narrowed slightly. "But you're incredibly intelligent."

"That's my point, Marti. One thing has nothing to do with the other. I met a teacher a few years ago one night at a bar. I was miserable and half-drunk, and this guy came in and sat down beside me. We started talking, and he said something to me that night that changed my life." He held her gaze with his own, willing her to accept the truth of what he was about to tell her. "He said that the school system caters to about eight different abilities. Only eight. And children who may be gifted in ways other than those eight often leave school feeling like failures."

Her eyes never left his, and the flicker of understanding he saw in their clear blue depths gave him the courage to go on. "Since our society stresses that those talents are the only way to measure success, ability and intelligence, those kids go through their whole lives feeling like failures." He put a hand over hers and prayed she wouldn't pull it away.

She didn't. Instead, she turned her hand over and laced her fingers through his.

His pulse stuttered, then picked up speed, and a comfortable warmth spread through him. "I see myself in Cameron. I've spent most of my life working in jobs that other people think are acceptable, but I've been miserable. Every day I go to work at my high-paying job and I hate it, but for a long time I've bought into the belief that there's something wrong with me."

She tightened her grip on his hand. "Oh, Rick. There's nothing wrong with you."

"I know that now. And there's nothing wrong with Cameron. Just because the traditional subjects in school aren't easy for him doesn't mean he's not a bright kid. He's loaded with brains. He's better than I am at deciding how to fix something. And I really think half of his frustration right now comes from believing that what comes naturally to him isn't good enough."

She nodded quickly and looked away but not before he saw the glimmer of tears in her eyes.

"Anyway," he said, trying to lighten the tone a little. "After talking to that teacher, I decided not to pretend to be something I wasn't any longer. I went home and told Jocelyn I wanted to leave my job at the court. A few weeks later, we bought the property from your dad and started building the cabins."

There. He'd said it, and she hadn't pulled away or argued or tried to justify her position the way Jocelyn always had. Marti was a remarkable woman.

But when she turned to face him, he saw a different kind of pain in her eyes. "You were so lucky to have Jocelyn. I love this place, but it's not for everyone. Not many women would have given up everything to follow you."

Her words sent a spiral of the all-too-familiar guilt through him. How could he respond to that? The truth would mean admitting aloud that he'd been guilty of selfishness in insisting on a lifestyle Jocelyn had hated.

The irony was, she probably wouldn't have married him if she'd known who he really was.

He spoke softly, admitting the truth aloud for the first time. "She didn't want to give up everything, and she desperately wanted me to go back to Denver. It wasn't her fault. She fell in love with someone who didn't exist. She only saw the ambitious legal-eagle who'd worked up the ladder within the court system. She didn't even know this side of me existed." He rubbed his forehead slowly. "I changed the rules on her partway through our marriage, and I was so anxious to finally become the real me that I didn't stop to think about what those changes would do to her—or to us. I think she honestly tried to like it here, but she couldn't."

Marti let her hand linger in his for another few seconds, then drew it away gently. "Thank you."

His hand felt strangely empty. He balled it into a fist. "For what?"

"For telling me the truth. For sharing that with me, even though it was obviously painful. I guess I have some work ahead of me with Cameron, don't I? Now all I have to do is figure out how to reach him."

"I promised Ashley and Kendra that I'd cut a Christmas tree tomorrow. Cameron's going with me. Would you like to join us?"

For a second he thought she'd refuse, but she smiled and some of the light crept back into her eyes. "You're serious?"

"Absolutely. It would give you a chance to talk to him alone—away from Gil and your dad. And you could do something fun with him. Something he enjoys."

Her eyes lightened a bit more. "Yes. Thank you. I think I'd like that." She leaned closer to brush a kiss across his cheek. Her lips felt warm against his skin, and it took all his self-control not to pull her into his arms and kiss her thoroughly right there on Main Street in front of half the town.

"Come on," he said, not at all surprised at the sudden gruffness in his voice. "You need to finish your Christmas shopping."

"You're right," she said. "I do."

He stood and offered his hand to help her up. She took it and let her hand linger in his again, and when their eyes met, he saw reflected at him desire and regret to match his own.

"Can I ask you one more favor?" she asked when they'd started back toward Morrison's.

"Anything."

"Come with me to the hardware store and help me pick out Cameron's Christmas present."

He grinned so broadly, his cheeks hurt. Wrapping one arm around her waist, he gave in to temptation and drew her close. He covered her mouth with his own and probed her lips gently with his tongue.

She parted her lips slightly, inviting him inside, but he forced himself to hold back. He let his tongue brush across the silk of her mouth for only an instant, then forced himself to end the kiss.

All at once, he felt sixteen again—full of hormones and horny as hell. Back then, he probably would have tried to find some private place where they could be together. Now he would wait—difficult though that might be. And he knew that if the day came when he could make Marti his, the wait would only make the moment sweeter.

MARTI REACHED the bottom of the stairs, pulled her coat from the closet and crossed to the window. Her heart danced with anticipation and her hands grew clammy. She took several deep breaths to calm herself, but when she saw Rick's truck turn off the road onto the Lazy M, all her efforts failed her.

She pulled back from the window and slipped on her coat, then stepped onto the front porch to wait. Praying Cameron hadn't refused to come along, she held her breath until the truck grew close enough for her to see more than one body inside.

Releasing the breath she held, she worked up a smile and stepped off the porch to meet them. Cameron sat on one side of the cab, looking miserable. In spite of her resolve, his obvious unhappiness sent a spiral of apprehension through her. But she forced it away. He might not be happy, but he'd hadn't refused to come along.

Kendra sat in the truck between Rick and Cameron. Marti's smile grew slowly. If they were all going, the ride into the hills would certainly be cozy.

Rick smiled when he saw her standing there, and the expression made Marti's heart jump. As she crossed the parking area toward them, Cameron threw open the truck's door, and scooted closer to Kendra to make room. He didn't look at Marti.

"Where's Ashley?" she asked.

"She didn't want to come," Kendra said. "She thinks it's too cold."

Marti climbed into the truck, settled herself in the

narrow space on the seat and shut the door. "It's a perfect day for cutting trees. I'm so glad you had the idea, Rick."

Rick put the truck into reverse and backed it around the parking area. "Actually, it was Cameron's idea."

"Really?" She arranged her gloves and scarf on her lap and braved a smile at her son. "Well, it's a great idea. It's been years since I've cut my own Christmas tree."

Cameron merely raised his eyebrows and looked back at her. "When did you ever do it? I never have."

"Years ago," she said again, "when I was a girl. My mother always sent Dad out to cut the tree on the day after Thanksgiving, and we would decorate the whole house that weekend."

Kendra leaned slightly forward to see around Cameron. "I love decorating Christmas trees."

"So do I," Marti admitted, and added, "We stopped cutting our own trees when the government tightened the regulations for getting permits to cut trees from the national forests."

Rick grunted, but Marti thought she detected a hint of a smile.

She laughed softly. "I hope one of you remembered to get permits to cut the trees."

"We got 'em," Cameron assured her.

"Good. It would take some of the fun out of the day if we ended up in jail."

"You can't go to jail for cutting a tree," Cameron said with a roll of his eyes. "They'd just slap us with a fine."

Marti had intended her comment as a joke. An explanation hovered on the tip of her tongue. She almost offered it, but an unwelcome flash of awareness stopped her. The response she'd been about to make to Cameron had been defensive and even a little angry. But if either Rick or Kendra had made the same comment, she probably would have laughed it off.

The realization left her more than a little uncomfortable and made her cheeks burn. She tried telling herself that her caution had grown from Cameron's never-ending anger, but the niggling suspicion that each of their attitudes had fed the other wouldn't go away.

Working up a change of tone, she said, "I know, but can you imagine what Grandpa would do if we did go to jail?"

It seemed to take forever for Cameron to realize she was speaking to him, and every passing second made her heart beat a little faster.

Rick laughed aloud as he turned onto the highway. "I can't think of anything I'd like less than to explain to Henry why his daughter and grandson wound up in jail after spending the morning with me."

Cameron scowled for a few seconds longer, but at long last a slow smile spread across his face. "He'd be *real* excited about that."

"Oh, yeah," Rick said with a grin. "It would probably earn me a lot of points in his book."

"No kidding." Cameron relaxed against the back of the seat and brushed shoulders with Marti.

She looked out the window and pretended to study the countryside, but was shaken by Cameron's response. She didn't like thinking she'd inadvertently fostered some of his hostility—after all, she'd grown comfortable with the image she carried of herself as the misunderstood mother—but she couldn't deny the evidence.

She turned back toward the windshield and sighed softly, but she could tell from the quick glance Rick darted in her direction that he'd heard it. She didn't want Cameron to misread her mood, so she nodded toward the pine-covered hill that loomed in front of them. "I'd forgotten how beautiful this place is."

"I hadn't," Cameron said under his breath.

Again, she had to soften her instinctive reaction. "I know. You really love it here, don't you?"

Surprise shot across his face, but he hid it well. "Yeah. I do."

"I do, too," Kendra said. "I wish my mom and dad would let us move here."

"Somehow, I can't picture your mom living here," Rick said gently.

"Can I visit sometimes? By myself?"

"I'm not planning to keep the cabins," Rick reminded her. "But if I did stay, you could visit whenever you wanted. And you could talk Cameron into teaching you how to fish."

Kendra sent a shy glance at Cameron, and to Marti's surprise the boy's cheeks reddened. Marti pretended not to notice, but she knew him too well not to understand that he had a crush on the girl. Luckily, Kendra seemed equally charmed. And why not? Cameron was a handsome young man.

Rick kept his gaze riveted on the road ahead, but when he turned off the highway onto a rutted dirt road, forcing Kendra to lean against Cameron for a few seconds, their cheeks turned an even deeper shade of red.

For the space of a heartbeat, Marti envied them the thrill of new love.

Rick looked away from the road a second later. Their eyes met, her heart skipped and her insides grew warm. And in that split second, she realized she had nothing to envy. Nothing at all.

CHAPTER ELEVEN

RICK CUT the motor on the chain saw and wiped sweat from his brow. He glanced over his shoulder at Marti and Kendra waiting beside the truck, but quickly looked away again. The morning had started out fine, but somewhere between Marti's house and this field of trees, something had happened to alter her mood. She'd grown quiet. Speculative. And something lurked just behind her eyes that Rick couldn't quite decipher.

He replayed the morning's conversation in his mind as he'd already done a dozen times or more. But he still couldn't remember anything that anyone had said to offend or upset her.

As if he could read Rick's thoughts, Cameron closed the distance between them and nodded toward Marti without looking at her. "So? What have I done wrong now?"

Rick rubbed his sleeve across his forehead again and thought about pretending not to understand. But Cameron would know he was lying. The change in Marti's attitude had been too abrupt. "I don't think it's anything you've done."

Cameron's eyebrows knit and his mouth puckered into a frown. "Yeah. Right. It's *always* something I've done."

Rick met his gaze with a steady one of his own. "I'm serious, Cameron."

"So am I."

"Why are you so certain it's you? Maybe it's me. Or maybe it's something else entirely."

Cameron snorted a laugh. "You? You didn't do anything."

Rick wished he could believe Cameron. He forced himself not to look at Marti again and nodded toward the blue spruce she'd chosen for Henry's living room. "It's just about to fall. Are you ready to help me get it into the truck?"

"Sure. Do you want me to cut down the one Kendra picked out?"

Rick glanced at him. Cameron's need to impress Kendra was written all over his face. "Sounds good to me. Do you know how to do it?"

Cameron hitched his jeans up by the belt loops. "I can figure it out. I've been watching you."

"Just make sure you cut so the tree falls away from the women and the truck."

"I will."

Cameron sounded slightly annoyed, but Rick didn't let that bother him. "All right," he said with a grin. "I'll finish up here, and then it's all yours."

Gratitude flashed across Cameron's expression as he pivoted away. Rick waited until the boy had put enough distance between himself and the tree for safety, then started the chain saw again. He got a kick out of watching Cameron and Kendra moon over each other, but he worried a little, too. After all, he could still recall what it felt like to be a fifteen-year-old boy.

The instant that thought hit him, another followed.

Maybe that's what was bothering Marti. Maybe she was worried about Cameron and Kendra. He couldn't blame her for being a bit concerned. None of them needed the complications and heartache that would inevitably follow if the kids got carried away with their new romance.

Rick didn't think they'd gone anywhere with it yet. They blushed too much to be more than newly aware of each other. He'd just have to keep an eye on them and make sure they didn't go too far. Maybe that would help set Marti's mind at ease.

He felled the tree, watching as it toppled. The impact sent snow billowing into the air, onto his hair and down the back of his neck.

Almost immediately, Cameron appeared at his side again. "You take the top," he said. "I'll carry the bottom."

Rick pulled on his gloves again and searched among the thick pine boughs for a sturdy branch. When he finally found one, he nodded at Cameron and hoisted his end of the tree off the ground.

He watched Kendra's smile grow and her eyes widen as they approached, and told himself this much admiration ought to be enough for any young man. He let Cameron take charge of getting the tree into the truck bed and refrained from offering helpful suggestions, which Cameron would almost certainly resent.

No, he thought, let the kid have his moment. He just hoped Marti wouldn't do or say something Cameron might misunderstand or misinterpret.

Hoping to send her a warning glance, he looked up at her. To his surprise, she wore a soft smile. When she met his gaze, he saw honest amusement dancing in her eyes.

Confused all over again, he waited while Cameron climbed into the truck bed and helped him arrange the tree in place. Maybe Marti wasn't worried about Cameron and Kendra. But if not that, then what?

Cameron climbed onto the side of the truck, jumped to the ground and jerked his head toward the stand of trees. "Come with me," he said to Kendra. "You can make sure I'm cutting the right one."

"*You're* going to cut it?" Kendra sounded adequately impressed.

"Sure."

Marti turned to hide her smile until the kids had moved away. Only then did she look back at them. "I've never seen him like this," she said. "He must like her a lot."

"I think the feeling's mutual." Rick watched her reaction, but he saw nothing unusual. No darkened eyes. No flush of concern on her cheeks. Nothing.

"It is. She's in awe of him." Marti flicked a glance at him, but she didn't let her gaze linger. "Obviously, he enjoys it."

"Of course he does. Every man wants to know he can impress the woman he likes."

The color in her cheeks deepened and her gaze faltered. "Does he?"

A thrill he couldn't ignore raced up his spine. "Oh, yes. Trouble is, it's more difficult for adults than it is for the young ones. After all, the adult females have already stopped being impressed by everything the males do."

She hesitated for an instant, then turned her gaze

back to his again. "They can still be impressed," she said. "They only pretend not to be as a defense mechanism."

"Really?" He took another step closer and touched the small of her back tentatively.

"Yes." She sent him a wan smile. "But you can't repeat that aloud. And you have to promise never to use it to your own advantage."

He sketched an X over his heart with one hand and inched the other a little farther around her waist. "Never. The true male doesn't use things to gain advantage." He pulled her a little closer. "So, did I impress you with my tree-felling abilities?"

"Were you trying to impress me?" She smiled, but her voice came out low and seductive.

Need coiled through him. "You have no idea how much." He leaned closer still, drawn by the look in her eyes and the compelling softness of her lips. He needed to kiss her again, to feel her against him, if only for a moment. But before he could close the remaining distance between them, the chain saw roared to life again.

She jerked away, then sent him an apologetic smile. "It startled me." She had to shout to make herself heard.

He nodded. It had done more than frighten him. It had doused his passion as effectively as a cold glass of water in his lap. He squeezed her waist gently and released her, then walked to a vantage point where he could reach Cameron quickly if anything went wrong. He tried to keep his mind on the boy, the saw and the tree. But his mind kept wandering back to that aborted kiss.

He told himself that he'd find some way soon to take up where they'd left off. But next time, he'd make sure Cameron and Kendra were nowhere around.

MARTI TILTED BACK her head and let soft snowflakes land on her face while she waited for Kendra and Cameron to climb inside the truck beside Rick. Logic told her she should be glad the kids would be seated between them for the return trip home. Everything else inside her yearned to sit beside him while he drove.

She couldn't remember ever being so aware of a man before—of the force of his personality, the texture of the air whenever he came near, the sound of his breathing. Even in the early days of her marriage, when she'd thought herself to be head over heels in love, she hadn't been quite so conscious of Gil.

Sighing softly, she made an effort to stop thinking that way. It had been a perfect morning so far—free from arguments, from hurt feelings, from innuendo and speculation. She'd had a wonderful time watching Cameron and Kendra together, and remembering that moment when she'd thought Rick would kiss her again made her heart race.

Cameron moved away from her side and stepped onto the truck's running board. He stopped before he climbed inside and glanced at her. Following her gaze, he looked up at the light gray clouds overhead. "Looks like we finished just in time. I'll bet it'll be snowing hard within half an hour."

"I think you're right." She pulled her gaze back from the clouds and sighed again. "I've missed the snow. Christmas without snow just doesn't feel right."

Cameron's eyes flickered. "No, it doesn't."

Kendra leaned across the seat of the truck and tweaked the sleeve of Cameron's coat. "Come on, you two. I'm cold, and it's snowing."

Two spots of color flamed to life on Cameron's cheeks, and he darted a glance at Marti. Obviously, he didn't want to disappoint Kendra by making her wait. "Are you ready?"

Marti smiled to set him at ease. "Yes, of course. Let's go before the snow gets worse. We don't want to get stuck up here." Climbing into the truck behind Cameron, she settled herself onto the seat and pulled the door shut.

She leaned back in her seat and tried to ignore Rick, but she found herself watching him from the corner of her eye as he maneuvered the truck to a wide spot on the narrow trail where he could turn around. The muscles in his arms worked as he cranked the steering wheel, and without warning she longed to feel them around her again.

He glanced at her as he shifted gears and let his gaze travel from her eyes to her mouth and linger there. Then, as if the moment had never passed between them, he cleared his throat and spoke. "Our tree's on top, so I guess we'd better drop it off first and take yours home last."

She tried to match his casual tone. "That's a good idea."

"I hear it's best to let the branches drop for a couple of days before you decorate."

Somehow, she managed to force out another word. "Yes." But she couldn't hold back the scene that flashed in front of her—a fantasy in which she and Rick cut a single Christmas tree and decorated it together. The image caught her off guard and brought a flush to her cheeks. She forced it away.

Beside her, Cameron's voice rose and fell as he talked with Kendra. The girl's voice rose to meet his, and the two blended for a moment, then drifted away again. Marti didn't listen closely. Instead, she watched the forest and the thickening snowfall as Rick drove slowly over the rutted road toward the highway.

"What do you think, Mom?" Cameron nudged her gently with one elbow, but the insistent tone of his voice warned her he'd been trying to capture her attention.

Marti turned from the window and met his gaze. "I'm sorry, I was thinking about something else. What do I think about what?"

Kendra leaned forward in the seat so Marti could see her eager young face. "About coming on the sleigh ride with our family."

Marti cursed herself for not paying attention and tried desperately to look as if she understood. "Sleigh ride? When did you say it was again?"

Obviously, she'd failed.

Cameron's face puckered into a slight scowl. "It's two days before Christmas." He enunciated each word carefully, as if she needed an interpreter.

Marti nodded, as though that helped. "Next Wednesday?"

Kendra bobbed her head so quickly her hair fell into her eyes. "Yeah. Everything's arranged. So, will you come? It'll be lots of fun."

It did sound like fun, but she knew Cameron wouldn't want her there. She shook her head and smiled an apology. "I don't think I can make it."

To her surprise, Cameron's pucker tightened. "Why not?"

"Well, I don't..." She let her voice trail away for a second while her gaze traveled from Kendra to Cameron to Rick. They all looked expectant and eager, and she couldn't help smiling. "Yes, of course. It sounds great."

An instant too late, she realized that Kendra had said "family," which meant Lynette would also be there. Marti had no desire to repeat the experience she'd had with Lynette in Rick's kitchen.

Unless Rick's sister-in-law had undergone a serious change in attitude, she wouldn't want Marti there. Marti had no doubt the woman would make her displeasure known. And if Cameron picked up on the reason for Lynette's antagonism, it would ruin everything.

No matter how much Marti wanted to go, somehow she'd have to find a way out of it. The price of being there would be just too high.

PLEASANTLY FULL from dinner, Rick relaxed in his favorite armchair and sipped a glass of wine while Tom, Lynette and Ashley admired the bare tree he and Kendra had set up near the front window. He felt good tonight. Damn good. Better than he'd felt in a long time.

A log in the fireplace popped, and the scent of apple wood—sweet and smoky-tart—drifted across the room. He sipped again, leaned his head against the back of the chair and let his imagination conjure up a picture of himself alone with Marti in front of the fire.

"You're looking awfully pleased with yourself." Lynette's voice drew him back to the moment.

He smiled. "We had a good day today, didn't we, Kendra?"

Just as he'd expected, Kendra blushed. "Yeah, we did." She ran one hand across the needles on the tree, took a deep breath and glanced at her mother from beneath lowered lids. "I forgot to tell you, we invited Marti and Cameron to come on the sleigh ride with us."

Lynette's face froze. Only her eyes moved as she sought Rick's gaze. "You didn't."

Her reaction surprised Rick. He hadn't expected her to object to Kendra's infatuation with Cameron. "Yes, we did. They've been good friends, and Cameron worked hard to help me get everything ready for your visit."

Oblivious to the sudden tension springing from his wife, Tom lowered himself onto the couch with a loud groan. "He seems like a good kid. I've never met his mother, though."

Kendra perched on the arm of the couch beside him. "She's really nice. You'll like her."

Lynette's eyes narrowed. "He's not a good kid, he's trouble. I can tell that from a mile away."

"No, he's not," Kendra protested.

But Lynette had already closed her ears. She stepped away from the tree and jerked her head toward the kitchen. "Can I talk to you, Rick? Alone?"

He thought about refusing. He knew what that look on her face meant, and he didn't want anything to spoil his mood. But he nodded and set his wineglass on the end table beside his chair. "Sure."

Tom's forehead creased into a scowl. "What's wrong now?"

"Nothing," Lynette snapped. "Rick? Now, please?"

With increasing wariness, Rick pushed out of the armchair and stood. He smiled encouragement at Kendra and followed Lynette into the kitchen.

She crossed to the counter before wheeling back to face him. "I can't believe you invited them to come along on the sleigh ride. What were you thinking?"

"I told you, they're friends. Why don't you want Cameron there? He's a good kid."

"Isn't it obvious? He's not the sort of boy I want my girls spending time with. And I most definitely don't want *her* there."

"Her?" Rick stared at Lynette for a second and tried to convince himself he hadn't heard right. "You mean Marti?"

Her face reddened. "Yes… Unless you've invited some other woman, too?"

"No, but—" He broke off and shook his head to clear away the confusion. "What's wrong with Marti?"

Lynette barked a brittle laugh. "I'm sure there's nothing *wrong* with her."

"Then, why don't you want her to come along?"

"Why do you *want* her to?"

Even if Rick hadn't seen the accusation flash across her face, he'd have heard it in her voice. "She's a friend," he said simply. "And I can use all the friends I can get."

"A friend."

"Yes, a friend."

"I'm sure she is." She paced to the window and rounded on him. "How can you do this?"

"Do what?"

"You know very well what."

Struggling to keep control over his patience, he took a step closer. He knew losing Jocelyn had hurt her deeply, and he didn't want to cause her more pain, but it was time for both of them to move on. "I'm not married, Lynette. Not anymore."

"I know that." She backed away from him quickly. "But I thought you loved Jocelyn."

"I did. I still do. But she's gone, Lynette." He softened his voice even further, knowing how difficult it would be for her to hear him say what came next. "She's dead."

Tears filled Lynette's eyes and spilled over onto her cheeks.

He closed the distance between them and took her gently by the shoulders. "Do you want me to spend the rest of my life alone?"

She shook her head. "No. But—" She glanced up at him. "Do you love that woman?"

Rick hesitated before answering. "I don't know," he said honestly. "But I think what I feel for her could turn into love."

Lynette jerked away from him and stood in front of the window. "You've forgotten all about Jocelyn, haven't you? As if she never even existed."

He gripped the back of a chair and resisted the urge to follow her. "Of course not. I'll never forget Jocelyn."

"Then how can you do this?"

"What am I doing that's so horrible?"

"I could *never* look at another man if something happened to Tom."

"Maybe not at first, but you might after some time had gone by. I'm a man, not a saint. I can't live the rest of my life alone."

Her eyes filled with contempt. "You're disgusting."

"Why?" His voice rose several notches. He couldn't control his anger any longer. "Because I'm normal? Because I want companionship? Because I want to love and be loved?"

"If you want sex, then go find it somewhere. But don't cheapen Jocelyn's memory by…by—"

"By what?" he demanded. "By falling in love?"

"How can you love someone else? You and Jocelyn were soul mates."

No we weren't. He knew the time had come for him to admit what he'd kept to himself all these years.

"We weren't," he said softly. "We were too different."

"Don't." The word snapped out of Lynette's mouth. "Don't make everything worse by denying it."

"It's the truth. The marriage was falling apart."

"It was not."

"It was." He kept his voice low and steady, and he gripped the chair a little tighter so his resolve wouldn't weaken. "I didn't have the courage to tell you the truth when she died."

She would have backed away another step, but the wall stopped her.

"I told you she was going into town to do some last-minute Christmas shopping, but that wasn't true. The truth is, she was leaving me."

"Don't!" Lynette shook her head frantically, as if she could keep his words from touching her.

But now that he'd started, he had to say the rest. She

needed to hear it so she could accept the truth at long last. And he needed to say it. "She hated living here. It wasn't what she expected when we got married. She'd been trying to talk me into moving back to Denver, but I didn't want to go back. She gave me an ultimatum that night—either I had to agree to go back, or she'd leave me."

"Jocelyn wouldn't have done that."

He heard the warning note in her voice, but he ignored it. "I refused to compromise with her. I couldn't. I was too full of my own needs. Now I understand that our problems were as much my fault as they were hers. I changed the rules by moving here. I wasn't the man she'd married anymore."

Unleashing her anger, Lynette turned on him. Her eyes flashed. Her mouth thinned. And she looked so much like Jocelyn the last time he'd seen her, his lungs refused to pull in his next breath. "You can make up any lies you want to excuse what you're doing, Rick. But I refuse to stand here and listen. And I'll never believe you. *Never.*"

Without giving him a chance to respond, she pushed past him through the door into the living room.

Shock kept him rooted to the spot while she ordered Ashley and Kendra to get their coats. Then Tom wasted a few more seconds asking what had happened. A minute later, he heard the front door slam behind them.

Slowly, he walked out of the kitchen and bolted the front door. He turned out the lights, secured the screen over the fireplace and climbed the stairs. He started to open the door to the spare room, but stopped himself before he went inside.

It was time, he thought. Time to lay all of the ghosts

to rest. He pulled fresh sheets and two heavy blankets from the linen closet, took a deep breath and crossed the narrow landing to the master bedroom.

YAWNING, Marti carried her first cup of coffee across the living room to her makeshift desk. She couldn't see out the window while she worked any longer—they'd moved the desk to make room for the Christmas tree the day before—but she didn't mind. She loved the fresh scent of pine and, silly though it seemed, the tree made her feel closer to Rick.

Laughing silently at herself, she lowered her cup to the desk and turned on the computer. She'd spent all day yesterday playing. Today, she had to work, so she could justify having lunch with Cherryl later in the week.

She pulled out the draft of her article and arranged it on the desk so she could read the edits she'd made the last time she'd worked on it. Even with them in front of her, it took several minutes to find the rhythm of the piece again and to feel the cadence of each sentence. And it wasn't until she registered the excited voices approaching the house that she even became aware that she'd finally drifted into the trancelike state she assumed when words and ideas began to flow together.

Jerking back to reality, she blinked rapidly and looked up from the computer. When she recognized Gil's voice, she frowned and turned around in her chair. A second later, the front door banged open and Gil tromped inside, followed by her father.

"I'll call the sheriff," Gil said. "You'd better stay outside and keep an eye on them."

Henry didn't even hesitate. He wheeled around and stepped outside again, muttering something under his breath Marti couldn't make out.

Out of long habit, she pressed the save key on her computer before leaving her work. "What's wrong?" she asked Gil.

He ignored her and walked quickly toward the kitchen to make his phone call.

Suddenly apprehensive, she hurried to the door and called to her father, "Who are you keeping an eye on?"

Henry jerked one arm toward the road. "Damn snowmobilers on the north field." He glared at her as if she'd personally driven a machine across his precious fields. "I *told* you that s.o.b. would be nothing but trouble."

She didn't need to ask. She already knew the answer. But she asked anyway. "What s.o.b.?"

Her father's eyebrows collided over his nose and he waved his arm toward the road again. "Dennehy."

"Rick? He doesn't even own snowmobiles."

"Well, he does now."

"No, he doesn't." Marti stepped onto the porch and crossed her arms against the chill. "His brother-in-law rented them."

"Same thing," her father said. Then, as if her words had finally penetrated, he whipped around to face her. "Did you know they were bringing snowmobiles onto my property?"

"He asked me if you'd give them permission to run on the north field," she admitted. "But I told him no."

Gil barked a hostile laugh in her ear. The sound startled her. She hadn't heard him come back outside. "Well, that shows how much he listens to you."

"If there are people running snowmobiles on the field, I'm sure Rick knows nothing about it."

"Oh, he knows, all right," Henry said.

Her heart slowed. "Is he one of them?"

"No," Gil admitted reluctantly. "But I'll bet my bottom dollar he told them to come over here."

Marti rounded on him. "That's ridiculous. Why would he do that?"

Her father scowled darkly. "Because he's a son of a bitch."

Marti's temper flared. "How can you say that? You don't even know him."

"I know enough."

"How?" she demanded. "Have you even bothered to meet him? Or are you basing your opinion on what Gil says?" She didn't try to disguise her disgust.

And it wasn't lost on her father. He abandoned his post at the edge of the porch and closed the distance between them. "I trust Gil's opinion. In this case, I trust his over yours."

"Yes, I know," she snapped. "That's been painfully obvious since I came back. But why?"

"Gil hasn't gone all doe-eyed over Dennehy," Henry said. "He hasn't lost his perspective."

"Are you sure he hasn't? Maybe he has a reason for trying to turn you against Rick." The accusation escaped before she could think about the wisdom of voicing it.

Gil jumped from the porch to the yard below and planted himself in front of her. "The only interest I have is what's best for your dad. I don't know what you see in Dennehy, Marti, but you're acting like a fool."

A week ago, his words would have hurt her. Two days ago, they would have made her angry. Today, a strange sense of calm filled her. "No, Gil, I'm not."

Before she could say anything else, her father's gaze locked on something in the distance. "There's the sheriff. We'll get this straightened out now, once and for all." Pushing past her, he strode across the yard to his truck.

But before Gil could follow, Marti stepped off the porch and blocked his path. "When do you plan to tell Dad what you want to do with the Lazy M?"

Gil's face didn't change, but his eyes hardened. "I don't know what you're talking about."

Any doubts she might have harbored about Cherryl's story evaporated as she met his icy blue stare. "Don't lie to me, Gil. I know all about the factory. And I can't tell you how sick it makes me to think you'd try to use Cameron and me to take advantage of Dad."

"What factory?" He put on the mask of innocence she'd seen him wear so often during their marriage.

She wouldn't play his game. Not anymore. She shook her head and nodded toward the truck. "You'd better get over there. He's waiting. But I suggest you talk him out of pressing charges, and while you're at it, tell him the truth about the Lazy M."

He snorted a laugh.

"I'm serious, Gil. If you don't, I will."

His smile froze in place, and his eyes narrowed. But his expression didn't faze her. Not this time. He must have sensed her determination, because something else flashed through his eyes a split second before he pushed past her and jogged toward the truck. She never would have believed it, but she would have sworn he'd looked apprehensive, if only for a moment.

And for the first time ever, she knew she could match him and beat him—even when it came to Cameron.

CHAPTER TWELVE

MARTI SAT on the floor in front of the Christmas tree and worked to untangle the cord on a set of multicolored lights. Heat from the fire she'd built after dinner and the occasional sound of logs popping teased her into believing all was right with her world.

She sipped from the glass of mulled wine at her side and stole a peek at Cameron. He sat on the couch, chin resting on one hand, as he watched Bing Crosby and Rosemary Clooney dance across the television screen in *White Christmas.* To her surprise, he looked interested in the movie and even amused by some of the dated bits of dialogue.

She loved seeing him so relaxed around her, but she wondered again, as she had several times during dinner, if she should tell him what she'd decided about her relationship with his father. But once again she talked herself out of it. She'd be a fool to ruin this new, easy camaraderie they shared. And she didn't want to ruin Christmas for everyone.

Whether she liked admitting it or not, the possibility that he'd want to stay in Gunnison while she went back to California frightened her. All her brave words to Rick in the cemetery about letting Cameron live with Gil had been only that—brave words. No matter how strained their relationship had been, she didn't want to lose Cameron.

Finally, working the last bit of cord free, she leaned up on her knees to plug the lights into the extension cord she'd stretched into the middle of the floor. Holding her breath, she willed the lights to work. But nothing happened. Not even a flicker. Sighing heavily, she unplugged the set and started gathering it together again.

"Let me see that." Cameron's voice sounded so unexpectedly loud behind her, she jumped and whipped around to look at him. He reached one hand out over the arm of the couch toward her and said again, "Let me see the lights. Maybe I can get them to work."

Smiling, she handed him the jumble of cord and lights. "I hope you can. This is the fifth set I've found that doesn't work, and I'm beginning to think I'll have to make a trip into Gunnison in the morning before I can decorate the tree."

"Yeah? Well, I'll see what I can do." He dropped the lights into his lap and began checking each bulb methodically.

She watched him work for a few minutes, then said, "Rick tells me you're very good at this sort of thing."

A pleased smile tugged at the corners of his mouth. "Yeah?"

"Yeah." She sat back on her heels and reached into the box at her side for one of the tiny Santas she'd carefully wrapped in tissue last time she'd packed them away. "He's quite impressed with your talents as a carpenter."

Cameron glanced at her again but his smile faded, as if he suspected her of some sort of trick. "Is he?"

Marti smiled encouragement. ''Is that the kind of work you'd like to do when you graduate?''

''Does it matter?''

''Of course it matters.''

''Well...'' He hesitated, then nodded slowly. ''Yeah.''

''You really don't want to go to college?''

Cameron let another long silence hang between them, and she could almost see him battling the urge to tell her the truth.

She tried to make it easier for him. ''You don't, do you?''

He pulled his head back and squared his shoulders as he always did when he anticipated an argument. ''No.''

The look on his face made Marti's heart sink. But she took a deep breath to fortify herself and tried to keep her smile warm and friendly. ''I know I've pushed you to get more education...''

He glanced away quickly and every muscle in his body seemed to tense.

''But that's only because I want you to be happy. I'm finally beginning to realize you *won't* be happy doing something just because I think it's the right thing to do.''

His gaze traveled slowly back to her face, and she could see curiosity mixed with disbelief in his eyes. ''What do you mean?''

''I mean, if you really like working with your hands, and if you have even half the talent Rick seems to think you have, maybe that's what you should be doing.''

''Are you serious?''

Nodding, she set the Santa aside and pulled another

from the box. "Yes. That doesn't mean you don't have to finish high school, just that maybe I've been wrong about college."

His smile reappeared, but it remained tentative. "Really?"

"Really. If you promise to do your best in school for the next two and a half years, I'll back off on the college thing."

His smile faltered. "What? You expect me to get straight A's?"

"No. I expect you to do your best, and I'll accept whatever grade that earns you. But you have to promise you'll try."

He tilted his head and gave that some thought. *Please,* Marti thought. *Please, don't get angry.*

Finally, as if in slow motion, he nodded. "Okay. I'll try."

She thought her heart might burst out of her chest. Instinctively, without giving herself time to think, she leaned forward and touched his hand. When he didn't withdraw it, tears filled her eyes. She tried to blink them away so he wouldn't see them, but as quickly as she could clear her vision, a new wave of tears took their place.

To her amazement, his expression softened a little more. She resisted the urge to scoot closer. She didn't want to push too hard and drive him off again.

He glanced down at his knees and opened his mouth as if he wanted to say something. But before he could speak, the front door banged open and her father stomped inside. He stood there, red-faced and breathing heavily, and glared at her.

Marti stood quickly and stepped over several sets of lights to reach him. "Dad? What's wrong?"

"I just finished talking to Gil. The sheriff isn't going to do anything about the trespassing this afternoon. Nothing." He narrowed his eyes and slammed the door shut behind him. "And if that's not bad enough, Gil tells me you've been saying some pretty harsh things to him, little girl."

Marti's pulse stuttered and shapeless dread filled her. She sensed more than heard Cameron tense behind her, but she didn't let herself look at him. "What did he tell you?"

Her father shrugged out of his coat and hung it in the closet, then slammed that door shut, too. He crossed the room and dropped heavily into his favorite armchair. "I thought things were goin' better between the two of you. But from the sound of things, you care more about Dennehy than your own husband."

"Gil's *not* my husband, Dad. Remember? We've been divorced for the past three years."

He waved her answer away with one hand as if it meant nothing. "And now I find out you've threatened Gil with lies if he didn't talk me out of calling the sheriff this afternoon."

Marti knew the time had come to tell her dad the truth, but she didn't want to have this argument in front of Cameron. She brushed a lock of hair off her cheek. "Can we finish this in your office?"

Her father shook his head, leaned back in his seat and gripped the armrests. "Cameron's not a child. He deserves to know what's going on. After all, you've let him believe you and Gil would get back together."

Frustration and anger flared within her. Cameron

stepped in front of her. The mellow expression he'd been wearing had disappeared and the old hostility had returned.

"I did try to work things out with your dad," she assured him. "But then I found out he wants to build a factory on the Lazy M."

"Gil wouldn't do that," her father interrupted.

"Of course he would," she insisted. "He's always looking for the quickest way to make a dollar."

Cameron tugged her around to face him again. "What factory?"

"I know Gil," her father said before she could respond. "I trust him."

"But you don't trust *me?*" The question came out harsh, bitter and angry. She took a deep breath and tried to temper her voice. "I'm your daughter. Why would *I* lie to you?"

"What factory?" Cameron demanded again.

Caught between the need to explain to Cameron and the growing urgency to convince her father of the truth, Marti met her son's gaze. "I found out that your dad only wants to marry me again so he can get Grandpa's property. He plans to sell it to a company from Kansas City that wants to build a factory along the river."

What little light remained in Cameron's eyes flickered out. "No way."

"Gil wouldn't do that," Henry said again.

Clenching her fists, Marti tried desperately to maintain some level of control. "Why would I make up something like that?"

"Why not?" Cameron demanded. "You're always trying to make him look bad."

"That's not true," she shouted. "He does that well enough by himself."

Making a noise low in his throat, Cameron spun away from her and jerked open the coat closet. "Go to hell."

"You're not leaving here—"

"Yes I am."

She couldn't let him leave. Not while he was this angry. "Cameron—"

He shoved his arms into his coat, yanked open the front door and stepped onto the porch. "Just leave me alone," he yelled, and slammed the door between them.

She raced across the room and followed him outside. She didn't even bother with her coat. She didn't have time. "Cameron, wait."

Ignoring her, he ran down the driveway toward the access road.

She followed him for several feet, but she couldn't hope to keep up. "Cameron! Come back. Let me explain."

She might as well have been talking to the trees. Frantic now, she turned back toward the house intending to grab her keys and follow him in the car. But her father stepped onto the porch and took her by the arm. "Get back inside, girl. I'll go after him."

Tears of anger filled her eyes. "Why did you have to bring this up in front of him? Didn't you know how he'd react?"

"This isn't *my* fault, girl. You should have been honest with him from the beginning."

"Honest?" The word tore from her throat. "I can't

be honest with either of you. Both of you only believe what you want to believe."

"Now, Marti, calm down—"

She started to push past him, but he caught her arms and held her in place. She tried to jerk away, but he only tightened his grip. "Let go of me," she snapped. "I need to go after Cameron."

"You're not in any condition to go anywhere." Her father's voice changed subtly, and she recognized the no-nonsense tone he'd used so often during her childhood. "Go back inside and wait there. I'll take care of Cameron."

But she wasn't a child any longer, and she was no longer afraid of that tone. "He's my son—"

"And he's my grandson." He led her through the door and released her to grab his coat from the closet. "I'll find him, don't worry. And I'll take him to Gil's to let him cool off."

Marti's heart almost stopped beating. "No. Don't take him to Gil. Bring him back here."

"Listen to me, Marti." Her father gripped her shoulders again and shook her. "Bringing him back tonight will only make things worse. You're both too upset and angry to talk."

The last thing she wanted was for Cameron to go to Gil's. She shook her head vehemently, but her father went on before she could speak. "Trust me." His voice dropped another notch, but this time his voice soothed her. "Let the boy spend the night with Gil. I'll drive back over in the morning to pick him up."

She pulled another step back from the edge of hysteria. She looked into her father's eyes, expecting to

"I'm not going back there," Cameron warned.

"I promised your mother I'd bring you home."

"I don't care. *Un*promise her. I'm not going back there. She hates me."

His grandfather frowned, and his wrinkles folded over on themselves. "She doesn't hate you."

Cameron snorted a laugh. "Oh, no? Well, she sure acts like she does."

Grandpa's frown deepened and his mouth disappeared in the folds of his skin. He glanced at Cameron again. "She loves you, boy."

Cameron wished he could believe that. But if she loved him, wouldn't she act like it? Wouldn't she hug him once in a while, or tell him he'd done something right, or...well, *something?*

Almost immediately, a voice in his head reminded him of the compliment his mother had paid him earlier that evening. Cameron ignored it. Didn't matter, anyway. One compliment. Big deal. She probably hadn't even meant it.

"Yeah," he said. "Sure. Whatever."

He didn't need his mom. He had his dad, who told him all the time how great he was, and how much he missed him. He talked all the time about things they'd do and places they'd go once Cameron lived with him for good. And he didn't have a bunch of dumb rules about how Cameron ought to behave.

Cameron couldn't wait. He was going to live with his dad, no matter what anyone said.

Grandpa slowed the truck to go around a curve. "It isn't easy for your mother to show people what she's feeling. Never has been."

There he went—sticking up for her, as usual. Cameron rolled his eyes in frustration. "That doesn't make it right."

Grandpa's eyes narrowed and his frown got bigger. "It's easier for some people than others."

"Yeah? Well, so's math. But she doesn't let me stop trying to do it."

His grandfather almost smiled at him. "No," he said slowly, "she doesn't, does she? I guess you can understand how tough it is for her, then. I mean, since you have to struggle with math and all."

That idea made Cameron uncomfortable, but he forced an angry laugh and tried not to think about it. "Not even." He flashed an annoyed glance at Grandpa. "Math's tough for me, okay?" He unbuckled his seat belt and let it snap back into the door. "So I guess that means I understand. But that still doesn't make it right." He pushed open his door and jumped to the ground before Grandpa even shut off the engine. He banged on the front door of his dad's house before Grandpa could even make it halfway up the front walk.

His dad answered just as Grandpa climbed the last of the steps onto the porch. He wore his good black jeans, his black boots and a white shirt—the same kind of clothes he always used to wear when he went out on the town.

Grandpa must have noticed that, too. "Did we catch you on your way out?"

His dad started to shake his head, then stopped himself with a shrug. "I was thinking about going down to the Lucky Jack for a couple of beers. Why? What's going on?"

"Cameron and Marti had a bit of a tiff," Grandpa

said. "They're both pretty upset still, so I thought it would be best if he stayed here with you tonight."

His dad nodded quickly and motioned them inside. "Of course. Sure." He stepped aside to let them enter and clapped one hand on Cameron's shoulder as he passed. "What happened? What did she do?"

Cameron stopped inside the door and unzipped his coat. The house looked different to him. Smaller. It didn't smell like home anymore, but it did smell like his dad. "She's been lying to us," he said. "And making up all sorts of crazy stuff about you."

His dad's expression sobered. He glanced at Grandpa and back again. "About the factory?"

Cameron nodded. "She says you want to marry her again to get the Lazy M and sell it so they can build the factory by the river."

His dad rolled his eyes and shut the door behind Grandpa and let out a heavy sigh. "I swear, I don't know what's gotten into her lately. See what I've been telling you, Henry? This is *exactly* why you don't want a woman running the place for you. They're too damn emotional."

Grandpa nodded. To Cameron's surprise, he didn't look angry. "You're right, of course. You always have been. But I can't help wishing things could be different. Marti was the only one of my kids who even wanted to take over the reins for me. I wonder sometimes if I'm making a mistake..."

Cameron sat in front of the fireplace and let the heat work its way over him. Everything was going to be all right now that he was in this house.

A second later, his grandpa's words hit him. He glanced at him and thought how funny it sounded for him to say that. He'd heard his mom complaining that Grandpa wouldn't let her run the Lazy M. Was she making that up, too?

His dad dropped into his favorite armchair and kicked his feet up on the footstool Cameron had sat on as a kid. "Well, she probably could if she had a steadying influence."

"Maybe," Grandpa said slowly. "I don't know anymore."

Cameron's dad shook his head slowly. "I know. I know. But I'm still here for you, Henry. Don't forget that."

Grandpa tried to smile, but it didn't work. He still looked sad. "I know, son. Don't think I don't appreciate it." He glanced at Cameron, tried once more to smile and turned back toward the door. "You two will be all right, won't you? I don't want to leave Marti alone for long."

"You bet." Groaning as if his jeans were too tight, Cameron's dad stood again and followed Grandpa to the door. "Don't worry about us."

"Good." Grandpa glanced at Cameron again, and this time he managed a smile. "I'll see you in the morning."

"Sure," Cameron said with a nod. But he didn't mean it. By morning, he'd have convinced his dad to let him stay here forever.

He waited inside while his dad walked Grandpa out to the truck, trying to rediscover the feel of home and replaying the argument with his mom over and over. He couldn't understand why she hated his dad so much or why she didn't realize that the whole divorce had been Cameron's fault in the first place, not his dad's.

It had been Cameron's stupidity that broke up his parents' marriage—that's why it was his responsibility to fix it.

His dad came back inside, but instead of coming back to the armchair, he put on his jacket and stood in the archway between the foyer and the living room, looking impatient. "I've got to go out for a little while," he said. "You know where the sheets and blankets are upstairs, don't you? Just make the bed in your old room."

Cameron couldn't believe his eyes or his ears. "But I want to talk to you."

With a shrug, his dad crossed to the front door and opened it. "And we will. In the morning."

"But, Dad—"

"Look, Cam." His dad didn't even let go of the doorknob. "You're tired and upset. Now's not the best time to talk about anything."

Was he kidding? He was really going to leave now? Cameron tried to look as if he didn't care. "Sure. Fine."

His dad smiled. "Good." He glanced at his watch and checked out the door, as if he expected to see someone there. "I've got to run. You'll be okay…right?"

"Yeah, right." Cameron's stomach ached, as if his dad had punched him in the gut. He knew how to keep his voice tough. He'd been doing it for years with his mom. But if his dad still went out all the time, his mom would *never* want to get back together with him. And everything Cameron had done would be for nothing.

He crossed to the bottom of the stairs and started up,

still wishing his dad would change his mind. Still thinking maybe—

The door closed with a solid click behind him. He held his breath for a second, until he heard his dad's footsteps going down the walk outside. He battled an almost overwhelming disappointment, but told himself to stop being a baby. His dad was right. He'd feel better tomorrow. They could talk about everything then.

When he reached the second-floor landing, he turned back and looked down the stairs. Without warning, a memory rolled over him. He could almost hear his mother crying and see himself as a child, standing in this same spot begging his dad to stay home, and listening to him walk away instead.

He tried to shake the images, tried to block the sounds from his mind, but instead of fading, they grew even louder. She'd sat on the bottom step with her face in her hands, her stomach swollen so large he couldn't even see her lap.

He'd been frightened, he remembered that. Especially when she'd arched her back and let out a scream that would have scared anybody—especially a ten-year-old kid. He remembered running down the steps to sit beside her. He'd cried like a baby, begging her over and over to be all right instead of helping her. Much later, when he noticed all the blood, he'd finally dialed the emergency number and asked somebody to help her. But it had been too late then. He'd waited too long.

That was the night his baby sister had come. He knew that, but he couldn't remember anything else except his father's face the next morning when he told Cameron the baby had been dead when she got here.

white. He must have been outside for some time. "What are you doing out at this time of night?"

Cameron didn't answer that. He wrapped his arms around himself and asked, "Can I stay here?"

"For the time being," Rick said, pulling a wool blanket from the coat closet and working it around Cameron's shoulders. "What did you do? Have another fight with your mom?"

Cameron glanced at him quickly, then nodded. He seemed hesitant to answer. "Yeah."

That didn't surprise Rick, but it did sadden him. He turned toward the kitchen. "I'd better call and let her know where you are."

"No!" The word shot out of Cameron's mouth like a bullet. "Don't." Rick turned to face him, but Cameron wouldn't meet his gaze, and his next words came out much softer. "She thinks I'm at my dad's house."

Rick tried not to look annoyed, but he didn't like being party to a lie, especially one told to Marti. "Is that where you told her you were going?"

Cameron shook his head quickly. "No. My grandpa took me there earlier—after the fight we had." He studied the pattern on the blanket. "I...I left."

Rick could only imagine how Gil would react when he found out Cameron had come here. But he also knew Cameron would not have left Gil's house unless something had driven him away. Relief for Marti's sake inched up his spine. Maybe Cameron had gotten a healthy dose of reality at his father's hands.

But he didn't say that aloud. He just shrugged casually and suggested, "Maybe I should call your dad, then."

"Don't bother. He's not home."

"He doesn't know you're gone?"

Cameron shook his head.

"How did you get here?"

"I walked."

"All the way from town? It's at least ten miles."

A faint smile tugged at Cameron's lips. "No, only partway. I walked about a mile, then some guy picked me up and gave me a ride."

"*Some guy?* Did you know him?"

Cameron shook his head.

"Well, that wasn't too smart." Rick's voice came out gruff with emotion.

Obviously, Cameron noticed. To Rick's surprise, the boy smiled. If he didn't know better, he'd swear Cameron liked seeing him worried.

"I know," Cameron said. "It was stupid. You don't have to tell me."

"The first thing we're going to do is warm you up," Rick said. "Let's get you into a hot shower. Then, I want you to tell me what's going on."

Cameron followed him up the stairs, and while the teenager showered, Rick found a pair of thermal underwear, sweatpants and shirt, and two pairs of thick wool socks. He left them on a small table outside the bathroom, called instructions to Cameron through the door and went back downstairs to wait.

Several long minutes later, Cameron joined him. But he still looked cold and weak, and Rick's concern grew. "Cover yourself with that blanket. I'll make something warm to drink."

Cameron didn't argue. In fact, a noise escaped him that sounded almost like a whimper. It twisted Rick's heart. Thank goodness Marti couldn't see him like this.

She'd go out of her mind with worry. Then the thought crossed his mind that when Gil realized Cameron was gone, he'd probably call Marti and she'd be frantic.

Rick thought about calling her from the kitchen, but before he could do anything, he heard Cameron's voice. "Don't get any ideas about calling my mom. I'll just take off if you do."

So much for that idea, Rick thought wryly. Okay, he'd wait until Cameron fell asleep. He just hoped Marti wouldn't find out Cameron had run away before Rick had a chance to reach her.

He spooned cocoa mix into two heavy mugs and tried to relax while water heated in the teakettle. But he couldn't stop wondering what had driven Cameron from his dad's house in the middle of the night. Why hadn't Gil been there with him? What could have been more important than taking care of his son?

After what felt like forever, the kettle began to whistle. Rick poured the hot water into the mugs and stirred in the cocoa mix, then carried the drinks into the living room.

Cameron had stretched out on the couch and covered himself with both blankets. Rick handed him a mug and lowered himself into a nearby chair. "Feeling better?"

Cameron sipped carefully and nodded. "Yeah. A little."

"Good. Now suppose you tell me what you're doing here."

Cameron looked at him over the rim of his mug. "I need a place to stay."

"You've got it. You know that. But tell me why you're not with your mother."

"We had a fight."

"You told me that much already," Rick said. "I need a little more detail."

Cameron didn't say anything for so long, Rick began to wonder if he'd pushed too hard. No, he told himself. Marti had spent the past three years trying to avoid confrontation with Cameron, and look where that had gotten her. Nowhere.

"Tell me, Cameron," Rick insisted.

Cameron took another sip of cocoa, and let out a heavy sigh. "She says my dad wants to get Grandpa's property so he can sell it to somebody else. And she says *they* want to build a factory on it."

"Is that what you fought with her about?"

"She's making it up—I know she is."

Rick tried to keep his expression impassive. "She didn't make it up, Cameron. I've heard the same thing."

"Where did you hear that? Who told you?"

Rick didn't want to involve Cherryl, so he shrugged casually. "I don't remember, exactly. Somewhere in town. But it was a pretty reliable source."

Cameron's frown deepened and two spots of color appeared in his pale cheeks. "It's a lie. My dad wouldn't do that."

"Are you sure?"

"Yeah. I am. I know my dad." Cameron sounded confident, but Rick could see a flicker of doubt in his eyes.

"You said earlier your dad wasn't home when you left. Where was he?"

Cameron sent him an angry glance, but he didn't answer.

"Yes. She's right here." Henry extended the receiver toward her. "It's Gil. Cameron's missing."

"Missing?" Marti's knees threatened to buckle. She steadied herself with one hand and nearly tore the receiver away from her father with the other. "Gil? What's happened to Cameron?"

"You tell me." Anger surged through the wire, and she could hear alcohol on his voice. "Where in the hell is he?"

"Why are you asking me? Dad dropped him off at your house."

"No kidding. He was here when I left, but he's gone now."

"Where did you go? How could you leave him?"

Her father put a gentle hand on her arm, and the gesture brought tears to her eyes.

"Don't start in on me, Marti." Gil's voice tightened. "Just tell me where Cameron is."

"I don't know. I haven't heard from him. Did he leave a note?"

"A note?" Gil let out a bitter laugh. "Hell, no. But there's a hole in the wall by his bed and there's stuff all over the floor. Are you telling me the truth? You really haven't seen him?"

"I really haven't." Marti glanced at her father. Panic coursed through her body with every beat of her heart. But panic wouldn't solve anything, and it wouldn't help her find Cameron.

She leaned against the wall and told herself to calm down. "Did someone break in?"

"No." Gil's voice rose a notch. "Nobody broke in."

"Then, where could he be?" She asked the question more of herself than of Gil, but he responded, anyway.

"How in the hell am I supposed to know?"

The question shattered the fragile hold she'd kept on her self-control. "You should know, you son of a bitch. He went there to be with you. Where were you?"

"Out."

His standard answer. Red-hot anger consumed her. All his past wrongs seemed to line up in front of her. "Out. You always go *out*." She nearly choked on the words and had to drag in several deep breaths before she could go on. "You've ignored Cameron for the past three years. He might as well not even have existed for all the attention you paid him. But for some reason, in spite of all that, he's kept you on a pedestal and thought you were some kind of Wonder Dad. But now, *finally,* maybe he's seen you for what you really are."

Without giving it a second thought, she slammed down the receiver and turned to her father. "I'm going to look for him."

"I'm coming with you."

She thought about refusing, but he looked so distraught she didn't have the heart to leave him behind. "All right. I'll get dressed and meet you downstairs."

She hurried to her bedroom, dressed quickly and raced downstairs. There, she yanked their coats from the closet, paced to the window and peered into the night. Clouds covered the moon and stars, making it impossible to see more than a few feet.

She glanced at the stairs and willed her dad to dress quickly. Sighing impatiently, she turned back to the window. This time, she thought she saw movement in the shadows. With her heart in her throat, she raced to the front door and wrenched it open. "Cameron?"

She ran to the edge of the porch and peered into the darkness. Yes. There it was again. This time, she made out the shape of someone walking up the driveway.

Tugging on her coat, she jumped from the porch and hurried toward the shadowy figure. Snow crunched beneath her feet as she closed the distance between them. "Cameron? Is that you?"

"No, Marti. It's me." Rick's deep voice drifted through the darkness toward her.

Surprise stopped her in her tracks. "Rick? What are you doing here? It's the middle of the night."

He stopped a few inches from her. "I came to let you know that Cameron's at my place."

Her knees buckled, as relief shot through her. The horrible fear that had propelled her during the past few minutes vaporized so suddenly, she felt weak. "At your place? Thank God. What happened? Is he all right? Why didn't you call me and let me know?"

Rick took hold of her arm and steadied her. "He's fine. In fact, he fell asleep on my couch. And I didn't call because I didn't want to do anything that might make him run again."

A sudden blast of icy wind curved around them. Rick shivered involuntarily. Marti looked behind him for his truck, but the driveway stood empty. "You didn't walk all the way over here, did you?"

He sent her that wonderful crooked smile of his. "No, I left the truck down the road. I didn't want to wake your dad." He let his gaze travel over the brightly lit house. "I guess I didn't need to worry about that."

"Only because Gil woke us both a few minutes ago. I've been frantic. We were just getting ready to start looking for Cameron. I'm so grateful you were there to take him in." She tugged on his arm, urging him toward the house. "Come inside where it's warm. I'll make something hot to drink, and you can tell me everything."

Rick's smile faded. He put one hand over hers where it touched his side. His expression grew serious. "Marti—"

Her breath caught. Something was wrong, she could see it in his face. But before he could say more, her father stepped onto the porch. "Who's out there?" he shouted. "Is it Cameron?"

Biting back frustration at the interruption, she called back, "No, Dad. It's Rick Dennehy. He came to let us know Cameron's at his place."

"*His* place? What's Cameron doing there?"

She hesitated, but this time Rick urged her forward. "I don't know yet," she said as she led Rick up the steps. "But I'm sure Rick will tell us."

Her father looked as if he'd like to say something more. To his credit, he clamped his mouth shut and stepped aside to let them pass, then followed them inside. He crossed the room and lowered himself into his chair without taking his eyes from Rick's face. "All right, we're waiting. What's Cameron doing at your place?"

Rick glanced at Marti and lifted one eyebrow in silent question.

She nodded toward the chair opposite her father's and sat on the couch between them. "What time did Cameron show up at your place?"

"A couple of hours ago," Rick said. "But he was so upset, and so insistent that I not call you, I couldn't let you know until he'd gone to sleep."

"You were wise," she said softly. "If you had called, he probably would have run off again."

"That's what I figured."

Her father leaned forward. "Why did he leave Gil's?"

"From what I've been able to piece together," Rick said, "Gil left almost immediately after you did."

Her father's scowl deepened. "That's what I don't understand. Gil said he came home and found Cameron missing. But where did he go?"

"Where do you think?" Marti couldn't keep the irritation from her voice. "Where does he always go? The Lucky Jack. And he probably went home with some woman after they closed."

Henry started to shake his head, but Rick spoke before he could say anything. "Cameron says that Gil didn't tell him where he was going. He says his dad was dressed to go out, and that he said they could talk about everything in the morning."

"Then, why didn't Cameron just stay put?" her father demanded. "It doesn't make any sense to me. No sense at all."

Rick glanced at Marti, and the same expression she'd seen outside crossed his face now. "Apparently, he started thinking about the past." He paused, drew in a long, slow, steadying breath and flashed another glance at Marti. "Did you know Cameron thinks it's his fault you and Gil got divorced?"

The words stunned her and everything inside grew numb. "*His* fault? Why?"

Rick glanced down at his hands. He seemed to be struggling with himself, perhaps deciding how to explain.

"Why?" Marti asked again, but the room felt suddenly very far away, and the moment almost surreal.

"That's ridiculous," Henry mumbled.

Rick met Marti's gaze, and she could see something odd lurking behind his eyes. "He told me about the night his sister was born."

"Chelsea?" Marti's breath caught painfully in her chest. "But what…" Words raced through her mind, but she couldn't seem to get them out. She'd tried so hard not to think about that night, and she'd convinced herself Cameron's silence meant he'd done the same. "Why did he tell you about that?"

"Because he thinks he's responsible."

No. The word echoed in her mind, but she couldn't seem to say it aloud. How could Cameron think that? He'd been a child—just ten years old. He was *still* a child, for heaven's sake.

Her father jerked out of his seat and paced toward the fireplace. "Responsible for what?"

"For his sister's death," Rick said. "For not getting help in time."

Tears filled Marti's eyes and a lump blocked her throat. Her hands trembled and she had to plant them on the couch cushions to hold herself up. The truth was, Cameron had saved her life by calling for help.

Her father snorted in response. "Nonsense."

"He was ten years old," Marti whispered. "He did everything he could. But nobody could have saved Chelsea." She tried to pull herself together, to push away the memory of that horrible night as she had so many times in the past, but this time it wouldn't leave. She remembered the pain, the blood, the horror on Cameron's face. She remembered how he'd cried and begged her to be all right.

Familiar anger coiled around the helpless anguish that always came with thoughts of Chelsea. Gil should have been there with them. He should have put his family first for once. If he had, Cameron wouldn't have blamed himself.

The marriage had been faltering for at least two years before that, but Chelsea's death and the blame she and Gil had heaped upon each other had ultimately led to its end. Surely Cameron remembered that. Surely he remembered all the arguments. How could he think *he* was responsible?

"For heaven's sake," Henry said. His voice sounded gruff, but this time, Marti recognized the emotion behind it. "If he hadn't called when he did, Marti might have died along with the baby. He knows that."

"No," Rick said firmly. "No, he doesn't. He thinks he waited too long. He's convinced that if he hadn't let his sister die, you and Gil would be happy together. That's why he's been so determined to get you back together. He's trying to make everything right again because he thinks it's his fault everything went wrong."

Marti felt the room slipping away and Rick's voice fading into unreality, as if he were on the other side of a thick wall.

"That's nonsense," her father insisted. But Marti could barely hear him over the sound of her internal voice crying out denial.

"You both know that," Rick said, "and I know that,

but what matters is that Cameron believes it. It's true in his mind.''

Odd noises seemed to grow louder—creaks and groans as the house settled, her mother's cuckoo clock on the mantel, the rustle of her father's jeans as he paced in front of the fireplace. Marti's heart turned to lead, her stomach twisted violently and she broke out in a cold sweat. She thought she might be sick, but she couldn't make herself move.

"Marti..." Rick's voice grew a little louder. "Are you all right?" His face floated in front of her, dipping and swaying, and making her stomach lurch.

She closed her eyes and tried to nod. But it was a lie. She wasn't all right. She should have talked to Cameron about that night, but it had been so painful for her, she'd been pathetically grateful that he'd never brought it up. She'd locked away her memories and tried to pretend that night had never happened. But she should have seen what the experience had done to Cameron. She *should* have known.

She opened her eyes and focused slowly. Rick's face wavered in front of her for a moment, then seemed to solidify. His eyes, deep and caring and frightened, locked on hers. "Are you all right?" he demanded again.

She managed to nod, but the movement made her stomach roll again. She opened her mouth to speak, but she couldn't form the words.

He sat beside her on the couch and wrapped an arm around her shoulders. When he moved, she saw her father beside the fireplace. His face had lost its color, his hands trembled, and Marti realized that the news had stunned him as much as it had her.

Rick tightened his hold on her. "Thank God. You're getting some of your color back."

She tried to smile reassurance, but her lips felt stiff and heavy. "I'm all right. I'm just…shocked. I've tried so hard to put that night behind me, I didn't realize Cameron ever thought about it."

Her father glared at Rick, at his arm around her shoulders and his nearness on the couch—the very things she needed most. "Why would he tell you about it and not one of us?"

Rick met his gaze steadily. "I don't know. We've become friends. Maybe he thought he could trust me."

Henry's frown tightened. "Why—"

Marti interrupted before he could finish. "I don't care who he told. I'm just glad he finally told someone."

She didn't add how glad she was that he'd chosen to tell Rick. Her father would never understand how much she'd come to care for Rick. How much peace the sight of his face gave her. How much comfort she derived from having him beside her at this moment.

But right now she didn't need her father to understand. The only person she needed to worry about was her son. The only person she needed to explain things to was Cameron.

CHAPTER FOURTEEN

MARTI STOOD outside Rick's front door, one hand poised to knock, heart hammering with apprehension. Rick's visit during the early-morning hours had left her too keyed up to sleep. She'd waited as long as she could, lying in bed and watching the sun turn the sky a pale winter gray. Cameron probably needed as much sleep as he could get. By the time she'd finally climbed out of bed, still without sleep, she'd known her emotional reserves were gone.

She hoped Lynette would still be in her own cabin. She didn't want to face her again. And she honestly didn't know if she could survive another rejection from Cameron.

With her eyes closed, she gulped several deep breaths to steady her nerves and to lessen the pounding in her head. In and out once, twice, three times. Finally, she found the strength to knock on the door.

It seemed like forever before Rick answered. But some corner of her brain still open to logic told her he'd actually answered almost immediately. He must have. If she'd had to wait, she probably would have let her nerves get the best of her.

Rick smiled when he saw her, a smile of genuine pleasure that touched her deeply. At least someone was glad to see her. She couldn't count on the same reaction from Cameron. She let herself enjoy the moment.

"He's waiting for you," Rick said. Simple words, but they struck a chord of fear inside her.

She tried to force a smile, but her lips felt thick and stiff. "You told him I was coming?"

Rick nodded and took her arm to lead her inside. "Yes, of course. And he knows that I told you about Chelsea. I wouldn't make you surprise him. That wouldn't be fair to either of you."

A wave of relief washed through her, and her smile came more easily. "Thank you."

He shrugged off her gratitude as if it were nothing. "He's willing to talk to you, but he's still pretty upset."

"I'll be careful."

Rick's hand caressed her arm. "I'm not trying to tell you what to do. After all, he's your son."

"You've been right about everything so far." And his obvious concern for Cameron touched her more than she could say.

"Only because I have emotional distance. You're too close. You have too much at stake."

He made it sound so easy. But half a dozen counselors had talked to Cameron over the years, and none had gotten to the root of his anger. Within just a few weeks, Rick had pulled confidences from Cameron nobody else had ever been able to.

"I talked to Gil after you left." She tried to sound normal, but just thinking about that phone call made her head ache and her hands tremble.

Rick's eyes clouded. "He upset you again."

"He's threatening to sue for custody."

"Custody? After Cameron ran away from him last night?"

"He blames me for that, too."

"You?" The word exploded between them. Rick shoved his hands onto his hips and paced a step away. "That's the most ridiculous thing I've ever heard. *He's* the one who left a very volatile kid alone. *He's* the one who couldn't even be bothered to see how much Cameron needed someone there with him."

"I'm the one Cameron was running from in the first place," she reminded him. "Cameron was only there because he'd already run away from me."

"Right. Because you told him the truth about the crap Gil's trying to pull with the Lazy M." He paced again, raked his fingers through his hair, and stopped a few feet away. "What in the hell does he think it will accomplish to sue for custody?"

Rick's reaction left her stunned and a little off balance. He seemed almost as upset as she was, herself. She opened her mouth to answer, but he didn't wait for her to speak.

"He's messing with you, Marti. That's all he's doing. He's using Cameron to keep you from pushing him about the Lazy M deal."

The truth in his words worked its way up her spine like a slow chill. The throbbing in her head grew worse. Even with all the ugliness there had been between her and Gil, could he really stoop that low?

Rick watched her, scowling so deeply a ridge formed on his forehead. "We won't let that happen, Marti. Cameron needs to be with you."

We, he'd said. As if he intended to stand beside her in the battle. Some of the heaviness lifted from her heart. His caring made her feel better even though she knew that ultimately it was her battle and she'd have to fight it alone.

"Thank you."

His eyes softened, and he pulled her into his arms. He didn't say anything, he just held her. He brushed her temple with his lips and heat spiraled through her. She closed her eyes and savored the moment. But she wasn't here for this, she reminded herself. She had to see Cameron, and she needed to have her head on straight when she did.

She pushed away from him gently.

He understood. "Are you ready?"

She made herself nod. Putting the moment off would only make it worse.

Still holding on to her, Rick led her through the living room with its huge Christmas tree, past the couch with its rumpled blankets and pillow. She imagined her son lying there, sad, grieving for his sister, blaming himself.

She averted her eyes, straightened her shoulders and followed Rick to the kitchen door. With one last encouraging smile, he pushed open the door.

Cameron sat at the table, staring out the window. He'd probably watched her drive across the bridge. He turned to face them as the door opened, and apprehension flickered in his eyes.

She took a hesitant step toward him. "Are you all right?"

He made a vain attempt to put on his usual surly expression, but it wouldn't latch on to his face.

Rick drew his hand away from her arm and backed

off a step. "I'll leave you two alone. You don't need me in here."

"That's all right," Cameron said. "You can stay." He sounded almost pathetically eager, but Marti didn't let it offend her. After all, she didn't want Rick to leave, either.

Rick shook his head and let the door start to close. "No, this is between the two of you. I'll be in the living room if you need me."

Marti laced her fingers together and held her hands in front of her. "I'm so nervous, I don't know what to say."

Cameron moved slightly. It might have been a nod of agreement, but she couldn't be sure.

"I guess Rick probably told you that he came to see me this morning. He wanted Grandpa and me to know where you were."

Cameron stiffened, and Marti guessed he was waiting for her to yell at him for coming here instead of to the Lazy M. She set his mind at ease. "I'm glad you came to Rick's."

He looked away quickly, as if he didn't want her to see his surprise, but he didn't say anything.

"I think it's time we tried talking to each other, don't you?" she said.

He glanced uncertainly at her. "We talk."

"Yes," she admitted, "but not honestly. Usually, I talk *at* you."

He didn't seem to know what to make of that. Pulling the saltshaker toward him, he began to twirl it on the table.

She took another step closer. "Sweetheart, I had no idea what was going on inside you. I wish you could have told me, but I understand why you didn't think you could.''

He shrugged as if it didn't matter and used both hands on the saltshaker.

But this time, she saw through the protective shell. She sat at the table across from him and rested her arms on its surface, barely resisting the urge to do something with her own hands. ''Rick says you blame yourself for what happened with Chelsea.''

Cameron didn't move, didn't look at her, didn't even seem to breathe, but she sensed his apprehension as if it were something tangible.

She pressed on. ''It wasn't your fault, Cameron. You did exactly what you should have that night.''

His gaze flicked over her quickly, then returned to the saltshaker. He rolled it between both hands, but his actions were jerky and agitated.

''Grandpa says you saved my life,'' she said. ''Did you know that? If you hadn't called for help when you did, I would have died.'' She decided to take a risk and reach for his hand.

He stiffened, but he didn't draw away.

She allowed herself a moment's hope. ''Tell me what you're thinking, Cameron. Please. Tell me what's going on inside of you so I can help. Don't leave me guessing. If you do, I'll probably say the wrong thing and make it all worse.''

His gaze shot to her face again. He hesitated, obviously struggling with himself, arguing against giving up the fight, against opening up to her. But she wouldn't let him hold back. She *couldn't* let him if she wanted to help him.

She tightened her grip on his hand. "I love you, Cameron. I want to help you."

This time, his gaze lingered a little longer. "I don't need help," he said, but his voice sounded almost plaintive.

"Maybe not," she conceded. "But I do. I need to tell you everything about the night Chelsea died. I need to get it out, so will you at least listen?"

He shrugged, but she thought she saw a spark of curiosity in his eyes and his hand tensed beneath hers.

She didn't let herself stop. "That night, things were especially bad. I didn't feel well. I was huge and bloated and uncomfortable, and I wanted your dad to stay home and help me. I'd gone to your baseball game that afternoon, remember? And out to the ranch to help my mom with something, so I was tired. I begged him to stay home, but he wanted to go to the Lucky Jack. I told him that if he walked out the door, he shouldn't come back." She tilted her head and tried to catch his gaze. "Do you remember that?"

Cameron gave his head an almost imperceptible shake.

"What do you remember?"

He stayed silent so long, she feared he wouldn't answer. But after a moment, he let a few, halting words slip out. "I remember you sitting at the bottom of the steps crying."

"What else?"

"I remember you screaming. And I remember blood."

"But not until later, right? And do you remember that as soon as you saw it, you called for help? You did everything you could, Cameron."

He nodded slowly, and uncertainty filled his eyes.

She leaned forward and touched his cheek with her other hand. "Cameron, none of it was your fault. Not what happened to Chelsea. Not the divorce. Your dad and I just aren't suited to one another. We want different lifestyles, and neither of us can give what the other needs to be happy. The marriage would have ended, even if Chelsea had lived. It was already in shreds."

She waited for him to say something—*anything*—that would let her know he understood this last part. But he looked away again, his shoulders sagged, and he pulled his hand from hers.

Standing quickly, he paced to the window.

"Cameron, please—"

He spoke, but he didn't look at her again. "I don't want to talk about it anymore. Please leave me alone."

Marti struggled not to let her hurt show. She realized Cameron needed time to think about what they had discussed.

She still had no way of knowing whether she'd reached him. She'd given it her best; now it was up to Cameron. Please God, she hadn't waited too long. Please God, she hadn't lost him forever.

CAMERON WATCHED his mom's reflection in the glass. She stood, hesitated as if she might touch him for a minute, then turned away. He thought about saying something, but he didn't know what to say. He didn't know what to think, or even how he felt.

She'd never talked to him that way before—like an adult. Like she was telling the truth. He didn't want to believe what she'd said about his dad, but her eyes had looked different this time—sad, the way they used to look when he was a kid.

He listened to the door close behind her, to the rumble of Rick's voice talking to her. Rick liked her, Cameron could tell. He didn't know what he thought about that, either. He liked Rick—a lot. And every once in a while, when he and Rick were working together, he wondered what life would be like if Rick was his dad. But that didn't mean he wanted his mom to get together with him. Not at all.

He shifted his gaze to his own reflection, sighed and rubbed his forehead. His head hurt, and he was still tired from walking so far in the cold last night. He didn't want to spend another night on Rick's couch, but he sure as hell couldn't go back to his dad's. Not now. His dad had probably flipped out when he found the hole Cameron had put in the wall. And Cameron wouldn't be able to explain to his dad what had happened. His dad wouldn't get it.

The thought made him stop rubbing his forehead. He looked outside at the snow-covered trees and frowned. He loved his dad. So why could he talk to Rick about stuff he couldn't tell his dad? It seemed stupid. But, then, everything he did seemed stupid. Wasn't that what the counselors that his mom kept dragging him to see had said? That he was stupid? Maybe not in those exact words, but that's what they'd meant.

They talked about accepting responsibility, and making wise choices, and "owning" his actions.

At first, he'd wanted to get to his mom because she'd acted as if she had nothing to live for after Chelsea died. But she had *him,* didn't she? *Didn't she?* Except that he wasn't enough for her. She only cared about losing Chelsea. Cameron hated the way she picked on him all the time, and the way she was never satisfied with what he did. Nothing about him was good enough for her. That's why he pretended not to care about her—because deep down inside, he knew she didn't care about him.

Hot tears burned his eyes. He wiped most of them away with his sleeve and blinked quickly to get rid of the rest. He didn't care. That's what he'd been telling himself, and that's what he'd keep telling himself.

He just wondered if he'd ever believe it.

RICK WORKED a thick wool sweater over his head and glanced outside his bedroom window at the gathering darkness. Any minute now, the sleigh would arrive. Any minute now, Marti would pull up in front of the cabin. His heart beat faster at the thought—it had taken some doing to persuade her to come. But Rick was sure it was the right thing to do. Maybe it would bring her and Cameron back together again.

He listened to Cameron moving around in the guest room. After that first night two days before when Cameron had fallen sleep in the living room, Rick had told him to move into the spare bedroom.

Cameron should be home with Marti for Christmas. Not that Rick minded having the kid around. In fact, he kind of liked having the company. He found himself growing closer to the kid every day. But Cameron wasn't his son. He belonged with Marti, and Rick knew how much it hurt her to have him staying here.

A noise outside drew his attention to the window again. This time, Lynette and Tom stood in front of the house, Kendra and Ashley stood a little way off watching four horses pull the sleigh into the clearing. A minute later, Marti's car rounded the last stand of trees before the parking area.

Tonight wouldn't be easy on any of them. Cameron and Marti had their problems. Rick was going to have to keep his feelings for Marti in check, and Lynette…Lynette would have to accept Marti's presence and the fact that she couldn't keep her sister's memory alive by pretending that Jocelyn and Rick had had a perfect marriage and that Rick would never look at another woman.

He grabbed his gloves, a hat and a muffler for his ears, then crossed the hall and knocked on the guest-room door.

"Cameron, the sleigh's here. I'll meet you outside."

"Okay. I'll be there in a minute." Before Rick made it to the top of the stairs, Cameron's door opened a crack and his face appeared in the opening. "Is my mom coming?"

Rick couldn't tell if he'd only imagined the hope in Cameron's voice. "She's coming," he said. "In fact, she just drove up."

Something shot through Cameron's eyes, but it disappeared too quickly for Rick to read it. "Oh. Okay." He pulled his head back and closed the door again.

Rick hurried down the stairs, snagged his coat and put it on as he stepped outside. Marti had parked near the end of the house, but she hadn't gotten out of her car. Rick started toward her, but Lynette stopped him before he'd gone even half a dozen steps.

Her face was tight with disapproval. "I thought you were going to tell her not to come."

Rick pulled on one glove. "I never agreed to that and you know it."

"I don't want her here."

"I'm sorry to hear that. But I *do* want her here, and so does Cameron."

"What am I supposed to tell the girls?"

"How about telling them I have a date?"

"A date?" Her displeasure made the air around them almost static. "This is supposed to be a family outing."

He leaned closer so no one else could hear. "I'll let you in on a little secret. If things work out right, Marti and Cameron *will* be family."

Lynette took a jerky step backward and horror painted her face. "You're making a big mistake. They're nothing but trouble—both of them."

"No, Lynette, they're not. And I don't think I'm making a mistake. I think it's the first intelligent thing I've done in years." Her nostrils flared slightly, but he didn't care. He'd been patient with her long enough. "Marti is here as my guest. I hope you can get along with her for a few hours, but if you can't, I suggest you stay behind." With that, he walked away.

He struggled all the way across the clearing to get his emotions under control. But he was still upset when he drew up beside Marti's car.

She climbed slowly out to meet him. She'd dressed for the weather in a stocking cap, scarf and heavy jacket. Thick gloves sheathed her hands and sturdy boots encased her feet. She smiled up at him and held out her arms as if presenting herself for inspection. "Think I'll stay warm enough?"

"You should." He'd hoped that his irritation with Lynette wouldn't show, but he could tell by the way

Marti's smile suddenly quavered that it had come out in his voice. He tempered his response with a smile and tried again. "Sorry. I just…" He didn't know how to explain without hurting her feelings.

"I saw you talking to Lynette. I take it she's not thrilled to see me here," Marti said.

"No, she's not," he admitted. "But it's not up to her."

"I don't want to intrude."

"You're not intruding. I want you here."

She smiled again, and this time the smile reached all the way to her eyes. The urge to pull her into his arms nearly overwhelmed him. He fought it away and reminded himself that tonight wasn't a time for them. "Besides, you and Cameron need some time together. Time having fun. Time spent *not* arguing."

"I wish I could be as certain as you that this will help."

He didn't admit that he wasn't certain at all. He didn't want to undermine what little confidence she had. He put one arm around her shoulder, but once he did he couldn't resist pulling her close.

Immediately, he realized he'd made a mistake. The feel of her in his arms and the look in her eyes roused desires that were better kept in check tonight. But he couldn't make himself release her or take his gaze from hers.

She melted against him for an instant, and he suddenly wanted the right to do this forever. No, he *needed* this forever. He needed her at his side and in his life. And he wondered just how long he could make himself wait.

She stiffened noticeably. "There's Cameron."

Reluctantly, he pulled his arm away. He turned to follow her gaze and saw Cameron on the front porch bundled up for the cold weather. He didn't appear to have seen Rick and Marti; his eyes had locked on Kendra standing near the horses.

"Young love," Rick said with a smile at Marti. Raw emotion filled her eyes. "It will be all right," he promised. "You'll see."

She nodded.

He couldn't help wishing he could do or say something to make tonight easier for her. Some part of him wished he could fix it for her. If he'd learned nothing else from his first marriage, he'd learned that he couldn't fix the world for anyone else. He could only help by offering his support.

He glanced down at Marti again, saw the emotions playing on her face as she watched Cameron, and pulled himself up sharply. He was here to help Marti and Cameron in any way he could. But ultimately it was up to the two of them to work out their differences.

He just hoped it wouldn't take them too long to come around. He didn't know if he could wait that long.

CHAPTER FIFTEEN

MARTI SAT in the sleigh beside Rick and watched Cameron laughing with Kendra and Ashley. A light wind lifted snow from the field as they rode through it and stars twinkled in the sky overhead. It was a perfect night. Not too cold. At least, it should have been peaceful. But every time they bounced over a rut, Marti brushed against some part of Rick—shoulder, arm, thigh, hip—and every time she touched him, the peace in her heart shattered.

She hadn't come here tonight to fall even more hopelessly in love with Rick or to let her ever-growing desire get the best of her. She'd come to try once more to mend her relationship with Cameron.

Shifting a little away from Rick, she told herself to ignore him and pay attention to Cameron. She had to reach him tonight. She didn't know how many more chances she'd get.

She glanced quickly at Lynette, sitting at the head of the sleigh beside Tom. Lynette scowled, but Marti didn't know whether she intended the scowl for her, for Cameron and Kendra, or for all of them. It didn't matter, she supposed. Lynette obviously didn't approve of something, and her attitude was throwing a pall over the entire party.

Every nerve in her body seemed painfully alive.

Every word, every laugh, every squeal of delight from Ashley or Kendra, every movement from Rick or shift of position by Cameron set her nerves jangling.

She closed her eyes and tried to find some comfort in the movement of the sleigh and the clip-clop of the horses' hooves on the road.

While she sat that way, someone began to sing softly. *"Silent night, holy night..."* Another voice joined in, both voices high and sweet. Kendra and Ashley. *"All is calm, all is bright..."* The music did what the rest of the night hadn't been able to and helped her relax slightly.

Someone else began to sing, this voice slightly deeper. It didn't sound low enough to be Tom's, and she knew Rick wasn't singing, which left Cameron as the only other possibility. Giving in to curiosity, she opened her eyes and focused on her son. He sat between Kendra and Ashley, a serious expression on his face, his mouth moving in time with theirs. *"...mother and child. Holy infant so tender and mild..."*

He'd been tender and mild once, she thought. He'd been a sweet little boy who'd run to her when something hurt him and who'd believed there was magic in her kiss. A vision of Cameron at about the age of eight flitted through her mind. He'd been in the elementary school's Christmas program, front row. He'd tilted his head back and let the music pour out of him, but that had been so long ago, she'd almost forgotten how much he'd liked to sing. Or how beautiful his voice had been during the solo the choir director had given him in the "Little Drummer Boy." It had been her favorite Christmas carol ever since. She couldn't hear it without getting tears in her eyes.

He looked so different now. His voice came softly and he seemed uncomfortable with himself. Regret for the little boy she'd lost tore through her and she blinked rapidly to clear the tears from her eyes. She couldn't let herself cry. Even as a little boy, Cameron had rolled his eyes when he caught her crying at his concerts. She'd tried explaining that she couldn't help herself, that the tears had been joyful ones that ought to tell him how proud she was of him, but it hadn't made any difference to him then. And she knew he'd hate her for losing control now.

Their voices drifted away, then almost immediately started again singing a chorus of "Jingle Bells." For just a moment, she thought she heard Rick humming along. Kendra must have heard him too, because she beamed across the sleigh at him. "Come on, Uncle Rick. Sing with us."

Rick shook his head. "I'm tone-deaf."

Ashley sat up on her knees. "So? Who cares? It's Christmas."

"*I* care," Rick said, but the ghost of a smile tugged at his lips.

Kendra giggled. "Well, nobody else does. Come on, Cameron's singing."

"Cameron can carry a tune," Rick argued.

Marti smiled at his obvious discomfort. She put a hand on his arm and patted him gently. "Don't be mean to your uncle Rick, girls. If he wants to be a party pooper, let him."

Ashley laughed aloud and scooped a handful of snow from a bush as they passed. She lobbed the powder playfully at Rick, but most of it drifted in different directions before it reached him. "All right. Fine," she said. "You sing something, Cam."

Cameron looked hesitant, but Ashley obviously didn't intend to let him follow Rick's example. "Sing 'Deck the Halls.'"

Kendra nodded. "Or 'Santa Claus is Coming to Town.'"

"No," Cameron said. "I don't want to sing those." He darted a quick glance at Marti. To her surprise, his eyes softened. He looked down at his hands for a second, then lifted his head and sang.

"Come, they told me..."

He sang at least an octave lower than he had in elementary school, but the song immediately transported her back in time. And, as it always did, brought tears to her eyes.

"...our newborn King to see..."

Did he know what hearing that song did to her? She tried to hold back the tears, but her emotions were too raw, too close to the surface. She couldn't stop them.

"...our finest gifts we bring...to place before our King..."

One of the girls joined in with him, her voice high and clear, but Marti couldn't focus well enough to see which of them had decided to sing along. It didn't matter, anyway. The only voice she could really hear was Cameron's.

Lynette shifted position and lifted a limp hand to her forehead. Immediately concerned, Tom put an arm around her. "Are you all right?"

"I'm fine," she whimpered. "I just have the most dreadful headache."

Tom waved a hand toward the kids. "Enough singing for now. Your mother's not feeling well."

Cameron fell silent, but the look on his face tore Marti up inside. Strong, maternal, protective anger raged within her.

She caught a glimpse of Rick's face from the corner of her eye. He frowned over at Lynette, who glanced away quickly.

Lynette leaned against Tom's shoulder with a satisfied smile. Suddenly Marti recalled the many times Gil had imposed his will on her. Marti had always given up the fight every time he showed the slightest sign of disapproval.

Anger surged again, but this time she wouldn't sit here silently and let Lynette manipulate the circumstances—especially at Cameron's expense.

"I'm sorry you don't feel well," she said. "Maybe we should take you home and let you rest while we finish the sleigh ride."

Ashley darted an anxious look at Kendra who sank back into the seat. Cameron glanced up at Marti from beneath knit eyebrows. Rick didn't say a word, but she could feel his eyes on her, watching, assessing silently. Tom just looked miserable.

"No," Lynette said, trying to sound weak. "I'll be all right if we can just be quiet for a few minutes."

She sent Lynette a tight smile. "But it would be a shame to ruin the sleigh ride for the kids just because you're not feeling well. It's almost impossible to be out on a night like this and be silent."

Lynette glared at her. "I'll be fine in a few minutes. In fact, I'm already starting to feel much better."

"I'm so glad."

Turning her smile on the kids, she took up the song where they'd left off. Cameron would probably hate her for losing control. She'd probably embarrassed him beyond forgiveness.

CAMERON LISTENED to his mom sing alone for a few seconds. She didn't have a very good voice, but for some weird reason, he didn't care. She sounded good tonight.

He watched as Rick put an arm around her shoulders and smiled at her. Cameron knew what that smile meant—he'd seen smiles like it often enough to know Rick *really* liked his mom. Maybe even loved her. But all of a sudden, he didn't mind that, either.

He'd felt like a dork when Kendra's mom said his singing gave her a headache. But his mom had stuck up for him. He couldn't remember her doing anything like that for a long, long time. But she'd done it tonight.

A few flakes of snow fell onto his eyelashes. He blinked them away and leaned back against the sleigh's side and smiled to himself. Weird, but she actually looked kind of pretty tonight. And she was lots nicer when she was around Rick than when she was around his dad—even Cameron had to admit that. Probably because Rick was so much nicer to her than his dad. Rick didn't talk to her like she was an idiot. And he didn't act annoyed by everything she did or said.

For the first time since the divorce, Cameron thought maybe he understood his mom a little. He didn't like people talking to him like he was stupid, so why would his mom like it?

She smiled at him from across the sleigh, but she

looked nervous, as if she thought he might be mad at her. He smiled back, just to show her he wasn't, and started singing with her.

"Then, he smiled at me, pa-rum-pa-pum-pum..."

Just like always, she got tears in her eyes. She looked away, as if she didn't want Cameron to see her crying. Funny, the way she did that, as if knowing that she was proud of him would make him mad. He didn't mind her crying. In fact, he kind of liked it. He'd just always figured it would sound dumb to admit it.

But maybe one of these days, he thought, he'd tell her. Maybe she'd like that. Maybe it would make her smile.

WHILE TOM AND LYNETTE hurried toward the cabin to start cocoa, Rick swung Ashley down from the sleigh then turned to give Marti a hand. Thick snowflakes drifted from the sky and landed on her cheeks and eyelashes. Her breath painted the night sky with frost. Her smile seemed to take the place of the stars. Looking at her like this made it harder than ever to remember his vow to give her time to work things out with Cameron. He wanted her—by his side and in his bed.

She took his hand almost shyly. "Thank you."

He glanced over his shoulder to make sure all the kids had moved out of earshot, then grinned up at her and held her in place beside the sleigh. "I've got to tell you, that was one of the best things I've seen in a long time."

"What was?"

"The way you handled Lynette. She's not used to having someone call her on something like that."

Marti laughed softly. "I wouldn't have said anything

if she hadn't been trying to get Cameron to stop singing.''

"It *was* pretty obvious, wasn't it?''

"Yes, it was.''

"Cameron seemed to appreciate what you did.''

Uncertainty filled her eyes. "Do you think so?''

"Of course he did,'' Rick insisted. "Didn't you see the way he looked at you? He knew what you did.''

"Maybe.''

Rick shook his head, suddenly irritated by her hesitation. "Hell, Marti. Give the kid a break. So, he didn't jump up and down and declare a truce. He smiled at you. He sang with you. What more do you want from him right now?''

She tensed and drew her hand away. "I don't know.''

"Are you going to ask him to go home with you tonight?''

"I don't know.''

He sighed heavily. "Ask him. He's ready.''

"I just don't think I can stand it if he says no.''

"Well, I don't think he could stand it if you didn't ask. Can't you see how much he wants to know you love him?''

She moved away from the sleigh, as if she wanted some space between them. "I *do* love him.''

"I know you do, but I'm not sure he does.''

"I've told him—''

"But you don't *show* him, Marti. You're always angry with him, or maybe you're too afraid to let him see what's in your heart.''

"If I am, it's because he's stomped on it so many times, I can't let him see.''

He swore softly. Softly enough that he didn't think she could hear him, but the sound obviously carried in the silence.

"I don't need this from you, Rick."

"What? Honesty?"

"No. Censure. Judgment." She started away from him.

He went after her and grabbed her arm. "I'm not judging you," he insisted. "I just think—"

"You think you know how to get through to my son just because he's not angry with you," she interrupted, whirling to face him again. "But you don't know, Rick. You don't know." She tried to jerk her arm away, but he held on.

"I know that he's just a kid," he said. "I know that you're the adult, and that it's your responsibility to take the risks in your relationship with him. Be his mother, Marti. Show him that you love him."

"I do love him, and he knows I do."

"When was the last time you hugged him?"

She shook her head without answering.

Rick's heart twisted. "Don't wait until it's too late to fix what's wrong between you. I waited too long to try with Jocelyn. I waited too long with my dad. I'll never get another chance with either of them. But you've got a chance with Cameron. For both your sakes, don't let anything stand in your way—especially not pride. Go find him and put your arms around him."

Anguish crept across her face. She shook her head and whispered, "I can't."

"Why not?"

"He'll push me away."

The agony in her voice went straight to his heart.

"Maybe," he conceded, "but only because he's so uncertain." Taking a chance, he pulled her into his own arms and cradled her against his chest. "If I said that I love you, would you believe me?"

She darted a frightened glance at him. "I don't..."

"Because I do love you, Marti. I do." He brushed her lips with his own. "But if I never held you, if I never touched you, if you thought I was angry with you all the time, would you believe me, even if I told you a hundred times?"

She didn't answer, but the tears that spilled onto her cheeks told him that she understood.

"I care about you," he whispered again. "And I think Cameron's one hell of a kid. I want both of you to be happy, but I know that neither of you will be until you work this out between you. So, go to him. Talk to him. *Show* him what you've been trying to say."

She lifted her gaze slowly, hesitantly.

"I know you're afraid." He brushed her mouth with his lips once more. "But so is he. And he needs you as much as you need him. Just be completely honest with him. Don't hold back. And remember, I'll be nearby if you need me." He tilted her chin and looked deep into her eyes. "All right?"

She nodded, but he could tell how much effort the simple gesture cost her.

"You'll do it?"

She nodded again.

"Good." He worked his hand over hers, lacing their fingers together. "Come on. Let's go make this the best Christmas you've ever had."

She clung to his hand and walked beside him. Every

step betrayed her uncertainty, but she didn't resist. Rick stopped in his tracks and pulled her into his arms once more. He lowered his lips to hers and kissed her deeply, wishing that somehow he could pour courage into her soul.

WITH HER HEART lodged firmly in her throat, Marti stepped into the cabin just ahead of Rick. Christmas music played softly in the background and the entire house smelled of pine and cinnamon. Cameron, Ashley and Kendra sat beneath the tree, but Marti couldn't see Lynette or Tom anywhere. Thank goodness.

Kendra handed Ashley a package from beneath the tree. Ashley smiled, held it to her ear and shook it gently. Cameron watched them, grinning, but the moment he saw Marti on the threshold, his grin faltered.

Desperate to believe Rick, Marti searched her son's face for some sign of what he was really feeling. The all-too-familiar expression crossed his face, but this time Marti thought maybe she did see apprehension there instead of anger. Clinging to that tiny ray of hope, she forced herself to walk into the room.

Rick turned a teasing scowl on his nieces, as if there was nothing unusual about the moment. ''Put down the presents, you two. Nobody opens anything until day after tomorrow.''

Kendra grinned up at him. ''We're not opening them. We're just checking to make sure the wrapping paper isn't loose.''

''I don't think you need to worry,'' Rick said. ''I'm pretty sure the tape's working. But if you keep getting into them, they'll all disappear before Christmas morning.'' His voice sounded gruff, but Marti could hear affection underlying the crustiness in his voice.

The realization stopped her in her tracks, and the full impact of what he'd said to her outside hit her again. It wasn't what he said to the girls, as much as the way he said it. Obviously, Ashley and Kendra could hear the love in his voice, just as Cameron must be able to hear the anxiety in hers whenever she spoke to him.

Summoning all of her courage, she smiled at her son. ''Can I talk to you for a minute while these two put everything back under the tree?''

Cameron stiffened and studied her expression intently. He glanced quickly at Rick. Apparently reassured, he shrugged and pushed to his feet. ''Yeah, I guess. Where?''

''Why don't you go upstairs to the room you've been using,'' Rick suggested, dropping onto the couch and ruffling Kendra's hair as if Cameron and Marti had private talks every day.

''Okay.'' Cameron sounded hesitant, but at least he didn't refuse.

With her heart thundering, Marti followed him up the narrow staircase, past an open door that led to a large, airy bedroom and into a smaller room just large enough to hold a single bed and a dresser. She shut the door behind them and turned to find Cameron sitting on the bed with his arms folded across his chest.

''What?'' he demanded.

She hesitated for a second, then gave in to her instinct and crossed the room to sit beside him. He tensed and shifted position to put a little more space between them.

''What?'' he demanded again.

"I want you to come home for Christmas."

His lips thinned and he pulled back slightly.
"Why?"

Half a dozen defensive responses rose to her lips,
but she pushed them all away and forced herself to find
the answer in her heart.

"Because I love you," she whispered.

Something she hadn't seen in a long time darted
through his eyes. As if he sensed that he'd given something away, he averted his gaze and studied the pattern
of the bedcover.

Somehow she found the strength to say what came
next. "I love you, Cameron. I miss you. I'd like to
spend Christmas together."

He traced the pattern on the bed with one finger.
"Yeah? Why? So you can be mad at me all day?"

The question stung and her defensive instincts rose
again to protect her. But, again, she forced them away.
"I'm not mad at you, Cam. Not really. I'm hurt, and I
guess that a lot of times I cover that up by acting mad."

He flicked a glance at her, the merest brush of his
gaze across her face before he looked back at the bed
again.

Holding her breath, she put her hand on top of his.
Her fingers trembled, and she prayed silently that he
wouldn't reject her. That he wouldn't pull away from
her touch.

His hand tensed and stopped moving, but he left it
under hers. Grateful tears flooded her eyes. Yesterday,
she would have considered them a show of weakness
and tried to hide them. Tonight, she let them come.

Cameron lifted his gaze to meet hers slowly. "What
about Dad?"

"I know you want to see him on Christmas, and that's fine. It's right. You *should* spend time with him. But I have to be honest with you, Cameron. I can't get back together with him." He glanced away again, but she'd come this far, she wouldn't back down now. "If I got back together with him just to make you happy, I'd be miserable. And if I'm miserable, I'd make you miserable, too. I know you want us to be a family again, but we'd be living a lie, and I don't think that would make any of us happy in the long run."

"But you only got divorced because of Chelsea—"

The agony in his eyes wrenched her heart. Lifting her other hand, she brushed his cheek with her fingertips. "No, Cameron. That's not why we got divorced. You were so young, you probably don't remember what things were like before that night. Maybe I was wrong to hide so much from you, I don't know. But your dad and I were having trouble before I even found out Chelsea was on her way. When I realized I was pregnant, I thought we could make things work. But I was wrong. It didn't work. And after we lost Chelsea, everything finally fell apart."

Cameron shook his head quickly. "But if Chelsea hadn't died..." He shuddered and looked away again. "If I'd called for help sooner—"

She tilted his chin and looked into his eyes again. "It was too late for Chelsea, before I started having the pains. The doctor said nothing we could have done would have saved her."

"Then why did Dad say—" He cut himself off, but Marti knew what he'd been about to ask.

"Why did your dad say it was my fault?"

He nodded miserably.

"For the same reason I blamed him in my heart. Because we were hurt, and because we thought we needed somebody to blame. People do that to each other sometimes when something terrible happens that they can't explain. I was angry with your dad for leaving us alone that night, but we couldn't have saved Chelsea even if he'd stayed home."

Cameron glanced at her, but he didn't say anything more.

"We've all been carrying the pain of that night around with us for a long time," she said. "We've even let it come between us, but I don't want it to anymore. We're still here, and we need each other—at least, *I* need *you.*"

She thought he might pull away from her then. Instead, his face crumpled and tears filled his eyes. Slowly, hesitantly, she worked her arms around his shoulders. "I want us to stop being angry with each other, Cameron. I love you, and it's hurting both of us too much."

To her surprise, he leaned against her almost as if he wanted her to hold him closer. Nearly choking on her own sobs, she tightened her arms around him.

After what felt like an eternity, Cameron slid his arms around her waist and held on. She rocked him gently, the way she had when he was little, and stroked his hair with one gentle hand. "I love you, Cameron."

"I love you, too, Mom," he whispered so softly she didn't even know if she'd heard him right.

But her heart told her she had, and for the first time in forever she listened.

CHAPTER SIXTEEN

RICK PUSHED AWAY his plate and rested his hands gently on his stomach. Candlelight flickered on the table, illuminating Lynette and Tom across from him. Kendra and Ashley had moved into the living room to sit beneath the tree and shake presents.

Rick groaned pleasurably. He'd eaten too much, but Lynette had fixed a Christmas Eve feast to rival anything he'd ever seen before, and he hadn't been able to pass up anything.

Tom put an arm around her shoulders and leaned back in his chair. "Good food."

Smiling, Lynette settled into the crook of his arm. "Thank you."

"It was wonderful," Rick said.

She sat up. "I'm glad you liked it." Her voice sounded frosty.

Things had been strained between them since the sleigh ride the night before, and Rick knew that when she found out what he'd been thinking all afternoon, they'd get even worse. He hadn't said anything yet. He hadn't wanted to ruin Christmas for her. But if he intended to follow through with his plan, he'd have to say something soon.

Tom arranged his silverware on his plate and handed it to her. "What's for dessert?"

Lynette stood, gathered a few dishes from the table and spoke over her shoulder as she carried them to the sink. "Pie. Your choice—pumpkin, mince or cherry."

Rick waved her back to her seat. "You cooked everything. Sit down and let Tom and me do the dishes."

Tom rocked back in his seat and put on a look of mock horror. "What do you mean, Tom and me? If you want to volunteer, speak for yourself."

"Come on, old man, it'll do you good."

Tom groaned and patted his stomach, as if it contained a precious cargo. "Sorry. I can't move."

"Yeah," Rick said with a laugh. "After all that hard work you did eating, I can just imagine."

"It *was* hard work."

"Exhausting," Rick agreed. "Now let's work a little of it off so we have room for the pie."

Shaking his head, Tom pushed to his feet. "First he makes me chop wood just to stay warm, then he volunteers me for kitchen duty." He took Lynette by the shoulders and guided her toward the door. "Go on, then. Go peek at your presents while we clean up."

She smiled up at him. "You don't mind?"

"Of course I mind," he said, "but I'll do it anyway. I can't let Rick show me up, can I?"

Her smile faded again, but she didn't say a word. She disappeared through the door and left them alone.

Tom leaned against the counter and fixed Rick with a steady gaze. "All right. Spit it out. What's bugging you?"

"Nothing. I just thought it would be nice if we did the dishes, since Lynette cooked everything."

"Yeah? Well, you're right about that, but I can see

right through you, my friend. Something's on your mind.''

Rick tore off a length of foil and covered a dish of leftover sweet potatoes. Maybe he *should* talk to Tom. If anyone could help him get through to Lynette, Tom could. He put the dish in the refrigerator and turned to face him. ''I'm going to ask Marti to marry me.''

''*Marry* you?'' Tom barked a laugh and shook his head in disbelief. ''No kidding?''

''No kidding.''

''Are you sure?''

''Positive.''

''You love her?''

''With all my heart,'' Rick said, lifting a bowl of mashed potatoes.

Tom tore off another sheet of foil and handed it to him. ''Isn't this kind of sudden?''

''Kind of.''

''Well, then, how can you be sure she's the right one for you? After all, she's the first woman you've even *looked* at since Jocelyn died.''

Rick leaned one hip against the counter. ''I know I haven't dated a lot—''

''A lot?'' Tom carried the platter of turkey to the counter and searched the cupboard for a container. ''You haven't dated at all. Maybe you're just horny.''

Rick laughed aloud. ''I am that, but that's not the reason I want to marry her.'' His smile faded slowly. ''She's genuine, Tom. She's real, and I feel better when I'm with her than I've felt for a very long time.'' He paused, and added, ''I love her. I can't imagine my life without her in it.''

Tom stopped searching and faced him. "You're serious, aren't you?"

"Yes, I am. In fact, I've already called Bix Mason and taken the property off the market. And I called the court and turned in my resignation this morning. I'm staying here, and I'm going to make a go of the cabins. I want her here with me."

"What about her dad? Won't he put up a fuss?"

"Maybe," Rick admitted. "But I'm hoping he'd rather have me here than a factory."

Tom let out a heavy sigh and hung his head. "You know how Lynette's going to react to this."

"I know. That's why I haven't said anything yet. I don't want to ruin Christmas for everyone."

Tom shook his head. "Don't worry about it. You've put off your life long enough, and you've done more than most men would have to keep their in-laws happy—more than I would have, anyway." He cocked an eyebrow at Rick. "Does Marti know how you feel about her?"

"I've told her."

"And? Does she love you?"

"I don't know," he admitted. "But I think she does."

Tom clapped one hand on Rick's shoulder. "Well, then, maybe you ought to go find out."

"I will."

"I mean now."

Rick stiffened. *"Now?"*

"Now."

"I don't—"

Tom sighed heavily and rolled his eyes. "You say you love her. You say you can't imagine your life without her in it. I've watched you with Cameron, and I know how much you like having him around. So, go ask her.''

Still hesitant, Rick glanced at the door into the living room.

Tom followed his gaze. "Go. I'll talk to Lynette. It'll take her some time to get used to the idea, but she'll come around...eventually.''

"Are you sure?''

"Positive. She's stubborn, willful and pigheaded, and part of the problem is she's loyal to a fault. She still misses Jocelyn very much. But underneath everything, she does care about you. Besides, what if she doesn't accept your decision? Are you going to let that stop you? Because if you are...''

He didn't finish, but he didn't have to. Rick knew what he meant. Tom was right. If he truly loved Marti, he wouldn't let anything—even Lynette's disapproval—stop him.

"All right," Rick said, turning toward the door. "I'll do it.''

Tom smiled. "Good. But I've got to warn you about one last thing.''

Suddenly wary, Rick halted and looked at his brother-in-law. "What?''

"You, my friend, are going to owe me one hellacious favor.''

"I'll talk to Lynette myself—''

But Tom waved the suggestion away with one hand. "Not for that. For volunteering me to help with the dishes and then leaving me to do them alone. One *hellacious* favor. Like a free weekend's stay in the cabins during the fishing season next year.''

Rick grinned. "Make it a week, and you've got a deal."

"All right." Tom nudged him toward the door. "Go on, then. Get out of here. You're so damn lovesick you're getting on my nerves."

Rick didn't need to be told again. He hurried through the living room and grabbed his coat from its hook near the door. Ashley and Kendra stopped shaking presents to watch him.

Lynette looked up from her seat near the fireplace and frowned. "Where are you going?"

"Don't leave," Ashley begged. "I thought we were going to unwrap one present each before bed."

Rick opened his mouth to answer, but Tom spoke before he could say a word. "He'll be back. He's got important business to take care of."

"On Christmas Eve?" Lynette's disapproval showed clearly on her face.

Tom crossed the room to sit beside her. "Yes, sweetheart. On Christmas Eve." Every muscle in Lynette's body stiffened and her face turned a deep shade of red. But when it looked as if she might say something else, he cut her off. "Let him go, Lynette. It's time." And to Rick, "Go on. Get out of here. You've lived in the past long enough. It's time for all of us to move on."

Rick knew Tom was right about one thing—it *was* time for him to move on. But he had one more thing to say. "Lyn, this doesn't change how I felt about Jocelyn," he said softly. "It doesn't mean I've forgotten her. But I can't hide from life anymore."

Lynette shook her head quickly. "But—"

"If I'd been the one who died, Jocelyn would have

gotten married again. I would have wanted her to. I would have wanted her to be happy.''

She stared at him, but didn't argue.

''I've finally realized that nobody can make it through this life alone, and only a fool would try.'' He drew in a deep breath and let it out slowly. ''I'm tired of being a fool, Lyn. And I'm tired of hiding behind you and the rest of the family, pretending that I have some sort of responsibility for making everyone else happy when the truth is, I'm afraid.''

''You're not afraid—''

''Oh, but I am. I'm afraid of needing somebody in my life. I was afraid the whole time Jocelyn and I were married, so I kept her at arm's length. I was afraid of the pain I felt when she died, so I ran back to Denver.'' He closed the distance between them and brushed a kiss to her forehead. ''But life's too short. It's too fragile. And I don't want to spend any more of it running away from what I'm feeling. So, I'm going to see Marti, and I'm going to ask her to marry me. And I'm going to pray she says yes.''

He heard Kendra's delighted gasp behind him, but he didn't turn around. ''I hope you'll be able to accept my decision,'' he went on. ''I hope you'll even be able to find it in your heart to be happy for me. But even if you can't, I'm going to ask her.''

Lynette averted her gaze, for a moment, but when she looked back at him, she was no longer frowning. Not exactly smiling, but who knew, maybe given time… Either way, the ball was in her court now.

MARTI SAT in front of the fireplace, relishing the heat from the blaze. Cameron had gone outside to bring in firewood after dinner. Her dad sat in his chair, head back, eyes closed.

It had been an easy evening. A wonderful evening so far, and Marti had Rick to thank for it. He'd been right about Cameron. If she'd needed any further proof, she'd gotten it tonight. She thought about calling to thank him again, but she told herself to forget it. She didn't want to destroy her family's relaxed mood, and she didn't want to disturb Rick's family celebration. Lynette and Tom and the girls would be gone soon, and Rick would be alone again.

She wondered, as she had since the sleigh ride, if he truly did love her, or if he'd only been trying to show her what she needed to do with Cameron.

She believed that he cared about her. She *knew* he cared about her. But she still didn't know whether he could put Jocelyn and their marriage behind him.

Her dad leaned forward in the easy chair, propping his elbows on his knees. "So, girl, have you made up your mind?"

Her heart dropped a little further in her chest. She didn't want to talk about Gil. Not tonight. She sighed softly. "About what? Staying in Gunnison?"

"About everything."

Which meant Gil. "I don't—"

"I'm not talking about you getting back with Gil." Her dad waved the idea away with one hand. "After what happened the other night, I know that's not going to happen. And I'm not sure it should."

That surprised her. "I thought you wanted me to get back together with him."

"I thought I did. I thought you should. But that's before I realized how bad things were between you...."

He let his voice trail away, obviously at a loss for words.

She didn't know what to say, so she let the silence hang between them for a moment.

"You know I loved your mother," her dad said after a long time.

Marti stiffened. She didn't want to talk about *that* anymore than she wanted to discuss Gil.

He stood slowly, and she realized with a start how old he looked. Old and tired and sad. "There was a time, right after you were born, when things were rough between your mother and me."

"Daddy, don't—"

But he ignored her. "I won't go into detail. You don't want to hear about it, and it's none of your concern, anyway. But I made a mistake." He met her gaze evenly. "*One* mistake."

She felt a little better knowing that it hadn't gone on forever. That he hadn't made a career of cheating.

"At first, I hoped she wouldn't find out. But she knew something was wrong, and in the end I decided to tell her what I'd done." He rubbed his face with his palm, and Marti could see how difficult it was for him to talk about it. But she didn't stop him. "Life was rough for a while. Real rough. I won't say that it wasn't. But she knew I was sorry, and she knew how much I loved her." He turned to face her again. "She forgave me, Marti. And because she was such a wonderful, kind, loving woman, we managed to keep the family together."

She tensed, wondering what was coming next. He'd already said he'd given up the idea of her and Gil getting together. So, what?

"For a long time, I thought you and Gil had the same sort of problem." He held up both hands to keep her from speaking. "I knew how much your mother's forgiveness meant to me, and I figured Gil..." He stopped, rubbed his face again, and spoke in a shaky voice. "I figured Gil felt the same way. I thought he loved you. And I thought he loved the Lazy M, but I was wrong."

Wrong? She couldn't have heard right. She didn't think she'd ever heard him admit to being wrong before.

He sent a miserable glance at her. "What I'm trying to say is, I'm sorry."

Tears filled her eyes. She whispered, "Oh, Daddy," but she couldn't force anything else past the lump in her throat.

"I don't want you to go back to California—" He broke off, blinked a couple of times, and turned away.

Marti pushed to her feet and crossed the room to stand behind him. She touched one tentative hand to his shoulder.

He didn't look at her. "You know how hard it is for me to say what I feel—"

She knew only too well.

"But I don't want you and Cameron to leave again. I want you to stay. I think it's about time you took over running the Lazy M."

His words robbed her of her next breath.

"Not all at once," he said quickly, and smiled at her. "But if anybody's going to run this place after I'm gone, I want it to be someone who loves it as much as I do."

She couldn't see through the tears. She couldn't

think. She couldn't do anything but wrap her arms around her father and hold on. "Really? Do you mean it?"

He chuckled softly. "Believe me, girl. I wouldn't say it if I didn't."

She might not know much, but she knew that was true. "I never thought I'd hear those words coming out of your mouth," she said with a shaky laugh.

"I suppose that's fair enough," he said, turning toward her and slipping one arm around her waist. "I never thought I would, either. So? Will you stay?"

"Say yes."

She whipped around, surprised by the sound of Cameron's voice behind her. He stood in the kitchen door, holding it partway open. Snowflakes dusted his hair and shoulders. His nose and cheeks were red from the cold. "Say yes, Mom. Please. I hate California. I don't want to go back."

She stared at her son. There was no sullenness, no anger on his face. He was merely stating a fact and waiting for her response.

"Besides." He came into the room and let the kitchen door swing shut behind him. "What about Rick?"

His easy tone shocked her. She never would have believed he'd accept Rick as part of her life. Turning slowly, she glanced at her father to gauge his reaction. To her surprise, he didn't look upset, either.

He lifted his eyebrows and met her gaze. "It's a good question. What about him?"

"I—"

"Come on, Mom." Cameron crossed the room and

came to a stop in front of her. "We're not stupid. We can see how much you like him."

"But I—"

"And I'd have to be a total idiot not to see how much he likes you."

Confused and more than a little off balance, she rubbed her forehead with the fingers of one hand. "But—" She smiled gently. She didn't want to disappoint Cameron again, but she couldn't make promises about a relationship with Rick. "I'll admit I like him. And I know he cares about both of us. But—"

"But nothing," Cameron said with a playful scowl. "He smiles all the time when he's around you, and you get this goofy grin on your face..."

She could feel herself blushing, but she couldn't stop it. "This isn't something you and I can decide," she protested. "Rick lost his wife a couple of years ago. He still loves her. I'm not sure he's ready for a new relationship."

Cameron's scowl deepened. "Yes he is."

"What makes you think that?"

"He told me so."

Whatever Rick had said, Cameron must have misunderstood him. "When?"

"A couple of minutes ago." Cameron grinned and hooked his thumbs into the waistband of his jeans. "He's outside on the porch waiting for you. He came to the back door first because he wanted to see what I thought about you two getting together."

Her pulse stuttered and her mouth dried. How like Rick to care so much for Cameron's feelings. Her love for him welled within her. She glanced at the window, and back at Cameron again. "Are you serious?"

"Dead serious." Cameron slipped off his jacket and hung it in the closet, pulling hers off its hanger and holding it out to her. "I told him I thought it would be okay, as long as you wanted to."

Her heart began to race, and she couldn't breathe.

Her father nudged her forward. "Go on. Don't keep the man waiting forever out there in the cold. Even I can see that you love him. I guess I'll just have to get used to the idea of losing you again."

Even the idea of leaving Gunnison, of losing the Lazy M for good, couldn't wipe the smile off her face. She'd give up everything for a life with Rick. She turned to her father. "No matter what happens, Daddy, you won't lose us. I promise."

As in a dream, she slipped on her coat. She could feel her father and Cameron watching as she crossed to the front door and slowly pulled it open.

Rick stood beside one of the porch pillars, head down, hands stuffed in the pockets of his down-filled jacket. When he heard the door open, he looked up quickly and smiled. "Marti."

She felt more than heard him speak, but it filled her heart with warmth. Such tenderness filled his eyes, tears threatened her own again. She pulled the door closed behind her and took a step toward him. "Cameron said you wanted to see me."

"I do." He closed the distance between them, lifted one hand and gently brushed her cheek with his fingers. "I came to ask you not to leave. I know we've only known each other a few weeks, but I've fallen head over heels in love with you. You're all I ever think about, and...and I think we deserve a chance to see where this will lead."

He looked so flustered, she couldn't help smiling. "You want to date me?"

"I want more than that," he said. "I want to spend the rest of my life with you. But I'm willing to take it slow if that's what you need." He let his gaze travel across her face, and she felt her pulse quicken.

"But I—"

"I'm not leaving," he said quickly. "I'm going to stay and run the cabins. I love it here, and I know you do, too."

He couldn't have said anything more perfect if he'd tried forever. "Yes," she whispered. "I do."

"So stay. Stay here with me."

She didn't know what to say. Everything had happened so fast, she hadn't even had time to catch her breath.

"I love you, Marti."

"And I love you, but—"

"No buts," he said. "As long as we can talk, as long as we're honest with each other, we can work everything out."

Slowly, hesitantly, he touched his lips to hers. Everything inside her seemed to thaw. All her reservations, all her fears, all her confusion melted away. She couldn't hold back the soft moan of pleasure. She didn't even try.

In answer, he wrapped his arms around her and pulled her closer. Her heart threatened to stop beating, then quickened. Her lungs refused to work for a moment, then filled with one deep, shuddering breath.

He deepened the kiss, working magic and ripping away the control she'd worked so hard to maintain. She let her hands travel slowly across his shoulders, then down the solid wall of his chest. He groaned and pulled her closer still. He probed her mouth with his tongue, and fire erupted within her.

"Say yes," he whispered into her mouth.

She smiled slowly and nibbled his bottom lip. "Convince me some more."

To her delight, he did.

EPILOGUE

CAMERON SCOWLED at the set of lights in his lap and worked the cord through the knot that had somehow tied itself while the decorations spent the year in the toolshed. Through the window, he could see snow falling, blanketing this land he'd loved all his life, and obscuring the guest cabins from view.

A mug of hot spiced apple cider sat on the coffee table in front of him, and Christmas music played softly on the stereo across the room. His grandpa dozed in the chair he always claimed when he came across the river to see them, oblivious to the popping logs, the music, the laughter that erupted from the kitchen every few minutes.

Cameron smiled. During the past four years, his mom had laughed a lot. He liked it. He liked knowing she was happy—with herself and with him.

He made another effort to untangle the lights. After all, he'd promised his mom he'd get the lights on the tree before Cherryl and her family showed up for dinner. But he couldn't make himself concentrate. Tomorrow, Kendra and her parents would be arriving for the holidays, just as they did every year now. This time, Ashley was bringing along a boyfriend, and Cameron was looking forward to meeting him.

Out of the corner of his eye, he spied a chubby hand

reaching for his mug of cider. Dropping the lights, he caught the tiny wrist gently with one hand. "Oh no you don't, kiddo."

The tiny face under the mop of curls as dark as Rick's puckered into a frown. "Mine."

"No," Cameron said gently. "Mine."

"Mine."

He scooped the little girl onto his lap and nuzzled her neck. Noelle pulled away from him with a scowl. "Ouch."

"Ouch? What—you don't like my whiskers?"

"No."

"Okay, I'll be nice." Smiling, he ran a hand across his chin. He liked the way his whiskers felt after a long day at the tech school and an afternoon working at Rick's side. But his sister didn't, and he couldn't say he blamed her. "Where's Mommy?"

Noelle pointed toward the kitchen door. "Wiv Daddy."

"Okay," Cameron said, and picked up the mug of cider. Blowing gently to cool it, he held the mug to his sister's tiny mouth. "I'll share this with you, but don't tell Mommy."

"Don't tell Mommy what?" His mother's voice caught him off guard.

He glanced over his shoulder again and grinned at the mock scowl on her face. She held the kitchen door open with one shoulder and balanced a tray of cookies with one hand. In the kitchen behind her, Rick held a bottle of wine and two stemmed glasses. Cameron grinned broadly. "Don't tell Mommy how pretty the tree is."

His mother's scowl deepened, but he could see the

laughter in her eyes. "You're giving her cider again, aren't you?"

"She likes it."

His mom sighed softly, but it didn't bother him the way it once had. "Just make sure it's not too hot for her."

"It's not." He held the mug toward her. "See?"

"Mine," Noelle said again, but this time she wrapped her tiny arms around Cameron's neck and gave him a slobbery wet kiss on his cheek.

He lowered the mug to the coffee table and ruffled her hair. "No, you're *mine*."

He felt as though she was his—his very own Christmas present from Santa two years before. The year before that, Rick and his mom had gotten married in his grandpa's living room and they'd all moved into Rick's place together. And the year before that, the year they'd met Rick, Cameron had finally stopped blaming himself for what happened to Chelsea—with his mom's help.

Looking at his mother now, he could barely remember how angry he'd once been with her. Watching her with Rick, seeing how much they truly loved each other, made him wonder why he'd ever thought she should get back together with his dad. Now he couldn't imagine two people less suited for each other. Or two people more perfect together than his mom and stepdad.

His grandpa had even mellowed. Just last night, he'd suggested that they turn the Lazy M into a guide service for horseback riding and hunters who stayed at the cabins. At first, Cameron hadn't believed him, but he liked the idea a lot, especially since Grandpa suggested that Rick make him the head guide.

The only thing that left Cameron unsatisfied was his dad. If you asked him, his dad still didn't know what he wanted. He'd quit his job at the feed store to work at the factory when they'd finally located twenty miles downriver on the other side of town. But even that didn't make him happy. He still spent most of his spare time at the Lucky Jack. And he'd had more girlfriends than Cameron had in the past four years. But Cameron had learned to live with it, and to make the best of the time they spent together. And he still hoped that someday his dad would find a nice woman who could make him happy and settle down.

He brushed another kiss to Noelle's soft cheek and put her gently on the floor. Lifting his mug, he offered a toast to Rick, his mom, his sister—to his life.

Once, he'd believed life was the pits. Now, he couldn't imagine it getting any better than it already was.

IN UNIFORM

There's something special about a man in uniform. Maybe because he's a man who takes charge, a man you can count on, and yes, maybe even love....

Superromance presents *In Uniform*, an occasional series that features men who live up to your every fantasy—and then some!

Look for:
Mad About the Major
by Roz Denny Fox
Superromance #821
Coming in January 1999

An Officer and a Gentleman
by Elizabeth Ashtree
Superromance #828
Coming in March 1999

SEAL It with a Kiss
by Rogenna Brewer
Superromance #833
Coming in April 1999

Available wherever Harlequin books are sold.

HARLEQUIN®
Makes any time special™

Dangerous, powerful and passionate...

THE AUSTRALIANS

Stories of romance Australian-style, guaranteed to
fulfill that sense of adventure!

This January 1999, look for

Her Outback Man

by **Margaret Way**

Logan Dangerfield, head of one of Australia's most affluent
families, had severe doubts about Dana Barry's motives.
Offering comfort to Logan's niece kept Dana on his cattle
station, but could she hide the fact that Logan was the only
Outback man she had ever loved?

*The Wonder from Down Under: where spirited women win
the hearts of Australia's most independent men!*

Available January 1999
at your favorite retail outlet.

HARLEQUIN®
Makes any time special ™